Vote for Murder

Jacqueline Beard

ISBN: 978-1-326-41498-6

PublishNation, London
www.publishnation.co.uk

CCBC
AMAZON
05/2017

To Lee, for his encouragement
and
to Jill, for her unwavering support

Also by this author

Beau Garnie & the Invisimin Mine

Contents

≈≈≈≈≈

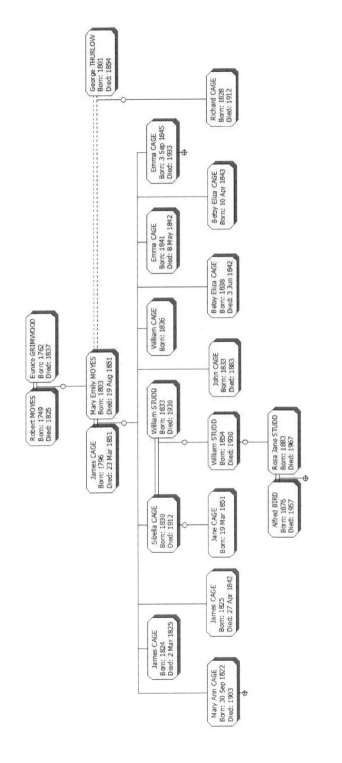

Prologue

Mary patted her belly and sighed. "How do I look?" she asked flattening the pleats of her stiff cotton skirts.

"As lovely as the finest lady, Mary Emily," replied Anna, ignoring the obvious baby bump distorting the pleated fabric. "Here," she continued lifting a worn red check cloth from her basket. "I made you a present."

She unwrapped another cloth revealing a head dress lovingly hand-crafted from bluebells and cowslips, each purple and pale yellow bell trembling as she passed it to her friend.

"Oh Annie," gasped Mary reaching for her gift. "It's exquisite."

She placed the headdress over her dark curls.

"How does it look?" she asked. "Never mind, I want to see for myself." She grabbed Anna's hand giving her no opportunity to reply. "Come with me."

Mary threw open the door of the gloomy cottage. They ran up the muddy track into a field where a group of bedraggled sheep chewed grass next to a stone trough.

"There," said Mary, peering into the trough of algae-infused water. A smiling, tousled-haired young woman returned her gaze.

"Annie," she exclaimed, "you have done me proud. James will think me the prettiest girl in the village."

"And rightly so," agreed Anna. "It is hard to believe you will be Mrs James Cage by the end of the day."

Mary took Anna's hands and pulled her onto the flat stone bench in front of the trough until they faced each other. "You have been patient Annie," she said. "You have reservations and you may be right, but James will love me in time and with the little one coming, I must marry."

"And marry you shall," said Anna. "I wish you nothing but joy." She kissed her friend on the cheek before turning towards the cottage.

Her smile slid into a frown as a recent memory stole back into her consciousness; an unwanted recollection of James Cage trying to

1

steal a kiss. She could almost smell the stale sweat and alcohol. A drunken kiss from an idle waster; poor choice Mary, a man not fit to speak your name in church.

Anna resolved to keep the incident secret. The truth could not help Mary. Her child was due in three or four months and her father determined to eject her from the house unless she was married before the baby arrived. There was no choice. Anna could only hope for the best outcome for her friend.

Mary sat alone by the stone trough swishing her fingers through the slimy water. Short and slight with dark lustrous hair and fine features, high cheek bones finished her delicate face. Her full lips set naturally in a wide smile but her eyes were sad as if something dark loomed in her future. Anna watched and wondered then embraced her friend.

"James will change when you are wed and the baby is here," she reassured. "He will become responsible and hard working. You will have lots of babies and live in a happy home. You start married life with rooms to yourselves. It is more than most couples have."

"We are lucky," beamed Mary. "Our home is not grand but we are blessed to have two rooms for our own use. I am fortunate, Annie and I know James likes a drink but I believe he cares for me."

"So do I," agreed Anna, "and you a wife and mother before you are even twenty."

"But what else could I be?" asked Mary, "I am not educated like you. We spent our days picking stones in the fields while you learned your letters."

"What of it?" asked Anna, straightening the headdress. She tucked a loose curl behind Mary's ear. "I will marry a local man and live close by. We will be neighbours and our children will grow up together and how will it matter I can read a book and you cannot? Besides, you sing like an angel and I cannot carry a tune in a pail."

Mary laughed, "I know," she said, "and I do not mind so very much. I do not wish to go anywhere and will be content so long as you do not leave to seek your fortune elsewhere."

"Never," said Anna scanning the fields as she heard voices in the distance. "No," she cried. "James is on his way. Run indoors. He cannot see you before the wedding."

Mary lifted her skirts and ran up the pathway laughing. Waving at Anna she slammed the door.

"I will see you later," called Anna picking her way up the stony path to the front of the cottage.

Set directly onto the road, the cream fronted cottage stood side by side with three similar dwellings. Dirt and debris covered the lower walls grey. Anna noticed another hole surrounded by a spider's web of cracked panes. Shabby red curtains were squashed into the holes in a vain attempt to retain the heat.

The sight of Mary's mother bustling along the street distracted Anna from her thoughts.

"Good day Mrs Moise," she said. "How are you?"

"I am well," said Mrs Moise. "Have you come to give Mary some last minute advice?"

"No," laughed Anna, "I made her a headdress for the wedding."

"That was kind," she replied. "Will you join us when we walk to church later?"

"Oh yes," replied Anna. "It will be an honour to walk with you and a joy to see Mary wed."

"It will," agreed Eunice Moise. "We may have peace in our home at last when Cage makes an honest woman of her." She smiled wryly. "Mr Moise has not been pleased of late."

"Today is a happy day," smiled Anna chatting for a few more minutes before taking her leave. She walked up the street towards the Ten Bells beer house swinging her basket.

A shadow loomed large in her path, "Hello Annie."

She looked up to see James Cage leaving the beer house with two of his friends, a quart of ale in each hand. He grinned. "Some well-earned lubrication," he added nodding at the beer.

"Be sensible with it," said Annie. "Mary is happy. Do not spoil her day."

"I will not," he said, "unless you decide to marry me instead. Then I will send Samuel to the church in my place."

"Not I," smirked Samuel, "You bring up your own bastard." He patted James on the back and they laughed.

Anna shook her head, "I know you do not mean a word of it," she said, "but you should not joke about such things. Now get yourself clean and ready for church. Off with you now."

The three men sauntered up the road swigging from ale jars. Anna followed keeping a safe distance behind until she reached her father's tidy detached cottage.

She was immensely proud of her ivy clad home painted in Suffolk pink with a smart, red-tiled porch, nestling its little patch of front garden. It was a happy family home in which she felt secure and loved. She opened the door and retired to her room until it was time to change into her Sunday best dress ready for church.

~~~~~~~

The bells pealed from the church tower as a snake of villagers meandered down the stony road towards the church. It was a bright, sunny June day. The softest breeze ruffled Mary's headdress and the flowers quivered. Mary walked at the head of the procession dressed in cream pleated skirts and a white laced bodice yellowing with age. She carried a posy of freshly picked wildflowers with the gentle scent of lavender just discernible when the wind changed direction. Anna followed behind holding the soft, warm hand of Mary's young niece. The little girl clutched a small basket filled with crimson rose petals.

The wedding party ambled towards the church, square flint tower sturdy in the distance. They continued up the path and into the vestibule leaving Mary and her father at the gate.

A few minutes passed, the pealing stopped and the sonorous tones of the organ filtered through the doors.

Robert Moise straightened his cravat. "Make me proud, Mary," he said, taking her arm before leading her into the flower-filled church.

They walked slowly up the aisle in time with the music until they reached the altar where James waited, leaning casually against a carved, wooden bench end. He grinned at Samuel who covered his mouth and whispered. James laughed aloud and slapped Samuel on the shoulder.

The vicar gestured for quiet. He peered at the congregation over horn-rimmed glasses. "Be seated," he commanded.

James pointed a dirty nail at the vicar. "You be seated," he slurred.

Anna gasped. A woman cried "shame," while others tutted and shook their heads.

James was drunk. He swayed from side to side grinning at the congregation. Mary stared blankly at the altar, face expressionless. She did not react.

James hiccupped and slapped a hand to his mouth reaching to Samuel for support.

Dressed in a faded worsted jacket, and the same breeches and boots he wore working in the fields, James cut an unkempt figure. His face was pallid, covered in a smear of grey and in no cleaner state than his nails. Anna wondered how she failed to notice the condition of his clothes earlier.

"I said sit down," boomed the vicar. James slumped upon a wooden seat, legs splayed in front.

The vicar embarked upon his sermon as Robert Moise rose from his seat. Silent as a cat, he picked his way across the floorboards until he reached James. Crouching over he whispered, but his voice was too low for Anna to hear.

James frowned and pursed his lips then sat up straight backed, watching the rector through narrowed eyes.

The rest of the service passed without incident. Anna held her breath as the vicar asked if anyone knew of any impediment to the marriage of James and Mary but, to her relief, there was no objection. They took their vows and exchanged wedding bands then Mary's niece Sarah tossed rose petals to the floor as the organ ground back to life. Mary and James walked up the aisle side by side; a newly married couple.

The wedding party strolled the short distance to the Ten Bells public house where Frederick Abbot grabbed his fiddle and scraped a tune. The younger people danced and frolicked but Mary remained sitting quietly beside Anna.

Anna smiled. "How are you feeling Mary?" she asked holding her hand.

"I am well," replied Mary softly.

"You are quiet."

"I cannot dance in my condition," replied Mary watching James in the distance.

5

"He is young and foolish," said Anna as James consumed another quart of ale.

"I can live with that," said Mary, "but he is twenty six and already drinks like a hardened lag. Is it too late for him to settle? Do I hope in vain?"

"It will change when the baby comes," said Anna, "Have faith."

"It must," replied Mary. "Or I must make it."

Mary's eyes flashed gimlet grey. Anna shuddered, acknowledging a steely resolve in her friend not previously apparent. For a moment she felt she did not know Mary at all.

Chapter One

A call to action

"If we must obey the law, should we not have a say in who makes the law?" The clear pitched voice cut across the buzz emanating from the crowd of women milling around a podium in Christchurch Park. The crowd, composed of middle-aged, smartly dressed women, moved reluctantly aside as two younger girls squeezed their way through the gathering. They pushed towards the front attracting unwelcome attention in their enthusiasm. When they reached the foot of the podium, the dark-haired girl stood in front of the stand with her hands on her hips leaning towards her shorter, fair-haired companion.

"Marvellous, isn't she?" she whispered, nodding towards a strident sounding woman standing high on the podium above. The woman was an expressive speaker, accompanying every word with an earnest gesture which made her argument passionate and sincere.

"She is inspiring, Louisa," replied Sophia, "but who is she?"

"Constance Andrews, leader of our Women's Freedom League. If she cannot get us closer to the vote, I do not know who can."

Louisa watched the throng of women listen to their figurehead with rapt attention. Her full voice carried across Christchurch Park and over the chatter of the assembled women. After a few moments the audience quietened, mesmerised by the eloquence of her argument. Constance Andrews talked with authority and confidence.

"I bring news from London," she declared, "from Millicent Fawcett. She plans a peaceful demonstration against the census. From north to south our suffragette sisters mean to boycott the census next Sunday. They refuse to be counted if their vote does not count. Whether they live in London or Scotland, many women will leave their homes on census night hiding from the enumerator so their presence will not be declared on Prime Minister Asquith's statistics." Her face contorted at the mention of the Prime Minister.

"The government cannot be trusted," she continued. "Even now, their promises, their mealy-mouthed words, count for nothing."

"Hear hear," trilled a fine-featured woman dressed in a soft plum hat and matching jacket. Her clothes were cut from the finest cloth but pinned with purple and green 'vote for women' buttons leaving no doubt of her commitment to the cause.

"That's Grace Roe," whispered Louisa. "She is beautiful but much more radical than Constance. She runs the Women's Social and Political Union office in Princes Street and is great friends with Emmeline Pankhurst."

Grace Roe spoke. "May I?" she asked gesturing to Constance Andrews. She nodded.

"I believe in this course of action," said Grace. "But is it enough? We have only empty promises from the government for all our negotiations though we kept our word and ceased militant action months ago. There have been no hunger strikes and no smashed windows, but what advantage has it bought?"

"Come now, Grace," Constance replied. "Radical action does not have to mean violence or self-harm. I still keep to my militant principles. I have not paid for Spartan's dog licence although they threaten me with prison."

"A dog licence indeed," said Grace shaking her head. "It is hardly going to bring the government down. We should do more."

"We will do more," agreed Constance. "But for now this is a valuable demonstration. The census is a historical document. Our action on Sunday night will skew the census forever. It can never be righted."

She addressed the crowd of women in front. "What say you ladies?" she cried. "Will you support us?"

A dozen women raised their hands chanting, "We will," in unison, but many more stared at the ground making no commitment.

"Lydia Marshall, shall you not join us?" asked Constance.

"I would if I could," replied Lydia. "But I cannot. My husband would not brook law-breaking of any kind. He tolerates my attendance at these meetings. He even expresses some level of understanding. But if he thought I intended to go against the government he would stop me."

Several other women nodded in empathy.

The two women on the podium fell quiet. The expression on Grace Roe's face left no doubt as to her feelings on the subject of husbands' claiming their authority, but Constance Andrews was more sympathetic.

"I understand your concerns," she said, "which is why it is important that those of us able to avoid the census do. I have secured premises at the Old Museum in Museum Street for Sunday night. I will provide food, shelter and warmth. We will be quite safe and away from the public eye. Again I ask; who will join me?"

This time more hands shot into the air. The realisation that shelter provided discretion and secrecy lifted their spirits.

"Oh I will, I will," cried Louisa enthusiastically.

"Thank you," said Constance singling Louisa out. "I welcome your enthusiasm."

Louisa blushed with pleasure at the attention.

"I too," said Sophia raising her hand uncertainly. She looked anxiously towards Louisa.

About forty hands were now raised, representing almost half of the women in attendance.

"We will meet at The Old Museum at 6pm Sunday night," said Constance. "Please come. If we can raise enough attention throughout the country our inconvenience will be worthwhile and helpful to the cause. I thank you for your attendance today and look forward to seeing you Sunday week"

A spontaneous round of applause erupted from the crowd. Constance waved and smiled until the crowd melted away. Once the park was almost empty, a smartly dressed man helped Constance from the podium.

"Thank you, Mr Bastian," she said. He released her gloved hand and smiled before returning to his waiting wife. Henry Bastian was one of half a dozen men standing in support of the suffrage cause. Many men attended in a show of solidarity to their wives but other liberal single men joined because it fitted their political beliefs. They were vocal in their support, clapping eagerly through the speeches. Constance approached the small group of men, shook hands and gave thanks to each individual for his time.

"I cannot wait until Sunday," said Louisa clasping her hands together. "I want to do my bit to help. What a great opportunity."

"But how will we get away?" asked Sophia. "My father will never give permission."

"Does he have no sympathy with suffrage?" asked Louisa.

"None at all," said Sophia shaking her head. "There is not the smallest chance he would allow me to go. And he is in a frightful rage with one of the servants at the moment and talking of dismissal so he is hardly in the right frame of mind to ask, even if there was a chance of his agreement. Surely your father would not allow you out at night unchaperoned?"

"My father will allow me anywhere as long as I am sensible and do not indulge in violence. It is a lost cause for papa. My cousin is married to Millicent Fawcett's sister so we are steeped in suffragist principles. Indeed, Millicent has visited us several times over the past few years. Mama has given her word that she will not get involved so he turns a blind eye to anything Charlotte or I wish to do."

"You are lucky," sighed Sophia. "Father has never allowed me much freedom. I would be in a great deal of trouble if he knew I was here and he has been much worse since we left Chippenham. I will not be able to join you, Louisa. I should not have raised my hand."

"Well you must say you are staying with me that evening," said Louisa. "We can invent a reason. With luck, we may not need to. My brother Albert is coming home in the next few days and he often brings friends. You must come to dinner. I will make a proper invitation."

"That might work," said Sophia, "A written invitation will make a lot of difference. Father is all about appearances and will undoubtedly give his approval to a dinner invitation. Mummy will not mind anyway."

The girls left the podium and walked along the pathway past the tall stone memorial to the Ipswich martyrs. The cross-topped monument stretched skywards casting a lanky shadow over the path ahead. Recently completed, the carved round pillars caught the light of the morning sun and the carved inscription stood fresh and clear.

"Do your sisters not support us?" asked Louisa.

"Oh no," laughed Sophia. "Ethel is too busy raising her children and has no time for such things. You may be surprised when I tell you about my sister, Catherine. She took holy orders two years' ago and lives in a convent in York."

"I had no idea," exclaimed Louisa, "but I forget how little time we have known each other. We are such good friends it seems we have been acquainted much longer. I did not realise your family were religious."

"We are not," said Sophia, "mother is somewhat but father not at all. Catherine has always been drawn to religion and there are other reasons why she has chosen to live in relative obscurity, but she has a simple life which does not involve speculating about women's politics".

"Understandably," agreed Louisa. "So shall I send you an invitation tomorrow and you can speak with your mother and father?"

"Yes, please," said Sophia. "My cousin Daniel will join us tomorrow but his arrival will not affect our plans for next week. He will have been with us for several days by then."

"Is he staying long?" asked Louisa.

"For the foreseeable future," said Sophia, "Which will hopefully please father. Some male company may improve his mood. Daniel is an engineer and begins a new career in Ipswich so he will board with us until he finds a permanent home. I am looking forward to some new conversation. I miss my sisters and John Edward is too young to be interesting company."

"Do you know Daniel well?" asked Louisa.

"Not at all," replied Sophia. "He was but fourteen when we last met, and I only ten. He dwelled in London until recently so he will have much to talk about. It will brighten up our dreary old house."

They left the park and walked up Ivry Street stopping outside Sophia's imposing gothic style house standing angularly at the end of a wide stone drive. Ivy clad, with mullioned windows and a turreted roof, it was bigger and grander than Louisa's red brick house next door, but for all the opulence it carried an air of gloom.

They reached the drive as Sophia's father emerged from the arched front door and strode towards a gleaming Ford automobile parked on the driveway.

"Sophia," he barked, nodding towards Louisa before climbing into a Model T parked at the foot of the drive. Sunlight glinted from the brightly polished chassis and the brass lamps gleamed like goldfish eyes. The vehicle purred into life and he pulled out of the drive turning left into Ivry Street.

"I should go in," said Sophia as the engine noise faded.

"Not before I thank you for coming to the rally with me," said Louisa. "I hope you enjoyed it. I will organise your dinner invitation tomorrow. You simply cannot miss the census night evasion."

Sophia smiled. "I will be there," she said waving to Louisa before entering the house.

A pair of familiar faces greeted Louisa on her return. "Ada, Bessie," she squealed seeing her two cousins standing on the front lawn of The Poplars. "You missed the rally in Christchurch Park."

"Yes, it was rather unfortunate," said Ada, "but we have been involved in the planning and will attend the evasion at the Old Museum next week. I guarantee you will not see the names of Ada and Bessie Ridley on the 1911 census return. Come inside. We have much to tell you."

Chapter Two

If women don't count, neither shall they be counted....

Sunday lunch at The Poplars was a merry affair with Louisa's father, Henry Russell his engaging, convivial self, providing much welcome and entertaining conversation to his dinner guest. Sophia, normally quieter than Louisa, was encouraged to chat about her family and enjoyed herself so much the afternoon slipped by.

Albert Russell was home, having returned from his lodgings in Camden Town and was charming and attentive to his sister's new friend. Charlotte Russell was equally welcoming.

At half past four Maggie, the housemaid, provided a platter of sandwiches, a selection of cakes and pots of steaming hot tea for the family.

The girls sat together in the drawing room watching Louisa's spaniels play on the flat rear lawn.

"This has been a wonderful day," whispered Sophia as she passed the cake stand to Louisa. Your family are so welcoming and your house lively. There are more of us than you, but we are quite gloomy in comparison.

"I am fortunate," said Louisa smiling.

"What are you girls plotting?" asked Henry Russell. "Are you involved in this suffragist business your cousin Ada mentioned?"

"We plan to go to the Old Museum with Ada and Bessie later," Louisa replied, "with your permission, of course."

Henry Russell placed his tea-cup down and spread jam on a scone with great precision. "I give my consent to you Louisa, as always, with the usual proviso that you do not place yourself in any danger or commit any act of violence. As I am assured this is a peaceful protest you may go but I cannot speak for Mr Drummond so assume that Sophia has obtained his permission."

Sophia stared at the floor as the colour rose in her cheeks.

"Indeed," said Louisa reaching for a pastry. She sat back into the seat with a bump and the pastry dropped onto the carpet.

"Oh, I'm so sorry," she said standing to pick it up while stepping on the edge of the sweetmeat, grinding it deep into the pile of the carpet.

"Oh Louisa," exclaimed her mother, "That was really careless. Look at my poor carpet."

She pressed a brass bell and before long the housemaid appeared.

"I'm sorry Maggie, but can you clear this mess up for me please?" she asked.

"Yes, ma'am," said Maggie returning with a dustpan, brush and damp cloth.

Louisa took the opportunity to excuse herself from the drawing room. Taking Sophia by the hand, they climbed the stairs to her bedroom on the first floor.

"Oh Louisa, you should not have made such a terrible mess on my account," admonished Sophia. "Your family have been so kind. Today was wonderful."

"It was necessary Sophia darling," said Louisa. "My father is indulgent where I am concerned but he would have felt obliged to check you had permission. He is suitably distracted now and will think no more of it. Let us get changed into warm clothes. It will take half an hour to walk and we do not want to catch a cold."

They donned coats, gloves and hats and left the house pausing only to say goodbye to Louisa's mother, Marianne, who waved them off from the hallway.

"Take care, Louisa," she said, "how I wish I could join you."

Louisa kissed her mother's cheek. "Thank you mama," she said softly.

Sophia murmured her thanks and they walked up the crunchy gravel drive into Ivry Street.

Louisa took Sophia's arm. "No talking until we are long past your house," she commanded.

They walked swiftly past Sophia's driveway but were no more than twenty yards past when a deep voice boomed, "Hello Sophia, where are you going at this time of day?"

A tall, dark-haired young man emerged from behind a dense bush at the top of the driveway where he had been enjoying an evening cigarette.

Sophia gasped. "It's cousin Daniel," she whispered, turning to Louisa before facing her cousin.

"Where is father?"

"Why are you whispering?" asked Daniel.

"Walk with us a little way," Louisa suggested, attempting to move the conversation away from the house.

They walked to the top of the road before Daniel stopped. "Enough now," he said. "Your reluctance to be seen outside your father's house is quite obvious Sophia. And as for you," he said turning to Louisa, "Who are you? Why do you endeavour to draw us away from Sophia's home?"

Sophia stared at Daniel, eyes brimming with tears. She trembled like a frightened child. "Please do not tell father," she implored.

"Do not tell Charles what, exactly?" asked Daniel. "There is nothing I could tell him even if I wanted to. I have no idea what you are doing or why you feel this apparent need for secrecy."

Louisa sighed. "We are visiting friends in Museum Street," she said, opting for a half-truth.

"Charles may be strict," said Daniel, "but even he would give permission for Sophia to visit friends. It must be more. Tell me the truth."

Sophia swallowed, staring at her gloved hands in abject misery. "We are going to the Woman's Freedom League meeting at the Old Museum," she confessed. "We are avoiding the census enumerator."

"For goodness sake, Sophia," Daniel exploded. "Your father would be appalled. I do not wonder you wish to hide this from him. What are you thinking?"

"She wants to be able to vote," snapped Louisa. "Furthermore, she is willing to do something about it."

Daniel glared. "What utter nonsense," he said. "Your father looks after your political interests." He pointed at Louisa, "and if you are lucky enough to marry, your husband will take over those responsibilities. What could you possibly know of parliament and politics? That is not your domain."

"How can you know better than us just because you were born a man," exclaimed Louisa, and then stopped herself pontificating further upon hearing Sophia's heavy sobs. She was crying with deep, undignified breaths.

"You have upset Sophia with your nonsense," thundered Daniel.

"My nonsense," Louisa responded, "she was perfectly happy until five minutes ago when we encountered you. You are to blame."

Daniel opened his mouth to reply then changed his mind before putting a protective arm around Sophia.

"Are you resolved to see this through?" he asked.

"I must," sniffed Sophia between sobs. "It matters, Daniel. It is the first time in my life I feel any purpose in my privileged existence".

"Your father will never give his permission," Daniel replied. "He will react badly if he ever hears of this." He exchanged a long look with Sophia who held his gaze. A mutual understanding passed between them. For a moment Louisa felt like an outsider watching a carefully crafted family tableau.

Daniel inhaled. A plume of smoke from his cigarette dissolved into the air. He tossed the cigarette butt on the path and ground it to dust with a well-polished shoe. "I was not here. I did not see you," he said walking away.

The girls watched wordlessly as he strode up the road, waiting in silence until he disappeared into the leafy driveway of The Rowans.

"Will he tell?" asked Louisa.

Sophia shook her head. "I do not believe he will," she replied. "But I cannot return home in any event. If he tells father I would welcome a few hours away before I have to confront him and if he does not tell, then all is well. Let us go as planned."

Louisa hooked her arm through Sophia's watching her friend's pale face as she stared back down the street. Sophia slowed, her eyes darting between Louisa and the road beyond.

"Do not worry. We will be discreet," said Louisa, pulling her forward. "The anti-suffragist's have heard of the planned evasion and may seek to stop us. As far as anyone is concerned we are taking an evening walk around The Park."

Sophia exhaled. "Then I shall enjoy our walk," she said.

Picking up the pace they continued through Ivry Street, passing the crossing to Constitution Hill. They walked alongside the Park until they reached the junction of Anglesea Road and Fonnereau Road. Dusk was falling and they heard whispered voices before several women emerged from the shadows.

"Louisa," a voice hissed through the air.

"Ada, Bessie, you have come," whispered Louisa. "This is my friend Sophia. She is coming with us. We will be a merry party."

"Welcome," said Bessie shaking Sophia's hand. "We are pleased to meet you."

"Not a merry party yet," warned Ada. "We have serious work to do tonight, and there are trouble-makers afoot."

"Yes," said Bessie. "There is a large group of people gathered at the other end of Fonnereau Road. "They are carrying banners, bells and whistles; no weaponry that we can see but they know of the proposed meeting and seek to disrupt it."

"Did they try to harm you?" asked Louisa, clutching her cousin's arm.

"No," Bessie reassured. "It is too difficult to tell a suffragist from any other respectable woman which rather hobbles them. They cannot tell whether we go about our normal, lawful business or not."

"We should hurry though," said Ada. "We do not want to take chances with such a crowd afoot. If they reach us and see us enter the Old Museum, they will know our business and have reason to do us harm."

They hurried into the High Street where the gas lamp lighters were starting their evening's work. The few lamps already ignited partly illuminated the way to Museum Street which they reached just before six o'clock.

"Stop," called Louisa, watching a group of men milling around the entrance to the Old Museum. "Do not go any further." She grabbed Sophia's hand and pulled her back.

"Don't worry," said Sophia. "They are friends. I recognise two of them from the meeting at the park."

Ada and Bessie strode forward, greeting the men in friendly voices. "Good evening to you Mr Tippett." Ada shook the hand of a smartly dressed gentleman in a bowler hat and double-breasted jacket. "Is Isobel inside?"

"She is," replied Mr Tippett gesturing to the doorway.

"It is good to see you here," said Bessie. "We met some of the anti-suffragist contingent en route."

Tippett raised an eyebrow. "We thought there might be trouble," he said. "We intend to stay here through the night. Whatever happens, we will make sure you are safe inside."

"Thank you," said Bessie. "We appreciate your support. "Come Louisa," she said beckoning the two younger girls.

Louisa smiled at the men as she walked towards the doorway of the stucco-fronted building with its fluted Doric pilasters standing sentry either side. The building had been retired as a museum long before Louisa was born and she did not know what it had subsequently become. With a frisson of excitement, she realised she might have an opportunity to explore the old building as well as participate in the night's events.

The doorway opened into a hall from which a staircase with a heavy balustrade rose into a galleried landing. Constance Andrews stood at the foot of the stairs with a jug in each hand which she placed on a neatly dressed trestle table containing glasses and a box of Huntley and Palmer's Royal Sovereign biscuits.

"My favourite," whispered Sophia.

"Good evening ladies," said Constance in clipped tones. "Please help yourself to refreshments and go through." She gestured to a door on the right. "There are several ladies here already and more expected from Felixstowe and Lowestoft shortly. Supper will be provided at 8 o'clock and you will have a good breakfast before you leave tomorrow."

"Thank you," said Ada leading the way.

Louisa was disappointed that the room, once full of interesting exhibits, had been converted into a boring office. The furniture had been rearranged for the night's events with dark wooden desks cleared to the side of the large room and a selection of wooden and leather chairs placed at intervals around the perimeter. A fire burned brightly beneath a marble mantelpiece and half a dozen women warmed themselves in front of the flickering flames chatting animatedly.

18

"I'll introduce you," said Ada, ushering the girls towards the group of women. "Isobel, Lilla, please meet my cousin, Louisa and her friend Sophia. They join us tonight."

Louisa shook hands with the well-dressed women to her front pleased to see Sophia's natural shyness evaporate as she joined the conversation.

More women entered until there were thirty or so present and the room filled with chatter until Constance joined them.

"Ladies," she began, "Everyone we expected has arrived and the doors are closed until tomorrow. We are protected and safe so let the revelry begin".

The evening passed in a happy medley of rousing speeches, songs and party games. Constance provided an excellent supper of sandwiches, salads and devilled chicken legs. Louisa particularly enjoyed a slice of raised game pie. Constance apologised for the lack of hot food but her apologies were dismissed by the other women who complimented her on a fine effort, considering the lack of facilities.

The clock was ticking towards midnight when Louisa finished the last of the strawberries in jelly. Her attempt to disguise a yawn beneath her hand failed and she turned to Sophia.

"I am so full and contented I will fall asleep if I do not move around soon," she said.

"Do not worry if you do," laughed Sophia. "Others have." She pointed to Mrs Vincent, a woman of sixty years or so, slumped in a leather armchair. Her ample bosom moved up and down in time with her audible snores. Louisa giggled.

"I know, but I would like to explore this fine old building. Do you mind?"

"Not at all," said Sophia. "Will you mind if I do not join you?"

Louisa smiled, "Of course not," she said. "I am pleased to see you enjoying the company of our new friends. May I take this candle?"

Sophia nodded finishing a small piece of cake before moving closer to Ada and Bessie. They huddled together around the brightly lit chimney breast, warmed by the well-stoked fire. Louisa carried the candle holder, guarding the flame with her hand.

She crossed the room and entered the hallway climbing stairs which creaked and groaned beneath her boots. The stairs opened onto a galleried landing occupied by sturdy dark wood cabinets. The glass framed, polished cabinets still contained remnants of fur and feathers, so Louisa guessed they once housed the museum's exhibits when it was still a museum. She passed the cabinets and opened a narrow, latched door leading to a corridor.

Louisa wrinkled her nose as the smell of damp assailed her nostrils but tip-toed through the corridor until a noise stopped her dead in her tracks. Tap, tap, tap – the noise was rhythmical like the tick-tock of a clock. Louisa shone the candle against the wall with a trembling hand. There was no timepiece; not even a piece of artwork - just white painted walls and four closed doors. For a second the only audible sound was Louisa's heart beating in time with the tapping. Too terrified to retreat up the corridor and downstairs to safety she waited as the seconds ticked by. Then a draught swished the curtain at the far end of the corridor and Louisa saw the branches of a tree tapping against the window.

With the source of the noise revealed, she exhaled and clutched a hand to her chest. "I should return and join the others," she whispered aloud.

When her hands stopped shaking she tried the first two doors at the top of the corridor. Both doors lead to identical offices with ornate desks positioned centrally on the far wall, a leather chair behind and two visitors' chairs to the front of each desk. The mirror-image rooms were devoid of character. Louisa was disappointed and her disappointment heightened as the third door failed to open. It was tightly locked.

The fourth and final door from the corridor squealed open. Louisa entered holding the candle high and almost dropped it at the sight of a skull staring sightlessly towards her from a crate at the end of the room. Logic triumphed before fear got the better of her as she realised the skull was a former exhibit and she must be inside a storage room. On further examination, she found other boxes; one containing frames filled with butterflies and another with a moth-eaten, stuffed polecat. She touched one of the tiny pointed teeth and the jaw wobbled.

"Perhaps not," she murmured, moving to another box.

This box was full of tin cups, spoons and other assorted pieces of household crockery. Sighing she turned to the final box housed on top of an iron safe lurking in the corner of the far wall.

This box appeared more promising. Hanging over the edge were several pairs of handcuffs and the largest bunch of rusted keys Louisa had ever seen. Underneath were pay books, files of minutes in shabby folders and a register of prison officers dating from the 1840's. The bottom of the box contained letters and a dog-eared, black leather diary with mould spores spotted across the spine. Louisa heaved the box to the floor, set her candle on the safe and pulled up a chair from the stacked pile in the corner. Blowing dust from the cover, she opened the front page of the diary. The flickering candle illuminated the fading letters. They read:

"The last days of Mary Emily Cage; a truthful record by Anna Tomkins"

Chapter Three

The Cracks Deepen

The shabby, battered diary commanded Louisa's full attention as she puzzled over the title. Who was Mary Cage? Why had her last days been recorded? She opened the diary and began to read.

"I scarcely know how to start this account, such is the shock of the news my dear Alfred bought home tonight. I am heartbroken to hear him say that one of his prisoners is my own dear childhood companion, Mary Moise. She is Mary Cage now, of course, having married in haste many years ago. I should know. I was there at her wedding, smiling and hoping she would have a good life even though all the portents implied not. She has been in the cells for a whole week and I did not know until today.

This week I returned from a long visit to Ireland where my cousin, Margaret, endured the last gruelling weeks of her pregnancy at her farm house in Galway Town. Of delicate health, Margaret was bed-bound in the final weeks, so my presence was fortunate as Patrick struggled to cope with a sick wife and two young children. He arrived at the station to collect me wearing undisguised relief across his face. He thanked me regularly and often. His unfailing appreciation of my efforts, while Margaret remained incapacitated, made me grateful and embarrassed in equal measures. Despite her frailty, Margaret birthed a fine son called Francis named after her father as he is the second son. Francis thrived and by six weeks of age had grown fat legs and a powerful pair of lungs. Margaret did not need me anymore so I returned home where Alfred greeted me with a beaming smile pleased to see me after an eight week absence. Mary, our eldest girl, is old enough to mind the younger two but Alfred said it was lonely without me and they are happy I am back and have told me not to venture away any time soon.

But what sort of home coming is this? My dear friend is confined in the cells and waiting to die. How will I bear it?

I was aware of the accusations. It was well-known that Mary had been charged with cruelly poisoning her husband but I knew just as well that she could not have done such a terrible thing. Not my Mary. So I expected they would find her innocent. The trial was last Saturday and the judge donned the black cap and found Mary guilty. They are wrong. They must be.

I will go to see Mary Emily tomorrow as early as I can. Alfred will make arrangements for my visit and I will do whatever I may to bring her comfort. I must atone for neglecting her these past twenty years.

But I am at a loss what to do with myself in the meantime. Since Alfred broke the news this evening, I have paced the floor and can find no peace. It is well past midnight and I sit penning this by candlelight as it helps to write about Mary if I cannot talk to her.

I have broken from this account to examine the bookcase in our back bedroom where I keep my old diaries. They are all there; every one I ever wrote. I stole into the room and removed them while the children slept, my youngest Alfred junior snoring quietly as I tip-toed past.

I was luckier than most. My father kept the village store so he learned to read and he sent me to school so I could learn to read too. I learned to count at school unlike most village girls. I signed my name in the parish register on our wedding day. We both did. All four of our children read. We made certain of it.

I am still a long way from sleep so have resolved to copy any entries from my childhood diary into this journal if Mary is mentioned in the narrative. Then I will remember properly ahead of our meeting tomorrow."

29 June 1822 – James and Mary wed yesterday morning. It was a fine day and many villagers attended, celebrating at the Ten Bells Inn after the wedding. James arrived at the church drunk and disrespectful, so Mr Moise admonished him and the rest of the ceremony passed without further incident. James recovered his usual good humour by the evening but Mary sat quietly complaining of tiredness so James took her home in an old cart dressed in bows and ribbons. He carried her ever so tenderly onto the seat and drove the cart home to their new rooms to start married life. I will give them some time together before I see them later in the week.

3 July 1822 – I visited Mary today and found her in good spirits. James has been very attentive since they married and she thinks he is over the worst of his bad behaviour and minded to be a good husband and father. She invited me into her small parlour furnished with a table, two wooden chairs and a carved rocking chair given by her godmother on the day of her wedding. Her bedroom is plain and empty, except for the bed and a small dresser but she says she is content and will make a happy home.

15th July 1822 – I watched Mary walk past our cottage today. She has grown bigger with child in the short time since I last saw her. She waved to me through the window but did not stop. Her arm was tied up with a bandage. I hope she has not had an accident. She will surely call on me if she needs my help.

30 Sep 1822 – Mary's first child is born. She has a new baby daughter called Mary Ann delivered by Mrs Woolner and her daughter, Kezia today. The tiny creature, wearing a permanent frown and a shock of dark hair, entered the world quickly for a first born. I visited Mary as soon as I heard the news to find her tired but eager for me to meet her new daughter. An absent James could not be persuaded away from his toil in the fields but was told of the birth and sent word he would see the baby on his return that night.

27 Oct 1822 – Poor Mary; she has scant milk to give and little Mary cries and cries. Mary Emily is exhausted. I have taken the baby to my rooms several times these last weeks so Mary may rest. James shouts and says he cannot be expected to work in the fields all day if he cannot sleep through the night.

11 November 1822 – Excellent news arrived for me today from Ipswich. Last month I applied to teach at the schoolrooms in Tuddenham Road and the headmistress has written to offer me the position. I travel to Ipswich in two weeks and will reside in nearby Christchuch Street. I work Monday to Friday and one in every three Saturdays, so will be able to visit home most weekends. It is no distance at all. Mother and father are delighted to see me in such a fortunate position.

16 Aug 1823 – I returned on Sunday, visiting Mary for the first time in several months. She is still aggrieved at my decision to move away from the village and we are not such good friends as we once were. I purchased a delicate navy ribbon in the haberdashers in Ipswich Butter Market and used it to trim my old bonnet as a gift for Mary. I called on her and presented her with my gift. She thanked me but put it on the side and did not try it on. Mary Ann is a lively baby and in good health, thank the Lord. Mary loves her but says she is in no rush to have another.

24 December 1823 – What a wonderful Christmas we are set to enjoy this year. Mother and Aunt Jane have talked of nothing else for weeks. I returned to Stonham Aspal Christmas Eve morning by carriage and spent the remainder of the day helping mother trim the house for Christmas Day. We gathered moss, holly, berries and pinecones from the woods behind our house, assembling a respectable wreath, which father hung on the front door. Father's fortunes have increased greatly of late since we acquired more space to stock our wares. He used some of this extra money to purchase a weighty turkey for dinner tomorrow. We are all looking forward to Christmas Day.

26 December 1823 – Christmas day passed in a haze of enjoyment with as much food as we could wish for and the best company. We attended church on Christmas morning, as always, but Mary was not there so I visited her today. She is with child again and not looking forward to carrying it for the next six months. There were no signs of Christmas festivities in her parlour and she looked thin and tired. She says James has been out of work for the last four weeks but will not consider any alternative to labouring in the fields preferring to spend his time in the ale house. She is glum and listless, depressed at James' suggestion that they move to Wetheringsett for farm work. It is but two miles from here but means I will see even less of her.

7 July 1824 – Back home again to see mother. Father was in Colchester these last weeks and mother tends the store alone. We enjoyed a happy few days together and expect Father back tomorrow. She will be exceedingly pleased to see him. Today I visited Mary in Wetheringsett. Her new baby arrived early in May, small and sickly. She named him James after his father and says she hopes James will show more interest in this child than he does in Mary, but so far this has not been the case. I invited Mary to take tea

with us but she declined; a great pity as she is thin and looks exhausted. I asked her if she gets any sleep and she says her mother minds the children from time to time, so she can rest when they are away. Mary says the men are to trim the old barn for a big dance after haysel. I asked her if I should return to the village so we could go together. She agreed providing she can find someone to watch the babies, so it is settled. Mary will be her old self again if she has some cheer in her life.

24 September 1824 – I returned for the harvest dance and it was a jolly affair. Mary's children were minded by her mother so we spent the afternoon together laughing and joking as we did when we were young. Mary wore the bonnet I gave her last year and her best blue dress with the flowered bodice. We danced and sang all evening. Mary laughed and was her former happy self. James grabbed my arm and tried to dance with me. I was polite and danced with him but he was drunk and touched me inappropriately. I did not tell Mary and she did not see as she was singing with the village girls at the time. James was not alone in his enjoyment of alcohol. I was surprised to see Mary drink too. She does not normally but seemed quite merry with it by the end of the evening.

5 April 1825 – Sad news followed my return to the village with the death of Robert Moise. At his age, and living so close to poverty, death is never wholly unexpected but Mary grieves so and her distress is terrible to behold. Mr Moise projected a natural authority in spite of his years and James was always mindful to appease him. There will be nobody to restrain his excesses now. Eunice Moise is head to toe in black. The curtains of her cottage are drawn. She cannot face the world, so Mary has little help with the children.

Baby James has grown little these last few months. He rarely cries but lies in the dresser seldom raising his tiny head. I lifted his frail body as soon as I entered Mary's parlour. He snuggled into my shoulder, shallow breathing in my ear. For such a scrap, he is a dear boy and the love I felt overwhelmed me as I held him, smelling his baby hair and concealing my teary eyes from Mary. In contrast, little Mary is as plump as a butterball and a happier little girl you never did see. With boundless energy and a child's natural curiosity, she tears round the house asking questions about everything she sees. I ruffled her hair as she ran to my side and thought how wonderful it would be to have my own children one day, if I ever meet a man who would marry me. Mary told me she will have another mouth to feed by the end of the year. She is with child again and three months gone already. There is no excitement in her for this child. She does not seem to relish motherhood.

2 May 1825 – I returned home at the behest of my mother. She hastened my return to tell me the awful news, so awful she would not send it in a letter. Baby James has died. My innocent little scrap faded to nothing and was cold and stiff in his dresser drawer one morning. Mother fears Mary is too isolated in Wetheringsett. It is only a short distance from our village but with small children and no means to travel, it might as well be London. I hailed a waggon that afternoon to visit Mary and console with her and I cried all the way to Wetheringsett, remembering little James' soft skin and his sweet baby smell when I last held him; chiding a God who would take such a dear boy for his own.

When Mary opened the door to me I held her close and told her how sorry I was for her loss. She was still numb with grief for she barely acknowledged my words, save to say she will name the new baby James if it is a boy. I tried to help her, offering to watch little Mary or perform some household chore, but our conversation was stilted and full of awkward silences. I felt unable to intrude upon her grief any further, so bid her goodbye.

As I left, her sleeve slid down as she reached for the door latch, revealing blotches and bruises stark against the pale skin of her arm. She dragged her sleeve over her forearm claiming the bruises were from a fall against the dresser. I wanted to believe her and did not pry.

When I returned to Stonham, I walked to St Lamberts and prayed for Little James at the altar. The Reverend approached me and we prayed together. He told me God will look after his little soul and it gave me comfort, so I am minded to tell Mary next time I see her. Perhaps she might benefit from the succour of the church.

22 December 1825 – I returned to the village for Christmas to catch up with the comings and goings in Stonham Aspal. Frederick Abbott is to be wed to the prettiest girl in the village, so we will have another celebration soon. Old Mrs Tydeman and the widow Wright have both died this quarter but neither death was unexpected. They were both poorly and Mrs Tydeman bed-bound these last two years. Another apprentice is employed at the blacksmith's and there is a new assistant at the butchers shop. I love meeting new people and will walk by later and introduce myself.

Mary's new baby is born and it was a boy much healthier and heartier than poor sickly James. They named him the same as his elder brother, as expected. I will visit her tomorrow and bring her all the village news.

23 December 1825 – I witnessed such horror today I scarcely believe my own memories. James Cage is the son of Satan with a dark hole where his heart should be. But I rush to get my words out and must form my sentences in an intelligible manner before I write them down, even though I cannot imagine wishing to recount them again.

I visited Mary today and found her tired and despondent, as is her usual demeanour these days. Mary Ann played contentedly in the corner but baby James bawled, red-faced and angry. Mary raised her eyes and scowled as she opened the door to me. She wasted no time on small talk but warned that James was lying in the bedroom and must have quiet. I picked up the baby, rocking him in the hope he might sleep but he continued to cry. Mary put him to her breast but he did not settle and the crying became a scream. I took him from Mary, inserting a fingertip into his angry mouth, when the door to the bedroom slammed open and James Cage strode into the room. Without uttering a word, he struck Mary about the face with one powerful blow. She reeled backwards, falling into the table. Crockery shattered onto the floor surrounded by a puddle of water from the jug. Mary lay where she fell with the broken items about her. She did not move and laid quite still, conscious but stationery.

"You cannot ill-treat her so," I cried but Cage raised his hand to me and told me I would get the same if I did not leave his house. Mary lifted her head and said 'go' in a firm voice, so I took the children and carried them all the way back to Stonham Aspal where I left them in my mother's care. I sought Mother's advice and she cautioned me to be careful not to get in between a husband and his wife, but the thought of Mary lying immobile on the floor for fear of making her husband angrier was unbearable. My conscience would not let me leave matters alone, so I hastened to the police house and *informed Constable Dawson. He told me he was familiar with the ructions between James Cage and his wife, but could do nothing unless grievous harm was perpetrated. I told him that in my opinion the harm was sufficiently heinous for police involvement but he said it was not. Must she be permanently damaged before they will act? Now I know how bad things are for Mary and I do not think she will thank me for bringing them to the attention of the authorities. Mother still has the little ones. I can only imagine what tomorrow will bring.*

24 December 1825 – Mary walked to our house from Wetheringsett today. She trudged through the sleet with holes in her boots, wrapped in a thin, fraying shawl. I invited her into my mother's parlour but she declined and stood shivering at the front door without stepping across the threshold. I asked whether James was violent towards her before yesterday's attack. She pursed her lips and stared sightlessly down the hallway without responding. I made another attempt. She shook her head then using a flat, monotone voice, told me not to visit again.

I do not know what made me act so impulsively but I pulled her through the door and pushed her into the chair by the fire. I knelt on the floor holding her frozen hand. "Do not ask that of me, Mary" I said. "I am your friend, and will not stand by and watch. Ask anything of me, but do not tell me I am unwelcome in your home." Her steel grey eyes momentarily filled with tears and then she recovered. She said she would not ask me to stay away forever but I should not return to her house soon. She picked up the baby and, taking little Mary's hand, marched from the parlour without further discourse. I ran straight round to John Firman's and asked if his cart was available for hire. It was and he agreed to collect Mary and take her to Wetheringsett so she would not have to walk across the fields in the bad weather again. I paid him the fare and he left to find Mary. I expect that is the last I will see of her until she is prepared to allow me to visit again.

13 April 1826 – Today I spoke with Mary for the first time this year after several abortive visits to Wetheringsett in January and February. On both occasions I knocked at her door but there was no answer. Whether the house was empty or not was impossible to deduce but I left Mary no opportunity to avoid me today when I spotted her leaving the chemist in Debenham. My aunt, Jane

Fairweather, lived there and I was in the town on a long overdue visit. We were taking tea in the parlour when I saw Mary through the window facing the High Street. Pausing only to ask my aunt if she minded me leaving her for a brief time, I ran up the street after Mary. I reached her towards the end of the High Street and tapped her on the shoulder. She turned and smiled; her old self for a moment. Then her face clouded and she turned away. "Talk to me Mary," I pleaded and she relented, suggesting we walk together to the churchyard. We settled on a wooden bench amongst the gravestones of our ancestors, for we both had kin in Debenham, and she began to talk.

She told me James mistreated her since the first days of their marriage. He was more restrained when her father was alive but since his death, had no fear of the consequences of his actions. James was tolerable when sober but a cruel drunk and as he was drunk most of the time, she was often the subject of his bad temper. I asked why she did not leave him but she pushed my hand away. "Where do you think I would go?" she asked scornfully. I suggested her mother might take her but she shook her head and said her mother can only feed herself because she receives poor relief. I said I was sorry to hear this. We sat in silence as she twirled a ringlet of hair round her finger, deep in thought. Then she took a deep breath, and talked frankly of James' meagre income and his inclination to spend the little he earned on ale.

As much as I tried to conceal my pity, a tear stole down my face as she talked of her troubles, but she remained aloof and distant; in complete command of her emotions. I recognised nothing of the warm, joyful girl who was my childhood friend and wondered at the change in a human soul when hope dies. We sat together a while longer but the conversation tailed away. I thought of my aunt waiting for my return, so bid Mary goodbye promising to visit early summer. She leaned towards me, dry lips pecking my cheek, and said she looked forward to my visit. Then we left the churchyard and walked our separate ways. Puckered furrows line this page where my tears fell into the ink while writing the day's events. I would offer money were Mary not too proud to accept. I want to help her, but do not know how.

30

Louisa broke from the diary at the sound of footsteps echoing down the corridor.

"Louisa, where are you?"

"I'm here, Sophia," she called watching as a shadow loomed large in the doorway, followed by Sophia bearing a lamp.

"You've been gone an age," said Sophia. "We were worried. It is past two o'clock in the morning, and many of the women are asleep. Are you not tired?"

"Not in the least," said Louisa. "I found a diary about a wretched woman and her cruel husband. It is a true story and I am only a small way through, so I want to know how it ends. From the inscription at the front, I fear it does not end well".

Sophia laughed. "Surely you do not favour this story over the tales of suffragette escapades we have enjoyed all evening?" she asked. "It is most unlike you, Louisa. You are the ringleader in our adventures."

"And will continue to be," smiled Louisa, "but I am in the grip of this diary. Let me have another half hour with it and I will return to you. I cannot read for much longer anyway. My hands are blocks of ice".

"Bring the book downstairs," suggested Sophia. "It is warm and cosy and Constance is about to make another urn of coffee."

"What a wonderful idea," smiled Louisa, "although I am not sure whether I ought to take the book downstairs. It is not mine and belongs to the Old Museum."

"It will not be missed for the remainder of the night," said Sophia. "Replace it after breakfast tomorrow and no one will be any the wiser."

"I shall," said Louisa, taking her candle in one hand and carrying the diary with her index finger marking her place in the other. Shrugging off the cold she headed back down the corridor and into the welcome warmth of the reception room.

Those women who previously laid claim to the leather chairs were dozing while those in the hard, wooden chairs were resigned to a sleepless night. An ever-diligent Constance Andrews kept the fire burning with flames, leaping and spluttering to provide a comfortable ambient temperature.

"Have my chair," said Sophia, directing Louisa to her seat next to the fire. "Your poor hands are freezing."

"Thank you," said Louisa. "Will you think me rude if I keep reading?"

"Only if you do not recount the story fully to me tomorrow," smiled Sophia, so Louisa continued.

9 July 1826 – The inevitable happened and Mary lies seriously ill in my mother's spare bedroom after a beating that left her black and blue. Her poor lips are swollen and her chest and neck a purple mess of bruising. Mary arrived at mother's door two days ago in the dark of night with her two bewildered children. They walked by moonlight with no candle or lantern to light the way, only seeking help because Mary lost so much blood she feared she would die, leaving her children alone with Cage.

Mother sent word to Ipswich and I arrived today to see her battered and broken in my home. I asked her to promise never to return to Cage but she has no other means to live and will not give her word. Fortunately both children are hearty creatures and have settled well. After much persuasion, Mary agreed to remain with us until the end of the month.

15 July 1826 – Mary is much recovered and relieved to be living in Stonham Aspal once again. Her health has improved, and she felt well enough to visit friends at Lasts' farm this morning. She was so much her old self when she returned it gladdened my heart. She says she will go again tomorrow and all the other days until she leaves us.

17 July 1826 – I feel uneasy today. Mary talks not just of her girlfriends, but of a young man she met at the farm. He is employed by Mr Last to repair a brick wall around the stable yard. She tells me they have talked together a great deal and she is very taken with him. Whatever her justification in staying apart from James Cage, she must remember she is a married woman. I have advised her to avoid this friendship.

25 July 1826 – Mary continues to see her bricklayer, George Thurlow. She says they only talk together but I know her well enough to be sure she is excessively fond of him. I made some discreet enquiries about the village to see what kind of character Mary has acquainted herself with. George was born in Stonham Aspal and, although I do not know him well, others do. They say he is charming and a bit of a rogue. He is a favourite with many of the village girls, but has shown no interest in any of them, or so I am told. I believe this friendship unwise and have been quite forthright in telling Mary my feelings. I have not mentioned George to my mother as she would not countenance this behaviour under her roof.

31 July 1826 – Mary tells me she is resolved to return to Wetheringsett. I wish she would not go but she knows she cannot remain here, and has no money to go anywhere else. She saw James Cage a few days ago and he says he will have her back and will mend his ways. He admits an excess of beer makes him violent and has told Mary he will not drink so much if she returns. She understands her friendship with George cannot continue and could lead to a great deal of trouble if she stays in our village. I said my goodbyes with a heavy heart. I do not trust James Cage. I do not believe a single word he utters. But Mary seems to love him still despite his heavy-handed ways, so I am resigned to her return to Wetheringsett.

8 November 1826 – This is surely the saddest day of my life. My gentle, loving mother passed away suddenly in her bed Sunday evening. She retired early feeling out of sorts and my poor father found her marble cold when he returned from the store. I will never feel her gentle touch or hear her words of comfort again. I cannot bear it. I am accustomed to the solitude of being an only child but the burden of trying to console my dear father alone while my own grief is so raw is more than I can endure.

Fortune favoured me with a kind and loving family and I have grown up with such affection that the loss of it makes me almost wish I never had it at all. Our homely kitchen is dark and cold, the fire unlit, the table bare. I sit beside mother's chair in the parlour at night, the arms worn away where she sat and sewed. Grandmother's old shawl lies across the back and carries the scent of my mother. The indentation where she sat remains but my mother will never occupy this chair again. Last night I woke after a fitful sleep, to muffled noises downstairs. I tip-toed in the hallway and saw father sitting at the kitchen table, head in hands, sobbing like a small boy. It broke my heart to see him but I could not comfort him for it would have made him feel worse to think I had witnessed his grief.

My mother will be interred at St Lamberts tomorrow. She will lie in the cold, frost-bitten ground and we will see her no more. I pray God will keep her safe and guide her to heaven.

9 November 1826 – I am numb. My heart is broken. I write because I cannot sleep. Perhaps I will never sleep again. We bade our final goodbyes to mother early this morning. It was even colder today and our breath hung heavy in the air. Many people joined us at church. Mother's kin arrived from Debenham and fathers' from Kenton. And in the cold November air we laid her to rest.

I am all cried out now. There are no more tears to fall even though I am sadder than I have ever been. My aunt Jane remained with us. She will keep house for the next week until she must return to Debenham. Mother was the last of her sisters, so her grief is considerable. She tried to persuade my father to eat a little for he has hardly touched a morsel in days. He tried some bread and butter, but pushed it away after a few bites. I have never seen him so upset. He has not opened the store since my mother was taken from us.

24 December 1826 – Christmas Eve is a hollow day this year; a mess of warm memories of Christmases past and the cold horror of our present reality. I travelled home to spread what Christmas cheer I may but father has lurched from one extreme to the other and keeps to his shop until late at night. It seems he cannot face Christmas without mother. Indeed, he seems reluctant to set foot in the house if he can avoid doing so.

I tried to make a Christmas wreath this morning. I ventured into the woods carrying mother's wicker basket and gathered ivy, moss and pinecones from the dewy forest floor. It was the loneliest walk I have ever taken but I knew mother would have wanted me to trim the house for father, so I persevered. I sat outside on the edge of the well fashioning a wreath of sorts from the collection of foliage and then tied a bright red ribbon about it. The wreath is not as good as the one mother and I made together. My sadness is woven into its very structure but I think mother would have been proud that I tried. I prepared a small chicken for tomorrow's dinner, as it is only for two of us. I usually look forward to Christmas but this year I dread it.

26 December 1826 – Christmas Day was an ordeal better forgotten. We tried to be cheerful as mother would have wished, but it was an impossible task. From the moment I saw father sitting in his chair in the parlour staring misty-eyed into the fire, I knew I did not have the strength to carry on. A lump grew tight in my throat and I could not swallow it down. I could not move, could not pretend. My father looked into my eyes and the grief seared through my body emerging in an agonised moan as the tears coursed down my face like drops of molten metal. I cried in great shuddering sobs until I could cry no more and my father cried with me.

When there were no tears left, we sat watching the rain streak down the windows. He talked of his life with mother before I was born, and of their courtship and her family and many things I never knew. By the end of the day so much grief was spent, we were exhausted; but it was cathartic. For the first time, I thought we could be happy again one day.

27 December 1827 - I visited Mary today as I had not seen her since mother's funeral. She came alone to the church that day leaving her children I know not where. I can hardly imagine they were with their father, but she spoke kindly of my mother at the funeral which gave me some small comfort. Her living quarters are unchanged. They are cold and spartan with her roof in a poor state of repair and leaking badly. I asked her how things were between her and James. She changed the direction of the conversation and talked of other things without answering my question, so I think they cannot be good.

She said she missed my mother dreadfully. Mother made her feel safe and our home had been a place of sanctuary. She held my hand, saying how sorry she was for my loss but that she also felt mother's absence keenly. I was grateful for her appreciation of my mother, but irritated that she mentioned the loss of her safe house despite her recognition of my loss and my grief. Perhaps this is unfair but I am not minded to be charitable while my own grief is so raw. I stayed at Mary's but half of an hour. She was not in a talking mood and the silence became uncomfortable. Mary Ann, normally so lively, was subdued and listless. Little James was quiet too. Mary seemed pre-occupied, so I took my leave.

5 May 1827 - I have returned from Ipswich four times so far this year to spend time with Father. Each time I leave, hoping his spirits will improve before the next visit, even if only a little. But his sorrow overwhelms him and he does nothing but work and sleep. He is

thinner than he should be, despite employing Mrs Johnson to cook and clean while he works. Even her renowned baking cannot tempt him to eat.

I decided to visit Mary today, so Mr Firman took me to Wetheringsett in his cart. Mary was not at home, so it is a good thing I did not walk all the way over for the visit to come to naught. When I returned from Wetheringsett I stopped at the church to pay my respects to mother and met Alice and Susan Hunt at the lychgate. They talked of village matters and told me that James Cage was making free with his fists again. Perhaps that is why Mary was so quiet during my last visit. I cannot be sure this is not idle gossip, so will try to put it from my mind. Mother has a gravestone at last. It is a fine granite stone with a simple inscription. "Florence Saunders, 1781 – 1826 - Well loved by all who knew her"

Chapter Four

A new acquaintance

20 August 1827 – I have not returned to Stonham Aspal this month, so father's letters bought the village news. Although I have been busy, truth to tell, I have become acquainted with a pleasant young man who walks with me from my lodgings to the school some mornings. He works at the prison here in Ipswich but lodges nearby, which is how we met. Alfred is kind and full of interesting stories about his work. I am reluctant to leave town so early in our acquaintance. Is this selfish? What would my mother think of me neglecting my father so?

27 August 1827 – I received a further letter from my father bringing alarming news. James Cage was caught stealing plate and silverware from The Old Hall, with three others. This is not the first time he has been charged with larceny, although he was treated leniently on the last occasion. This time is a different matter. He has stolen from powerful people and I cannot think that he will escape without a custodial sentence.

How will poor Mary live? James squanders much of what he earns but if he is gaoled she will be dependent upon poor relief, possibly even the workhouse. We must hope they show mercy but he has come to the attention of the authorities too many times to expend much hope.

1 November 1827 – I returned to Stonham Aspal last night with Alfred. We travelled together in the wagon all the way to the village, but decided it was too soon for him to meet my father. My mother has not lain in the earth a whole year yet and we think it insensitive for him to make father's acquaintance this soon even though we are walking out together. Perhaps next year would be better.

My father was pleased to see me and confessed his loneliness in the absence of my mother even with the comings and goings of people in his store. As soon as I reached the village, I learned that James Cage had been committed to trial and sentenced to nine months hard labour inside Ipswich Gaol. This is irony indeed, for Alfred works in the gaol and will no doubt encounter Cage in the course of his duties. I am saddened for Mary and do not know how she will cope without his income, however small. I am resolved to visit her tomorrow and offer her what little comfort I may.

2 Nov 1827 – Mary was at home when I visited earlier and in good spirits. Though James is absent and she has no income, her mother agreed, after much persuasion, to let her live at her house in Stonham Aspal for a few months. It will be a tight squeeze for her and the children in the cramped little cottage and I do not know how they will manage, but it is an improvement for Mary to be back in the village where people know her and can help. James is two years old now and Mary Ann five, so they are less demanding. Mary Emily seems happier and is excited about the prospect of returning to Stonham. A cart is due to collect her and her scant possessions on Sunday, so she will be installed at Mrs Moises' house by the end of this weekend.

She was in such good spirits I felt able to tell her about Alfred and how much I like him and what a gentleman he is. She asked if I might marry him and I told her I could not say, for he had not asked me and I did not know whether he ever would. But I do like him, so very much, and Mary is the one person I can tell.

21 December 1827 – I arrived early for Christmas this year to be met with the most scandalous news. Mary resolved her problem of how to live without an income by taking up with George Thurlow who she met last year. Upon hearing this information, I hastened down the street to Mary's mother's cottage and asked to see Mary at once. The children were still living with Eunice, but Mary had moved into George Thurlow's lodgings by the Green where she dwells with him in sin.

I found her there some half an hour later in a state of great contentment and fully cognisant of the damage to her reputation. "I love him," she told me, " and he loves me." When I asked her what she would do when James left prison she put her nose in the air and told me she did not care. She said George would look after her and see that no harm came to her when James returned. I asked her if she was sure of this and she said he had told her so. I met George when I returned later that evening. He is an affable chap and good company but he is young with no ties. I cannot see why he would wish to take on a married woman and her children. I have not told my father I visited Mary. Her name is blackened in the village and I am sure he would prefer me not to associate with her scandal.

4 April 1828 – I took much pleasure in visiting Stonham accompanied by Alfred who was meeting my father for the first time. Alfred lodged at the Ten Bells for the sake of propriety while I stayed with my dear father as usual. Mrs Johnson cooked a hearty supper today and father invited Alfred to dine. My aunt Jane arrived from Debenham and joined us. Father talked at length with Alfred. It appears that Alfred's aunt is distant kin to us by marriage. This first meeting seems to have gone well. Father asked Alfred to join us for lunch tomorrow, so I am exceedingly happy that the people I care most about seem easy in each other's company.

5 April 1828 – Today was good and bad in equal measures. Alfred, Aunt Jane and I spent a pleasant morning in Debenham later returning to Stonham by cart where we joined father for lunch. He seemed much taken with Alfred and shut the store for an extra half hour when they went to the Ten Bells together for a drink, while Aunt Jane and I helped Mrs Johnson clear the dinner dishes away. I cannot remember the last time father went to the public house and though I am not a great lover of beer drinking I think it will do him good to be sociable and join the other men, for once.

On their return, father re-opened the shop and I asked Alfred if he would mind if I visited my friend, Mary. He asked if he might join me but I made my excuses in case George Thurlow was present. I do not want him to know any detail about Mary's life or wish him to judge her only on this recent misdemeanour, so I made an excuse about Mary being shy and Alfred returned to the Ten Bells to read the local newspaper, as was his inclination.

It turned out to be a wise course of action as I quickly discovered the extent of Mary's shame. How it is not public knowledge about the village, I know not, but Mary's stomach is much pronounced and she is quite obviously with child. It is equally obviously not the child of her husband who has been incarcerated since October. Anxious to avoid an argument but unable to pretend I had not noticed, I asked outright whether she carried George Thurlow's child. She said she did but it was of no consequence as they would continue to live together as husband and wife when James Cage returned from gaol. She cared nothing for public opinion and was content for the first time in many years. George treated her kindly and she had known only cruelty from James. Her behaviour is morally wrong but her logic impeccable. How can I condemn her for her shameful conduct when living with her husband would surely be harmful? I told her I understood but did not invite her to meet Alfred. There is too much potential for trouble.

1 July 1828 – I was delighted to see my father when he visited my lodgings in Christchurch Street today. We spent an enjoyable time together joining Alfred in Christchurch Park where we lunched on sandwiches and fruit. It was a beautiful, cloudless day and the sun shone so brightly we were quite burnt by the end of it. Father walked me back to my lodgings at the end of the afternoon before boarding the coach to Stonham Aspal.

On the way to the coach he said two things both of which caused me great discomfort. Firstly, he asked if Alfred intended to make an honest woman of me. I could not answer as Alfred has never spoken of it. I know he likes me a great deal and treats me with the utmost respect. He holds my hands, kisses my cheek and has dined more than once with my beloved father but has never discussed a future with me. Perhaps he does not love me and sees this more as a friendship. As I write this diary I am in a state of considerable confusion.

The second disconcerting utterance from my father was the news that James Cage had returned to the village. I might have known this sooner had I risked speaking to Alfred about Cage but I did not want Mary's shame reflected upon me, so have said nothing of it. It turns out that James returned over a month ago to find his wife taken up with another man and big with child. He confronted George Thurlow, hit him hard and chased him off. George Thurlow has not been seen in the village since and is rumoured to be here in Ipswich. Cage took Mary and the children back to Wetheringsett. I dread to think what treatment she will endure at his hands after this and am even more surprised that he has taken her back at all and not abandoned her to the workhouse. I asked father if there was any word of Mary's condition and he said he had heard nothing, but would make enquiries.

40

5 July 1828 – I could not rest for worrying about Mary and ventured back to Stonham Aspal for one night only. Father was most surprised to see me but pleased as it gives him company. Father had business in Wetheringsett, so we rode by cart together and I went to Mary's rooms while he visited Mr Allen, the blacksmith.

Mary was there but James was not, thank the lord, so we were able to speak undisturbed. But she is broken. She is but a shadow of how she was only a few short months ago. She sat upon one of her hard wooden chairs for her rocking chair is gone and I know not where, and dare not ask; staring at the dying embers of the fire through faraway eyes. Her hair is unkempt, her clothes dirty and, God forgive me for noticing it, but she smells badly. The whole dwelling, leaking and musty, gave an air of melancholy that bought me low. A depression was settled across the household and even the children lay still on the floor, perfectly subdued by the all-pervading atmosphere of gloom.

I must have gasped aloud for she asked me how I was without moving her gaze from the fireplace. I took her hands and, ignoring the smell of her, looked into her eyes and asked her to tell me what ailed her so. She stared back, eyes unfocussed. "He is gone," she said. I asked her who was gone and she answered George and then she cried and I held her close until her sobbing ceased. Not since she was a young child have I known Mary to cry. A mistress of composure, she has never given in to tears before no matter how justified her circumstance. She must be distraught at the loss of her man.

I asked her where George had gone and whether he would come back. She said she did not know where he had gone but he would not come back and she knew because he sent one of his kin to tell her. He said she should remain with her husband and their love could be no more. He was not cruel in the words that he sent but he was firm, and resolved never to return to the village to live.

I watched as she stood from the chair and dropped two dirty white pills into a cup of liquid, gulping it down with such a lack of care that the liquid fell about her clothing. She told me that James intended to raise the child as his own. I professed surprise at this news which appeared out of character. She further surprised me by saying that James was not wholly bad and that although he did not

41

take time with the children, neither was he cruel or neglectful to them. He reserved that behaviour for her. She said he had not been violent since her return. She is due to birth her new child imminently, so I pray this state of affairs continues.

15 August 1828 – Father writes to tell me that Mary's child is born; she has a little boy who she named Richard. I mentioned Mary's baby to Alfred, but have not told him the circumstances of the birth. As far as he is concerned it is a child born of wedlock. I asked Alfred if he ever thought to have a child of his own one day. He smiled at me and said that he hoped fate would give him the opportunity. I do not know how to interpret this.

18 September 1828 – I arrived back in the village late this evening, as father had written to say he wished to discuss a matter of great importance, but did not wish to do so by post. We dined together, and he disclosed that he proposed to sell the store and use the proceeds to retire to Ipswich; but only with my blessing. I was taken aback by this news. Not only I have lived in Stonham Aspal my entire life but father has lived there the vast majority of his. He tells me what I already knew. He is lonely without my mother, and the house holds too many memories of happier times. He has a few kinsmen and a good friend in Ipswich and with my residing there too, thinks he could be happy in this altered location. I said, of course, he must do whatever is necessary for his fulfilment and that I would support him in this endeavour. He anticipates it will take a good many months to find a purchaser for the store and the cottage, so it will be sometime in the next year before he moves.

We sat by the fire and talked of happier days, remembering my childhood and our precious time with mother and then he asked after Alfred. I did not want him to ask about Alfred's intentions towards me, so I feigned tiredness and went to bed. Out of earshot of father, I curled up in my blankets and cried for my mother, the loss of her and now the loss of my childhood home where her love and kindness still lingers.

19 September 1828 – It was a warm, if slightly breezy autumn day, so I walked across the fields to Wetheringsett passing several others along the way. The door to Mary's house was wide open but I knocked before entering, to find her sitting on the wooden chair nursing her new son. She looked tired and wan. Mary Ann stood beside her stroking the baby's head and patting his cheek. He has a head of dark hair just like George. There is no doubting the father as James is fair-haired, as are their other two children. I asked her if she felt any better and she replied she felt somewhat better and that she would be fully recovered before long. I did not believe her but she has re-gained a little of her steely determination, so perhaps she will. I asked about George but she said never to mention his name again. He is gone from her thoughts forever.

22 December 1828 – I have returned to Stonham Aspal for Christmastide, as is my custom, to find father no further forward with his sale of the store and quite despondent about his prospects. He longs to leave the village now and says he cannot face another year here amidst his memories. I asked him if he would not miss the proximity of mother lying in the churchyard so close by. He replied that she was not there anymore. She was with him and would always be with him wherever he was settled. I was glad to hear that as he has suffered enough.

My Aunt Jane joins us for Christmas again this year. She arrived a few days since and has trimmed the house for us in time for Yule. There is a wreath upon the door which is a considerable improvement on my poor attempt last year. I was pleased to be spared this task, as it upset me sorely Christmas last. I intend to visit Mary tomorrow although I cannot profess to be looking forward to seeing her. She has been in such low spirits of late.

23 December 1828 – I did not visit Mary for such a momentous event occurred it went right out of my mind. All my hopes and prayers have come to fruition and I am truly happy for the first time since mother was taken from us. Father is overjoyed; but I digress and must write this down chronologically for my future pleasure.

Father and I breakfasted early this morning and I walked to the butchers at his bequest to purchase our supper. On my return I was most surprised to see a carriage at our front door. I entered our home to find Alfred and my father in conference in the parlour. Father saw me and waved me away, so I stood in the garden puzzled and upset to think that Alfred was here unexpectedly and father did not wish me to be privy to their conversation. I paced the garden in my confusion watching the chickens, only half hearing their throaty clucks, when the kitchen door opened and Alfred strode towards me, a big smile on his handsome face.

He approached me and said, "my dearest Anna, how I love you so." Those were his exact words, recorded here for posterity. "My dearest Anna..." I could listen to those words for ever more. Then he knelt down on the frozen earth, and asked me if I would have him for a husband and he reached into his pocket and pulled out a golden ring. I cannot say how surprised I was and how much I had longed to hear those words. At first I could not answer for the tears streamed down my face but once I composed myself, I said 'yes' so loudly and firmly he could have been in no doubt of my devotion. So we are now betrothed and I am sublimely happy.

I told him I did not think he wanted to marry me and he said that he had wanted to almost since the day we first met but he did not feel his prospects were good enough. Mr Bowden, his superior, retired last week and they have given him extra duties at the prison, together with a greater salary. He has enquired about property and should be able to acquire a small house for us to live in. My father has given his consent with much pleasure and will re-locate close by so we might see him regularly. I cannot believe my good fortune. Alfred stayed for supper and father opened a bottle of his best port and a merry time was had by all. Alfred left for the Ten Bells where he will stay for the Christmas period and in two days he will join us for our first Christmas lunch together. I am overjoyed.

25 December 1828 – We rose early and made our way to church where Alfred joined us for the Christmas morning service. After the sermon, father approached the reverend and asked him if he would marry us which he agreed to do most eagerly. Alfred wishes us to marry late next year so he may save enough to acquire our property before we are wed giving father ample time to sell the store and his cottage.

Aunt Jane and Alfred walked back to our house while father and I tended to my mother's grave. I whispered my news while I cleaned the tombstone as I wanted her to know from me. Father took my arm as we returned to the cottage, and told me how happy he was and what a sensible young man he thought Alfred to be. Father, Aunt Jane, Alfred and I ate a hearty Christmas dinner after saying grace. It was a happier and more substantial repast than last Christmas.

29 December 1828 – I returned to my lodgings in Christchurch Road and soon realised that I had forgotten to visit Mary in all the excitement of Christmas. I write this as an aide to memory. I will arrange to see Mary at the first opportunity in the New Year. I must not forget my obligation to my old friend.

15 March 1829 – Alfred and I arrived in Stonham Aspal on a beautiful spring day to cobalt blue skies and a welcoming procession of daffodils along the roadside. I love my village but especially in the spring. It is a magical season invoking boundless optimism for the year ahead. The weather was so alluring that virtually all able-bodied villagers found reason to be outside. Women bustled around the village carrying out errands while the fields were full of working men in shirt sleeves; jackets and smocks lying in heaps on the ground.

Alfred lodged at the Ten Bells as usual; glad to re-acquaint himself with Mr Pepper, the proprietor, with whom he has built a steady and enduring friendship. Alfred tells me they talk into the small hours when he visits but what they find to speak of for so long, I do not know. Alfred took his bag into the inn while I sought Father in his shop. He was in high spirits having secured a buyer for the store who will purchase it imminently. Father also found a separate purchaser for the cottage who is willing to wait until October which enables father to settle in Ipswich after we are married.

Mindful that I had not visited Mary for some considerable time, I stopped at Mr Firman's on the way back to the cottage and asked him to drive me to Wetheringsett on the morrow. He told me that Mary has moved to another smaller abode within Wetheringsett as James could not find work over winter and money was scarce.

16 March 1829 – I travelled to Wetheringsett today with Mr Firman. Alfred was dismayed that I did not ask him to join me but was too polite to ask my reasons. I am not entirely sure what they are myself. I am not ashamed of Mary, so why do I feel unable to introduce her to my betrothed? Suffice it to say I did visit Mary, but alone.

Neither Mr Firman nor I knew the location of Mary's new dwelling, so I asked a passing villager and he pointed towards a little wooden structure leaning against the crumbling wall of a nearby cottage. My heart sank. Mary's former rooms were of the most basic kind, leaking and cold but this shack was barely standing and I dreaded what I might find inside. I knocked on the pitted wooden door. Mary was home and answered the door to me. She stood at the doorway, dusty and unkempt with the same glazed eyes I had grown accustomed to.

"What do you want?" she growled. I was taken aback at her hostility but said I had come to visit her and was sorry that I had not seen her at Christmas but time had been pressing. She replied, saying that it was a shame I had not told her about my engagement and that she was hurt to hear it from one of the village gossips. She asked me if I was too grand for my old friends now that I was to be married. I said "No, not at all," and she said if that was the case, why did I not introduce her to my intended? And I had nothing to counter her with. Nothing at all, because I had battled with this thought myself and did not know or could not admit the reason why. Then she told me to go and slammed the door in my face. I stood, shocked for several moments, then knocked again but she did not reply. I believe I have lost her, my childhood friend. I have been careless of her feelings and now she is gone.

14 October 1829 – I marry in a few days and have returned to my village for the last time as Anna Saunders. Soon I will be Mrs Anna Tomkins. How wonderful those words sound. My father took leave of his store in early summer and since then has lived a work-free life as a man of means. His cottage is sold but will not be vacated until the end of this month when he follows us back to Ipswich forever. I attempted to visit Mary yesterday in the hope of repairing our friendship before I leave the village. She was not at home but a neighbour asked what I wanted with her and told me she was about the village somewhere. The neighbour spoke disparagingly of Mary and told me that she had lately been called to the overseers who quizzed her for confirmation of her bastard son's father, so they might claim maintenance for the child. James Cage has worked little these last months and the household is in extreme poverty and want. I walked the streets of Wetheringsett for half an hour but could not see Mary, so left with an unfinished task and a heavy heart.

18 October 1829 – I was married today and now carry the name Mrs Alfred Tomkins. My heart is full of love for my husband and I am excited to return to Ipswich tomorrow to make our new life at our

home in Woodbridge Road. I could not be happier save for one thing. I hoped against hope that Mary would attend my wedding, as I did hers, but she did not appear. Nor has she sent me good wishes or congratulations. I have lost her forever. I start tomorrow with a bright new future and a heart full of hope, so do not wish to be reminded of things I cannot change. This, my first diary entry as a married woman, will also be my last. I pray I shall have a happy life and I wish Mary all the love and luck in the world.

Chapter Five

Come the Dawn

"But that cannot be the end of it," exclaimed Louisa. "There is a substantial part of the journal still to be read."

"You are back with us," said Sophia, smiling indulgently at her friend. "And just in time too. Breakfast is not far off and I am exceedingly hungry"

"I am hungry too, "said Louisa, as the aroma of coffee filled the air and her stomach growled in an unladylike manner. "I quite lost myself in this diary, Sophia," she confessed. "There is much more to read but I do not have time to indulge in it now."

"No you cannot," agreed Sophia. "We have lost you to your reading most of the night and you have missed some chilling stories of the suffering of our comrades in London. Bessie gave a harrowing account of the conditions endured by her friend, Marion, when she was arrested in Kensington. The violence and language used by the police is barely imaginable."

"I have heard of it," said Louisa, "but not the whole account. I have been self-indulgent tonight and left you on your own with women you do not know well. Forgive me, Sophia."

"There is nothing to forgive. I have been perfectly at ease with my new friends. Life has bought me few challenges, Louisa. My family have means and I have never known a day of hunger in my life. I may not always be happy but I enjoy a privileged existence. You have opened my eyes to politics and the enfranchisement of women and I have never felt more alive. I will always be grateful to you for introducing me to these wonderful women and their noble mission."

"You are truly altered Sophia. Where is my shy friend who would not say boo to a goose?" teased Louisa.

"She is still here," said Sophia, "but now she has a purpose."

"Coffee, ladies?" asked the bright, authoritative voice of Constance Andrews. She bustled into the room and passed the girls two delicate china tea cups full of steaming hot liquid, which clattered against the saucers with the speed of her delivery.

"Thank you," they said in unison.

"She is marvellous," sighed Sophia again. "She has been awake all night long, given speeches, kept our spirits high and she makes breakfast with her own hands and very little help from anyone else. Is there anything she cannot do?"

"She amply demonstrates the importance of the suffrage movement," agreed Louisa. "There are many strong and capable women like her who should be allowed to take the lead in national matters."

"What are you ladies discussing?" asked Ada Ridley as she joined the two girls at their seats by the dwindling fire.

"Louisa has finally taken her nose out of the book," said Sophia wickedly. "She remembers why we are here today."

"A good thing too," said Ada. "We have much progress to make. This is only the middle part of a long journey and we have far to go."

They looked up to see Constance Andrews standing at the entrance to the doorway clapping her hands. "Breakfast is served," she said, gesturing to the hallway where pastries and breads were neatly arranged on trays. A delicious aroma of bacon pervaded the room and Louisa was left wondering how on earth Constance had found the means to cook food.

"I will only keep you for a few moments," announced Constance. "I do not want the food you have earned so well to go cold, but I would like to express my heartfelt-gratitude for your attendance here tonight. I hope it has not been too uncomfortable. There is a small gift for each of you," she continued, gesturing towards a square metal tray upon which thirty or forty button badges in the purple and green colours of the suffragette movement, had been placed. "It is not much, I know, but I hope you will wear it with pride and remember our night of peaceful protest."

Another woman well past her prime creaked unsteadily to her feet. She was unfamiliar to Louisa who realised what an opportunity she had missed by failing to become acquainted with the other local suffragists during the night.

"We thank you for your endeavours, Constance," the woman said in a deep, hearty voice. "This protest was successful due to your planning and efficiency. We are indebted to you, as always."

Louisa jumped to her feet, "Hear, hear," she cried. The elderly woman acknowledged her with a nod before asking the women to express their appreciation properly. Applause echoed round the room and a red-faced Constance clapped her hands again asking for everyone's attention.

"Breakfast is getting cold. Go and eat," she commanded.

After breakfast small groups of women began to leave until there were only half a dozen left in the building.

"I must return this journal," said Louisa. "But how can I finish the tale?"

"It is highly unlikely you will return," said Sophia. "If you put the book back you will never know how the story ends."

Louisa bit her lip and considered the matter for a few moments. She studied the journal and thrust it into the pocket of her coat.

"Finish your coffee and let us go," she said.

The girls emerged from the Old Museum into the chill April morning. The sky was a gloomy grey and raindrops danced along the sodden pavements. Two men stood by the door smoking pipes under a large black umbrella. "Good morning ladies," they said, doffing their hats.

"Good morning," said Louisa smiling, "and thank you for your protection."

"Our pleasure," said the taller of the two men.

Louisa and Sophia waited momentarily for the Ridley sisters but the sky seemed to darken and they left lest the light drizzle turned into a downpour.

"We should leave immediately," said Sophia. "My father believes I am safely ensconced at your house. If I arrive home soaked to the skin it will give the game away."

"Yes, we will go straight to The Poplars," said Louisa. "We cannot avoid getting wet as we have no umbrella but we can hasten back and dry ourselves by the fire before you go home."

The two girls hurried through town glad to take advantage of a sudden break in the rain. By the time they walked to the bottom of Christchurch Park the drizzle had virtually stopped and a feeble sun pushed through the clouds. But the sun was no indicator of a change of fortune. From the moment they turned the corner into Ivry Street, it was clear that something was awry.

"Who is that?" asked Louisa, pointing to the shiny black carriage of a hansom cab. A man tickled the ears of chestnut-coloured horse, as it pawed nervously at the ground.

"I do not know," said Sophia. "But it has stopped outside The Rowans and we are not expecting visitors."

"Perhaps they visit us?" suggested Louisa, "or they have settled in the wrong location. They could be visiting Mrs Elliot at The Laburnums."

"No, I think not," protested Sophia. She stopped in the street. "I hope they have not discovered my absence from your house. Perhaps they know I did not reside with you last night. I will be in a great deal of trouble and not permitted to see you again."

"Stop," said Louisa. "It is not the police, if that is what you think. There is no insignia on the carriage and the cabman wears a bowler hat, not a policeman's helmet. Stay calm; do not worry."

Louisa slipped her arm through Sophia's. They crossed the road to the opposite side walking hastily towards the cab in the hope that it would mask them from Sophia's family when they passed the drive. But they could not resist glancing towards the house as they tiptoed past noticing Daniel and several of the servants waiting in the turning circle of the driveway. Sophia stopped suddenly as Minnie ran towards her.

"Miss Sophia," she called. "Come quickly."

"What is it?" asked Sophia. "What is wrong?"

"Come here Minnie," commanded a hard voice in an unmistakable Suffolk accent. "Don't interfere. Mr Daniel will deal with this."

"Sorry miss," said Minnie, lowering her head. She scurried towards the upright figure of Jane Piggott, the cook.

Daniel strode down the driveway towards Sophia who flinched as he came closer.

Louisa instinctively walked in front of her friend. "Leave her alone," she said.

Daniel ignored her, turned to face Sophia and gently took her hand.

"What is wrong?" asked Sophia. "You are not angry with me. Has something happened?"

"Dear Sophia, try not to worry," said Daniel. "Your father was taken ill last night and has been in a great deal of pain and distress ever since. The doctor was called at first light and is treating your father as best he can. Your mother would appreciate some support, so you should come home immediately."

"Poor mother," exclaimed Sophia. "She must be very worried."

"She is more at ease now the doctor has arrived," said Daniel, "but she has had little sleep and will be pleased to see you."

"Do they know where I was last night?" asked Sophia.

Daniel pursed his lips. "They have better things to think about," he admonished. "Your secret is safe. I have no wish to make trouble for your parents at this difficult time though I must insist you do your duty and return with me now. Please leave all this nonsense alone, at least until your father has recovered."

Louisa opened her mouth to protest but stopped as Daniel put his finger to his lips.

"I am sure you agree that Sophia should return and comfort her mother," he said abruptly.

"You should," conceded Louisa. "I will look in on you tomorrow, Sophia, and hope to hear good news of your father."

She watched as Daniel escorted Sophia up the driveway and into the house then rushed towards The Poplars, bursting through the door and into the path of her sister Charlotte.

"Take care, Louisa," exclaimed Charlotte. "You nearly had me over."

"Charles Drummond is sick," said Louisa. "The doctor has been called."

"Hold the front page," said Charlotte. "This is hardly big news. What ails him?"

"I do not know but it is serious and painful," said Louisa.

"How unpleasant," replied her sister, "though I am sure he will soon recover. Do not worry yourself."

"You are right," said Louisa, "it will pass. You should have come with us last night though," she continued. "It was everything I hoped for with speeches and songs and horrifying tales of arrests and beatings. Constance was astounding. We were warm and well-fed through the night although I feel tired to the bone now." She put her hand to her mouth and yawned.

"I cannot feel as you do about such things," said Charlotte. "Good luck to you and the others, but count me out of it."

"I am going to my room", said Louisa. "I cannot go another minute without sleep. Let mother know I am back and will be down for dinner," she continued, trudging wearily up the stairs.

It was several days later, when she finally found the time to visit Sophia to enquire about her father's health. Knocking on the front door of the Rowans, she waited anxiously for the door to open hoping that Daniel would not be at home.

Louisa watched the slouching, grey-frocked form of Jane Piggott through the bevelled glass of the door, frustrated at the inordinate amount of time it took to walk the short distance down the hallway. She answered the door eventually and stood, arms crossed, on the doorstep with her hair pulled back into a tight bun secured with a white hat and pins. She looked disdainfully towards Louisa. "Good day miss," she said in her thick Suffolk drawl.

"Good day Mrs Piggott," said Louisa. "May I see Sophia?"

The housekeeper frowned. "You had best come in," she replied, and ushered Louisa into the oak-panelled library at the front of the house.

Louisa untied her bonnet and sat in the red leather armchair by the globe in the corner, spinning it absent-mindedly. She stopped and then wiped her dusty finger on the cushion behind. She examined the room. Heavy red drapes covered most of the windows, and the dark panelling did nothing to alleviate the gloomy air inside the room. She heard footsteps echo down the tiled hallway and the door swung open revealing the tall, suited form of Daniel Bannister.

"Good morning, Louisa," he said entering the room.

Louisa rose from the chair. "Where is Sophia?" she asked.

"Sophia is in the morning room," he replied, "and there she will stay."

"Does she not wish to see me?" asked Louisa.

"She has no knowledge of your presence," replied Daniel. "Louisa, please do not think me unduly harsh, but Sophia's father, though considerably improved, remains unwell. Sophia is needed here, and she must not be tempted to embark upon any more of your schemes. You cannot know how difficult it would be if her father came to know of her recent transgressions."

"You must tell her I am here," cried Louisa. "She will think I do not care. You cannot wish her to think herself friendless at such a time?"

"I do not," said Daniel, "and I will tell her you called upon her when you are safely away."

"But she is expecting my visit," said Louisa plaintively.

"She was expecting your visit yesterday," chided Daniel.

"I could not see her yesterday," said Louisa, "my godmother visited without warning. I was duty-bound to attend to my own family."

"As Sophia is to hers," said Daniel. "You will not see her today or any other day this week, and you should reconcile yourself to this. I will ring for Mrs Piggott to show you out. I wish you good day."

Daniel nodded his head and left the room without looking back. Mrs Piggott appeared almost immediately from the nearby dining room. Her thin-lipped faced was set into a stony stare. She opened the door without further discourse and waved Louisa outside.

Louisa stood open-mouthed on the doorstep of The Rowans and then stomped up the driveway, striding through the door of The Poplars where she knocked impatiently at the door of her father's study.

The deep voice of Henry Russell boomed through the door. "Come," he said.

Louisa entered the room to see the usual pile of papers strewn across his desk, each paper marked with diagrams and drawings of things she did not understand. Across the room the door to his laboratory stood ajar and she detected the unmistakable odour of sulphur.

"That smells dreadful," she said.

"I doubt you have come to discuss the condition of the air in my quarters," Henry said, smiling benevolently. He closed the door to the laboratory. "Sit down Louisa," he said, gesturing to the window seat beside his desk. "What troubles you?"

"I have been refused entry to The Rowans," she complained.

"They left you on the doorstep?" Henry intoned.

"No, they did not do that. They let me in but would not allow me to see Sophia."

"Why so?" said Henry Russell.

"Because her father is unwell and her cousin thinks her duties lie with the family," said Louisa.

"As they do," said Henry. "With Charles' health in such sharp decline, she must surely be needed by her mother."

"But I only wanted to ask after her father and let her know she was in my thoughts."

"Louisa, you must abide by the rules of their household," said Henry reasonably. "You may not like it but you must do as you are bid."

Louisa sighed and gazed at her father mournfully. "We were becoming such good friends," she said.

"Why do you not use this opportunity to visit your aunt and uncle in Kensington?" enquired Henry Russell. They have asked you to stay several times recently. Perhaps this would take your mind off your friend and allow her time to minister to her father."

"Perhaps I shall," said Louisa, staring at the floor. If she was enthusiastic about the prospect of a trip to Kensington, there were no visible signs.

"Then I will write to them tonight," said her father firmly. "We will settle it."

Louisa thanked him politely then wandered back into the hallway.

Charlotte was standing by the dresser removing browning leaves from a vase of flowers. "There is a letter for you," she gestured, nodding towards the dresser. A creamy-white envelope leaned against the ink stand. It was post-marked London. Louisa picked it up and took it to the morning room where she pulled up a chair and sat down at the round breakfast table.

"Would you like coffee, Miss Louisa?" asked their new cook and housekeeper, Janet McGowan, in clipped Scottish tones.

"Thank you," said Louisa and Janet returned moments later with a tray of coffee and a small plate of shortbread.

"I do not suppose you are acquainted with the housekeeper at The Rowans?" asked Louisa.

"Jane Piggott? Janet replied. Louisa nodded.

"A little," she said. "Harold is better acquainted."

"Does she know how Mr Drummond fares since the doctor's visit?"

"He is much improved," said Janet. "Maggie is friendly with their young housemaid, Minnie Cole. She keeps us quite well informed of their news."

"Did they find out what troubled him?" asked Louisa.

"They think it was a stomach ailment," replied Janet. "He is still in his bed but much better than he was."

"I am glad to hear it," said Louisa. "And Miss Sophia, is she well?"

"As far as I am aware, Miss," said Janet. "She will probably appreciate the peace for a few days until Mr Drummond is back on his feet."

"Thank you," said Louisa. She reached for the drawer of the morning room dresser and removed a letter opener, deftly slitting the envelope. The letter was in a familiar hand.

"Dear Louisa, We were glad to see you at the Old Museum on Sunday night and wondered if you might be interested in a forthcoming Suffragette debate at Caxton Hall, Westminster in two weeks' time. Bessie and I are staying at our club in London for the next month, and hope that you can join us at the debate. There will be a number of influential suffragette speakers and it will give you an even better understanding of this great and noble cause. Do feel free to bring your friend along, if you wish. Write to me, at The Empress Club in Dover Street and let me know if you can join us. Yours ever, Ada Ridley"

"How marvellous," said Louisa aloud.

"What's that darling," asked Charlotte, who had joined her sister in the morning room.

"Ada and Bessie have invited me to a suffragist meeting in London and father has just written to our Aunt and Uncle Cowell in Kensington, so I will be wonderfully well-placed to join them. How fortunate."

"Take care," warned Charlotte. "Father is resigned to you pursuing your political aims when he is nearby to watch over you. I do not believe he would give his permission for a visit to

Westminster when he is so far away. I think Ada and Bessie forget how young you are sometimes. This visit is unwise."

"It's only an idea," said Louisa. "Do not tell father, please. In any case, he has not received a reply from my aunt and uncle yet. Perhaps it would not be convenient for me to visit."

Charlotte sighed. "Just stay out of trouble, Louisa," she said. "The whole idea fills me with foreboding."

The next days passed in a blur of boredom for Louisa as she waited for the post to find out whether she would go to London, or not. It rained heavily outside and she did not dare try to see Sophia again for fear of Daniel preventing access.

She wandered aimlessly around the house recalling the camaraderie of the census evasion night when she remembered the diary was still in her possession.

Louisa ran to her closet, felt around inside her coat pocket and removed the journal with a sigh of relief. Sitting on her bed, she opened the book where she had left off. The next page was blank so she opened the one after and read.

Chapter Six

From bad to worse

Saturday 9th August 1851 – This is my first diary entry since my frenzied attempt last night to reproduce those former entries concerning my dear friend, Mary Emily Cage. The writing of those entries focussed my mind on previous times in my life causing me to re-examine my past conduct, of which I am not at all proud. How selfish I was, thinking only of my life and carelessly disregarding the needs of my best friend. As Mary's life descended into a hell, not always of her own making, mine rose accordingly until I was happily married and had sufficient food and shelter for all my needs. How it must have hurt Mary that her life was in turmoil while mine was always comfortable. How did I neglect her so and not consider how she might compare our fortunes and suffer more by it?

I visited Mary in her cell today. Before I left home, Alfred bid me sit down. Looking straight into my eyes, he watched me with tender concern, stroking my hand as he spoke. He said I must be in possession of all the facts before meeting Mary as I may not wish to re-acquaint myself with her when I knew to what depths she had sunk. I told him it did not matter what the facts were, I would not desert her now, nor would I take her own account any less seriously than the official accounts of her misdemeanour. Alfred said he was afraid of this but continued without preamble stating that Mary had been found guilty of murder by poison and would die within a week. There was nothing that could prevent her execution, so any renewal of our friendship would inevitably be of short and painful duration. I reminded Alfred that I had abandoned Mary once and must do all I could to make up for this past disloyalty. He kissed me tenderly and told me he had arranged a visit and would take me there right away, but warned me that the conditions inside the prison were not what I was used to and that I should not be shocked at anything I saw.

Clutching Alfred's arm, I walked the twenty minutes to the gaol with my husband, my rock, by my side. We did not talk but every so often he stopped and smiled at me, his hand firmly grasping mine. Poor Mary – how sad she never knew the love and care of a good man. Eventually we arrived at the gaol; a vast, brick building surrounded by a high wall. Atop the roof, tall chimneys stood stark against the skyline. Our entryway, through a large wooden gate, was positioned where the straight side wall met the curved wall to the front of the structure. Alfred escorted me through the gates and up the long pathway to the front of the building. He nodded to the guards at the front door and was granted easy access, as a man in his position should be.

I did not know what to expect of the prison for in all the years we were married, I never went near the place. From the outside, the grounds were pleasant. The door through which we entered was located to the side and a large, mullioned arch-window stood centrally about it occupying several floors. The sun shone brightly and I thought perhaps it would not be as bad as Alfred described but that thought only lasted until I gained access to the inside. Alfred escorted me through the dark reception hall and through the first of many heavy, metal gates, each with a prison warder within easy sight. We weaved through corridors away from the men's cells as Alfred did not wish to expose me to the worst of the prison, then we descended down dank, shallow stairs and through whitewashed corridors beneath the ground floor. Each side of the corridor contained a succession of single cells. Alfred explained that these were the condemned cells and it was unusual for a prisoner not to share a cell, however, this was a privilege granted to prisoners condemned to death. Many of the cells were empty. Alfred propelled me past two cells occupied by men and I did not have the opportunity to even glimpse inside despite the lack of private space, then we went through a further door and Alfred gestured to a cell on the left.

Fully exposed to the prying eyes of anyone who might pass by through floor to ceiling bars, the small cell was whitewashed brick with a clay tiled floor. A barred window was set high atop the end wall and illuminated a hard wooden bed pushed firm against the back wall upon which a small figure was sitting, clutching a book.

59

Her lips moved silently as if she was reading aloud; but the book was, in fact, closed.

"Mary," I whispered, for it was she and she looked up and smiled the most radiant smile and walked to the barred walls of the cell, reaching towards me. She said my name over and over and grasped my hand and I sobbed so hard I could not speak for some ten minutes. Alfred called the guard, took the keys to the cell and allowed me access. The guard picked up his chair and set it down for me beside Mary's bed and we talked for the first time in twenty years. Before I had the chance to ask her anything at all she said she had something she must say to me. Alfred sent word in advance of my intended visit, which allowed Mary the opportunity to think about our impending meeting and she had planned what she would say. Without further preamble she told me she was sincerely sorry for her past conduct, her dissolute life and, above all, her resentment of me. I said there was nothing to apologise for and that I should say sorry to her for my lack of consideration. She disagreed and said that I should not.

Mary had not aged as one would expect of a person having experienced such a difficult life. She was still small and relatively slight; no more than five foot, if that, with only a slight thickening of the body through age. Her face was quite un-lined. Her black hair was now peppered with grey but her eyes were kinder and less hard than I remembered. She was dressed in the black garb of prison and her hair was pinned back though not at all neatly and rebellious tendrils escaped through the pins, so the effect was softened. In her hand she grasped a bible as if her life depended upon it.

Even as I uttered the words I realised what an absurd question I was asking, but still felt moved to enquire how Mary fared. It seemed only polite to ask. She said she fared well under the circumstances; that the prison chaplain was a frequent visitor during her incarceration, and had provided her with much comfort. She was not afraid to face the next life and was fully reconciled to her fate. She told me she had been a most grievous sinner and regretted her actions completely. She wished God would grant her mercy and hoped that she would die forgiven. She asked for details of my life, which I gave with a degree of reluctance as I have fared so much better than she.

Mary confessed she stayed away from my wedding for spite, resenting that I never bought Alfred to meet her and I apologised for making her feel she was not good enough to meet him. But she said the fault was hers alone. I told her about my four children and her eyes filled with tears when she discovered my eldest girl, Mary Elizabeth, was named in her honour. She asked after my father and I smiled, remembering how he had enjoyed ten happy years in Ipswich in close proximity to our home before passing away leaving the proceeds of the sale of his house to Alfred and me. We talked about Alfred's progression within the prison system and I explained how he came to occupy his current senior position in Ipswich Gaol. Whilst not wishing to cause any further resentment, I felt moved to honesty and revealed that our good fortune allowed us to purchase a larger house in Christchurch Street where my original lodgings were when I was a teacher. She did not seem to mind though, and said she was pleased my life was comfortable and would not wish it otherwise just because hers was not.

I asked if there was anything I could do for her to bring some comfort in these last weeks and she said that there was. She had three sons and four daughters left living, who would dwell in the shadow of her misdemeanour forever and she was sorry and ashamed for the notoriety her conduct bought. She would ask for their forgiveness but also wanted God's forgiveness and to attain that she felt it necessary to give as true an account as possible as part of her redemption. She was adamant that this account could never be made public for the sake of her children. Mary asked if I might listen to her story and write it down as she could not read or write and that even after so long a time, she could trust me with her story as she could trust no other. She said that it may be difficult for me to hear her words, especially those narratives involving me, but that a true account must contain both bad and good. I did not have to think too long and said of course I would do this for her no matter how harrowing the detail. So it is settled. I come tomorrow and will sit with her and write what she tells me.

I left the damp confines of Mary's cell, and, at my request, Alfred took me to the prison chapel. I knelt at the front pew praying fervently for Mary's soul, while Alfred conducted some business in the nearby reception hall. Presently, I heard footsteps and the prison

61

chaplain joined me in prayer. When we finished I stood, and he engaged me in conversation, so I asked him about Mary and told him of our friendship. He said Mary was a most guilty sinner but that she had confessed to her loose conduct and depraved way of life and wholeheartedly wished to atone for her misdemeanours in the eyes of the lord. The chaplain said he told her that she must confess to all her sins including the murder of her husband to be truly repentant, but that she would not. If she did not confess before she died, God would not forgive her. He asked me to help her understand the importance of a full confession and I said I would do anything for her as I had failed her too many times before.

Then we left the gaol and I write this at home now. The next entry in this journal will be Mary's story in Mary's own words.

I, Mary Emily Cage, was born to good but poor parents at the turn of the century in the village of Stonham Aspal, where I dwelled for most of my life. My childhood was hard; none of us were schooled and we all went to work for our living from the age of seven years. A seven year old child cannot do much else of worth but pick stones from the fields and this back-breaking work is what we did until the boys were old enough to labour and the girls old enough go into service. We never had new clothes or any clothes that fit properly. Everything we owned was handed down, patched and worn. I never owned a pair of boots that did not leak nor had a dress without a stain. I would like to say we were happy despite our poverty, but it would not be true. It was a hard, cruel life and we were always hungry and frequently cold. Accidents and deaths were commonplace and became increasingly more so as we grew older. One of my brothers fell out of a cart, broke his head and died. Another lost three fingers to a scythe when he was but ten. But those of us who lived eventually went our own ways and at least our father was well-regarded in the village in spite of our lack of money, which is more than can be said for most.

Anna Saunders was my friend from as long back as I can remember. I cannot recollect how we met – it was not at school because I never went, but we were always friends and our friendship grew stronger and stronger as we approached the age that we would expect to leave our father's homes and be married. Anna's father was not rich but he owned property and a store, so I always knew she was better than me. I thought it would not matter but it came to matter a great deal.

I was not quite twenty when I married James Cage. We had known each other before we were wed and he agreed to make an honest woman of me. I loved him in the beginning which is why I let him bed me in the freezing cold of the hayloft one frosty January when he was the worse for ale, and I, desperate to show him I could love him like a grown woman. He was older than I and had other women before me, so I had much to prove.

After a short life as hard as mine, I ought to have known better than to think we would be happily wed and life would be easy for it was not easy at all. Indeed, but for the intervention of my father, I do not think in hindsight that James would have wed me. I birthed my first girl in my twentieth year and a boy two years after that. Those intervening years were hard, but not as hard as those that followed. If I knew then what I know now, I would have considered those the easiest of times, for I had the support of family and friends even though I did not enjoy the respect of my husband, whose violence to me increased as his love of the grain grew ever stronger.

My boy, James, died before he reached the age of one. He had been small and frail from birth and his death came almost as a relief, as it was wholly inevitable. I did not grieve and already carried his replacement, a boy we also named James. I never loved either of the children named James. Whether this was because they were named for their father, I could not say. I have loved other of my children, although not all, so why not these first two boys? It made their deaths easier though, so perhaps it was as well.

The boy child I loved best of all was called Richard. I am sure it was because I loved his father the best for he was the only of my children not fathered by James Cage. 1827 was the year I thought to be free of James and headed towards a newer, happier life. After the death of my father James became progressively more violent whenever he returned from the ale house. At first the violence was contained but then he began to beat me in front of the children and on one sickening occasion, in front of Anna. The pity in her eyes hurt me more than the bruises. The beatings were bad enough but James was often laid-off work because of his drinking. He became increasingly unreliable, so we had no money to eat or heat our rooms. Then James began to look for other ways to find beer money, indulging in poaching and burglary. He was caught and charged on more than one occasion, so when he was given a gaol sentence for larceny I was part relieved and part concerned about how I would manage without going into the workhouse. I begged my mother to let us stay with her, even though she had no money either. But I thought if she could mind the children for me I might get work labouring in the fields to earn enough for all of us to eat.

I applied to Mr Last's farm where my friend Kitty was a dairymaid, and he employed me. The labour was long and arduous but it suited me well, particularly as George Thurlow had returned to the farm to finish some buildings for Mr Last. I was pleased to re-acquaint myself with him, now James was away.

I did not intend to co-habit with George Thurlow. I thought only to enjoy myself and have some freedom from the children and the grind of my daily life but after only a few weeks, I fell in love.

He was kind to me; kind in a way that I had never known from James. Perhaps it was because he had steady work and no inclination towards excesses of alcohol. His industrious nature and sobriety gave him time to show me kindnesses that were only small but meant a great deal. He would not let me carry a load in his presence and he stroked my hair and told me I looked pretty even when I did not. After the beatings I had endured, these words and deeds warmed my heart and I would have done anything he asked of me.

One day he asked me to go to his lodgings and I did, full well knowing what was likely to happen. We lay together but it was different because he asked me first unlike my husband who took it whether it was offered or not. And his breath was fresh and sweet; not rancid with the sour taste of stale alcohol and sweat. After that first time, I returned every night leaving the children with my mother. To begin with she was angry and asked me what I thought my father would have said, had he been alive to witness my disgrace, but I asked her what she thought he would say if he saw all the bruises caused by James Cage, not to mention the larceny. She did not answer because she knew what he would have said and what he would have done. We did not speak of it again and she turned a blind eye to my living arrangements so long as I gave her money for the children's keep and came to see them every day, which I did.

I lived six months with George and for the first time in my life I had no need to worry about food and shelter. My bruises healed and instead of dreading the door opening, I welcomed it. I knew I was living on borrowed time and soon enough James Cage returned from gaol and came to claim his possession. It was May of 1828 and I was returning from the top field with Sally when I saw him stalking towards me. I discovered later that he had come to Stonham Aspal by cart following his release from Ipswich gaol, heading straight to the ale house where he was greeted with cat calls and derision by his friends. They told him I was full with George Thurlow's child and that he was no man to have such a wife.

What he did and said to George Thurlow, I will never know but I never saw George again except once from afar. James dragged me by the arm and told me I was to return to Wetheringsett that night and should forget about George or I would be the worst for it. I did not know he had spoken to George at that time, so broke free from his grasp and ran to George's lodgings. They were empty and cleared of all his possessions. I visited every of his kin folk that evening and there were many. Some would not speak to me and the others did not know where he was.

I returned to my mother's house and passed the night there but she would not let me stay any longer as she did not want any trouble from James. I took the children and made to leave the next day but just as I reached the front door of the house, Charlotte Thurlow appeared and told me that her husband, David, had seen George and that he had gone to Ipswich never to return and I should not think of him anymore. I had nowhere else to go, so heavily pregnant and with two small children in tow, I walked back across the fields to Wetheringsett and home to James.

The rooms stank when I returned. He had not set a fire or opened a window and the rooms, which had lain empty all winter, were heavy with damp and mildew and cold as the grave. James was sitting at the table when I returned sharpening a knife. He got to his feet and, taking the hands of Mary and James, set them outside the door. Then he pushed me into the bedroom and threw me onto the bed, stained and damp from the endless leaking. He claimed me right there, marking me as a dog may scent his bitch, then climbed off and said he would keep the Thurlow bastard as his trophy. There was nothing I could do and nowhere to go as without money there are no choices, so I stayed, spending the next months in fear for my unborn child. But when Richard arrived James was at worst, ambivalent and sometimes kinder to Richard than to his own children. I never understood why. Perhaps he did indeed feel that the child was his reward for the slight George Thurlow had caused.

While James appeared to forget his time in gaol quickly, I did not. I tried to put George Thurlow far from my mind but missed him every day. When Richard was born I was so low I could not rise to feed the children, nor care for them or myself. I missed him so much, I could not even cry. One day my mother visited and was so concerned she applied to the doctor in Debenham for some help for me. The doctor gave her some small, cream-coloured pills which I took with water. They made me feel a great deal better though tired and lethargic the next day but they dulled the pain. I took them until the packet was empty, by which time the worst of it was over.

Anna Saunders married and left the village the year before my daughter, Sibella was born. I had loved Anna for a long time but the more she prospered, the worse my prospects became. I thought she was ashamed of me. Forgive me Anna, but I still think that although I forgive you now. I was never as clever as Anna but even I am of sufficient intelligence that I could tell she was holding back from me. I met her husband for the first time this week in a condemned cell, twenty years after she married him. No, I do not think I have imagined the snub.

I wanted to be Anna Saunders. I wanted to read and write. I wanted to live in a proper house. There was only one child in the Saunders family and there were thirteen of us; all those mouths to feed. I do not think Anna has ever gone hungry or understood what it was like to have no shoes. I think she would have helped me more if she had known how bad things were with James but I did not want to be pitied by Anna. I loved her and I wanted her respect and admiration, not her charity. I remember when Kitty told me that Anna was to be married. I was devastated to find out second-hand; so much I was almost doubled over with the pain of it. I was her best friend and I had no idea of an engagement. I thought I might, at least, meet her intended but it never happened. You will not have known this until this very moment, Anna, but I did come to your wedding. I came as far as the Lychgate at the church bringing a horseshoe decorated by my niece Sarah, to wish you luck and joy. But I was so overwhelmed with jealousy, I could not enter. I hung the horseshoe from a tree and left. I wonder if you ever saw it? From that day to yesterday, I never saw you again. For what it is worth, I thought of you often.

The loss of Anna was tempered by the birth of my favourite daughter, Sibella. I was told I should not have favourites but I did and make no apology for it. Her birth was quick and pain-free. She was an easy baby, cried very little and fed contentedly from me. I loved this girl child very much. My life continued in the same vein; hard, grinding poverty, loveless copulation and the resumption of the beatings which had stopped for a while after Richard was born. By the time my son John arrived in 1833, I was weary to the bone. I could not eat, which is just as well as there was little food, and I could not feed John who nearly died. We were both so unwell in the winter of that year that the vicar relented and agreed to baptise my three youngest children for fear we would die outside of God's grace. The vicar must have been well-disposed that month as even Richard was baptised and he was the reason they refused to baptise my other children, as I had sinned in the eyes of the Lord.

I was so tired of life by then I cared nothing for baptisms and would happily have met my maker and sung at my own funeral; but it was not to be. I rallied and recovered, but not before I had taken myself to the village pond at Stonham and thought to drown myself. I got as far as entering the freezing, fetid water but Mrs Tebbing saw me and took me to Ursula Rainor who gave me some pills like those I had been given when George left me. I felt much recovered after that and returned to her whenever I needed to replenish my supply. They bought me down hard the next day but I could get through the worst of things, as long as I had my pills.

A few years later, we returned to Stonham Aspal never to leave again. James only worked sporadically at Wetheringsett and we would have starved had we not moved. There was no improvement in our living conditions. We dwelled in a wooden house with rotting floorboards, one living room and one bedroom for all of us and a privy outside. It was a very small space for so many, and not long after we returned another boy, William, was born and two years later a girl, Betsy Eliza, followed. They were both difficult children but I had remembered the power of the pills, by then. When Richard was born and everything was so raw I used the pills to quieten the children, so I might grieve my lost love in peace. When the pills were gone, as time went by, I forgot that use for them. But two nights with no sleep has a remembering effect and I crushed the pills down and the children lay torpid and quiet about me as Mary Ann and James had done those many years before. The same year Betsy was born, my mother died at last. She was a long way past seventy when she died and it was time for her to go. Her mind wandered often and she did not know me anymore, so I was not sorrowful at her departure. Besides, my days passed in a blur and I cared little for anything except my opium pills.

James died suddenly in 1842. Not James my husband unfortunately, for that would have been too much to hope for, but James my son. Nobody could account for it. He just fell down at home one day and was quite dead before he hit the ground. He was but 17 years old. His father James had continued his relentless taking of me, so I was heavily pregnant again and had Emma early, less than one week after my son James died. Although he was not a child of whom I was especially fond, neither was I glad about his death. So a demanding baby in his place, before his body was cold in the ground, was a burden beyond my ability to cope. Do not hate me for this Anna, for there are murders I can confess to, but I knew as I ground those pills up that I was using too many and I did it anyway. Emma lived but a week. And in early June, I did it again and buried little Betsy Eliza.

You may judge me but do not until you have walked a mile in my shoes. What prospect did these children have? Emma was early and never likely to thrive. Betsy Eliza had no future but stone picking in fields only to marry a drunken wretch. I started with 8 children and ended with 5, all seven years and above and all able to support themselves and relieve us of the burden of filling so many mouths. I like to think of it as a sacrifice – the few for the many. Unfortunately the rest of the village did not see it that way. Three children dead in as many months was never likely to be overlooked. I was the subject of relentless, cruel gossip lasting many months. Poor James was dug from his grave and opened up; but they did not find anything as I had not done anything to him. The gossip never went away but the accusations did. I was well-used to being judged unkindly by the villagers, so their endless chatter did not concern me. I had hoped that would be the end of my child-bearing years but as usual James could not leave me in peace and I bore another two girls in the following four years. I called them Betsy Eliza and Emma again as I could not find it in me to think up another two names.

Louisa turned the page, shocked at what she had read. Black ink turned to faded blue and Louisa realised it was written on different days and that it would be a good time to take a break. Besides, there was too much information to assimilate. Mary Emily, the hopeful young girl starting a new life as a married woman, had become so embittered by circumstance she admitted to killing her youngest two children, if not quite deliberately, then by extreme and calculated carelessness. Utterly shocked, Louisa's first thought was to tell Sophia. She ran down the wide stairs two at a time, tripping over her skirts as she fled into the hallway.

"Slow down, young lady," said her father, emerging from the study with a letter in his hand. "Where are you going in such a hurry?"

"I'm going to visit Sophia," she said breathlessly.

"Not without an invitation," he replied with a twinkle.

"Really father," Louisa said, "no invitation is likely to be forthcoming while that insufferable cousin of hers commands her every deed. What sort of independent woman is she?"

"Do not be too hard on her," Henry Russell replied. "She is torn between duty and friendship. If you are a true friend to her you will go to London and give her time to attend to her family matters here."

"Oh, have you heard from my uncle?" asked Louisa eagerly.

"I have," said her father. "You are invited to Kensington for two weeks and will travel Friday. We have planned a treat for you, Louisa. You will travel by motor carriage. Your uncle under-takes a business trip to Bury St Edmunds and will call in for you on his return. How do you like that idea to take your mind off your friend?"

"What a wonderful plan," she said. "It will do very well to distract me from Sophia. Thank you," she continued and kissed him on the cheek, before walking downstairs to the kitchen.

"Maggie," she called from the foot of the stairs. Maggie emerged from the kitchen clutching a tureen which she was busy drying.

"Can you bring my cases to my room when you have a moment? I go to London in two days. Bring my hat box too."

"Of course, Miss," said Maggie. "Will you need all of them?"

"Yes please," said Louisa. "I may not take them all, but I will have them all upstairs with me. Perhaps you can help me to pack later?"

"Yes, Miss," said Maggie. "I am not taking my half day today after all, so I can help you."

"Sorry Maggie, I forgot today was your day off," said Louisa. "Have you plans another day instead?" she asked.

"I do not know Miss," said Maggie. "I was going into town with Minnie Cole, but she cannot come. Mr Drummond is taken sick again."

"I thought he was better," exclaimed Louisa.

"Far from it," said Maggie, gravely. "The doctor visited in the early hours of the morning. Mr Drummond is so unwell they are not sure he will recover at all."

Chapter Seven

An unexpected encounter

By the end of the week, Louisa was happily settled in her aunt and uncle's large townhouse in Harrington Gardens, Kensington. She occupied a generous bedroom on the second floor looking out over beautifully-tended formal gardens with a window seat perfect for watching the comings and goings to the front.

The Park was frequented by smartly-dressed nannies walking their charges or pushing perambulators if the children were too small to walk. Midday, like clockwork each day they arrived, exchanging stories and, no doubt, discussing the machinations of their employers. Occasionally, smart-looking gentlemen hurried by on their way to the city, but The Park, by and large, was a relaxed area and helped Louisa appreciate her privileged position. She was immensely proud to have a wealthy uncle who could afford to live in such idyllic surroundings.

Within a few short days, Louisa had slipped into a routine of eating, shopping and people-watching interspersed with the occasional visit to a theatre with her aunt. Aunt Beatrice was older than her father and had no children of her own. Married to a successful banker, she enjoyed a fortunate but sometimes lonely life seeming to take great joy at having Louisa at home and treating her with kindness.

One of the first things Louisa arranged, on her arrival in Kensington, was a response to Ada at The Empress Club. Ada replied by return of post and Louisa read the letter with great excitement as she anticipated meeting her cousins at Caxton Hall in a few days' time. Try as she might, she could not remember her aunt's stance on suffragists. Her mother's family were mainly supportive but her father's kin were a different matter. As it happened, she need not have worried. As soon as she asked her aunt for leave to visit her cousins, her aunt made the connection.

"Are they the Ridley girls?" asked her aunt, on hearing their names.

"They are, Aunt Beatrice," Louisa replied biting her lip.

Aunt Beatrice put her hands on Louisa's shoulders and looked into her face wearing a serious expression.

"You should know that your uncle does not approve of suffragists," she said, "and as much as he dislikes their mainly peaceful actions, he vehemently hates the violence of the suffragettes.

Louisa sighed and lowered her head but her aunt placed a gentle hand beneath her head and lifted her chin until Louisa's eyes met her own green orbs.

"However, what he does not know cannot disturb him," she said with a twinkle.

Louisa threw her arms about her aunt, beaming in gratitude.

When her aunt disentangled herself, she continued. "I, Louisa, admire them greatly but do be careful. Everything is magnified in London. I hope you can assure me that you are a suffragist of the peaceful kind."

"Very much so," said Louisa. "I would never seek to hurt anyone or anything. You know my second cousin is Millicent Fawcett. We follow her methods not those of the Pankhurst's"

"Thank you for your reassurance," said Aunt Beatrice, "so we will discuss it no further except to make arrangements for your travel. Where do you intend to meet your cousins?"

"There is no need for me to go to their club although I am invited," said Louisa. "They have given me a contact number, so perhaps I may use your telephone to finalise our arrangements?" Then I can plan to meet them at Caxton Hall."

"Do that," replied her Aunt. "I will arrange a hansom cab for your journey."

Louisa took leave of Aunt Beatrice and rang the Empress Club. Neither Ada nor Bessie were present to take the call, but she left a message in the care of the receptionist for them, requesting that they meet her outside Caxton Hall the following night. With her aunt having no further need of her that afternoon, Louisa decided to take a walk as she had explored very little since her arrival.

It was warm and breezy for April, so Louisa dressed in a light cream smocked and embroidered silk dress with a matching wide-brimmed hat before setting off for her walk. She wore low-heeled, sensible shoes and felt that she did her aunt and uncle justice with her smart attire while ensuring her own comfort. She wandered down Collingham Gardens and through a pretty mews road, before finding herself on The Earls Court Road with its imposing brick houses and rows of bustling shops and banks. Outside the post office she happened across a railway arch and from there noticed a sign for the underground. Intrigued, she entered, determined to catch sight of one of the new moving staircases but had not gone more than a few yards inside when she heard a voice.

"What are you doing here?" asked Daniel Bannister.

Louisa stood open-mouthed. For a moment she did not recognise Sophia's cousin, out of the usual context.

"Never mind me, what are you doing here - and where is Sophia?"

"She is at home looking after her mother," said Daniel. "I would be with her, but for this infernal problem with the electricity supply," he nodded vaguely in the direction of the doorway. "It is uncommon for a young lady to travel alone on the underground railway system. Are you lost?"

"No I am not," protested Louisa. "I went for a walk and thought to explore the new moving walkways."

"It is not very pleasant down there," said Daniel, "and not at all the place for you to be. Let me escort you home," he said.

"I do not wish you to," said Louisa churlishly. "You would not let me see Sophia when I needed to. Why would I wish to walk with you now?"

"Because if Sophia were here she would wish it so," replied Daniel. "She would expect me to keep you safe."

"That is cruel," exclaimed Louisa, "you must know I could not refuse Sophia."

"Exactly," he smiled. "Now, where shall I take you? I must go to the power station, but I have half an hour to spare."

"I reside in Harrington Gardens with my aunt and uncle.

"I know it," said Daniel. "Come."

He escorted her from the station and they walked back through a succession of small parks and gardens using a much prettier route than the one Louisa had taken on the outward journey.

"How is Sophia?" asked Louisa presently after the silence grew too stifling to bear.

Daniel sighed, stumbled on his words and said, "If I did not have to be here, I would not have travelled today. Sophia's father has taken another turn. He is very sick indeed. If I did not know better....." the words trailed away.

"What do you know?" asked Louisa, alarmed.

"Nothing, it is not for me to speculate. Sophia is well. She is well. They all cope well with it." He stared into the distance momentarily. Louisa wished she knew him better so she could decipher the meaning behind the words he had not said.

"What is your occupation?" asked Louisa, trying to divert another bout of excruciating silence.

"I studied engineering," said Daniel, "and now electricity. I learned my trade in London and came to Ipswich from here. Now there is a problem with the electricity company and they seek to consult with me at this most inconvenient of times."

"Will you be in London long?" asked Louisa.

"Not if I can avoid it," replied Daniel. "I must return to my aunt's house at the earliest opportunity. I expect to be here no more than two days."

It seemed little time had passed when they reached Harrington Gardens. They walked through the park and then Daniel escorted Louisa up the steps of her uncle's house.

"What do you intend to do with your time in London?" he asked.

"I am going to Caxton Hall tomorrow," she said excitedly, the words flying from her mouth before she had time to think.

"More of this suffragette nonsense," said Daniel, shaking his head. "I am surprised at your father for allowing you to roam around London alone. It is not provincial, Louisa. There are parts of London where a young lady simply cannot go."

"My aunt has arranged a cab for me," said Louisa, "not that it is any concern of yours."

"At least one of your relatives has some sense," he countered.

"Please, do not speak to my father of this," begged Louisa. "You will return before me."

"So he does not know," said Daniel. "At least he is not complicit in this."

"It's only a debate," cried Louisa. "I intend to meet my cousins there. I am perfectly safe."

"You are correct. It will be safe, as long as you stay with your cousins and remain close to the road. But please, for Sophia's sake, do not wander off on your own, Louisa. She has enough to worry about."

"I will be careful," said Louisa petulantly, "but not because of you; for Sophia."

"Very well," said Daniel. He fleetingly touched the brim of his hat and then set off up the road with long, measured strides.

"Insufferable man," said Louisa aloud. "He is quite intolerable".

She stalked up to her room and sat down heavily on the window seat, watching over the park.

"I can look after myself without his help," she said aloud. She watched the park for a while. A young boy and his sister played with a spinning top in the dry earth of the walkway. While she did not know why, it put her in mind of Mary Cage's children and she thought of the diary carefully packed away at the bottom of her luggage. It seemed as good a way as any to distract herself from her annoyance, even if she was reluctant to read on after the last, horrifying instalment. Nevertheless, she unclipped her case, extracted the diary and began to read.

Chapter Eight

The only way out

Elizabeth Lambert came to live with us in the summer of 1846. She was a simple girl and not the type I would normally befriend but we were distantly related through a relative in Wetheringsett, so a connection already existed. She made an unfortunate marriage in Debenham and never lived with her husband even though she bore him children. She could not abide him and quite why she married him, defeated me. She was but twenty with a young daughter, and her mother would not have her. She reminded me of me, when I was young and hopeful and yearned for a better life, so I took her in even though there were eight of us sharing two squalid rooms. But she was grateful; at least I thought so at the time.

She looked after the younger children and it gave me a chance to get away from the house I had come to hate. I grasped the opportunity and I confess I spent a great deal of time in the company of others like me; women and men hardened with despair, none of us careful in our conduct. It shames me now, how we behaved, but you cannot understand what it is like to live without hope.

I knew my time without responsibility would be limited, so I lived life hard. James had taken quite a liking to young Elizabeth, to which I turned a blind eye. Far be it from me to cast aspersions, but the year after she left us she bore another child and I cannot say who the father was; nor do I care. It was James who told her to go in the end. I know not why but within four short months my freedom was curtailed again and I came home.

I could never rest easy after that. The horror of domestic life with James Cage was enough to make me weep with despair. But for my pills, I would have tried to do away with myself again. I could see no end to it. Then after a year, I met a man. I did not love him. He was tolerable, but to his credit he was not James and that was good enough. Robert was younger than me. I never did look my age - though how I escaped looking haggard and careworn after the life I lead, I do not know. Robert had little money but he had a place to stay, so I left with him. We did not live much of a life but he was not free with his fists and I thought well enough of him. Then Mary Ann came to find me and everything changed.

Mary Ann married out of our hell-house in 1845 to a poor but kind man. She bore three little urchins of her own and when she came to see me, it was evident another was on the way. She confided that Sibella was in the family way too. I do not know why Sibella did not tell me herself. I would have understood. So I left Robert and came back to Sibella before her father found out as I did not know whether he would be angry or ambivalent.

Sibella had lain with one of the village lads and was not long gone, but enough for Mary to notice. Poor naïve Sibella thought she was in love with the boy and continued to see him knowing full well that her father would disapprove. Inevitably James came to hear of it. I returned with the idea of protecting Sibella although I did not know how I could offer her the protection I had never sought myself.

Naturally, James laid the blame at my door. He called me a harlot and a whore and said I had corrupted my daughter and made her in my image. Then he beat me harder than he had ever beaten me before. I could not walk for two days. My tongue was so swollen, I could not speak or eat. It was so bad that Constable Whitehead saw fit to report James and held him at the station. I was not yet up and about, when he was sentenced to two months in Ipswich gaol for assaulting me. As I lay there freezing cold in blood-stained rags, pained and angry, I swore I would have my revenge on him; the brute.

When I could finally walk, I took Sibella and her young man, who she would not leave and journeyed to Ipswich with Robert and we all lived there together. I imagined how the village gossips would enjoy this latest evidence of my misconduct, not to mention the corruption of my daughter but I did not care a fig for their prejudice. I had spent the last thirty years beaten by my pig of a husband and not one of them ever lifted a hand to help me. They had no right to judge.

Sibella thrived in this environment of shame. This disgusting arrangement, in which she lived in close proximity to her wicked mother and her lover, but witnessing no violence and no rage, was calming for her contrary to the expectation of the gossips. She flourished and grew large and round. I cannot profess these were happy times. I was not in love with Robert as I had been with George but although hunger was never far from me, I was not in pain.

With all I had suffered, if there was one deed that would finally finish me, I thought it would be an act of violence; but it did not happen that way. Towards the end of summer, Sibella and I hastened from our lodgings in Ipswich High Street to the Butter Market to see what we might purchase with our paltry allowance, when I glanced at a familiar looking man across the thoroughfare. Even though twenty two years had passed, I recognised him at once. It was George Thurlow and he was still a handsome man with dark, wavy hair, peppered with grey. He was better dressed than when I knew him and the young woman to his side was clean and attractive. She held the hand of a boy about six years old who looked just like George.

I stood on the opposite side of the road, in my late forties, badly-clothed with a pregnant daughter, ill-used by my husband and watched what my future could have been. I stood and stared until they were far in the distance never saying a word until Sibella caught my arm and asked me, 'what in God's name was wrong.' I thrust the coins at her, stumbled back to our lodgings alone and cried and cried at the injustice of it.

A few days later, I found out that James Cage was soon to be released from gaol, so I marched straight to the prison and waited for him until he finally emerged. When I saw that evil bastard of a man, I launched at him and scratched his face and bit his chest and struck him over and over until the guards dragged me off him and took me away. I was still screaming profanities inside the cell at the police station over an hour later. Never have I hated anyone in my life as I hated James Cage that day.

They made me stay there through the night until I calmed down, so I pretended I had and the next day they released me. I returned to my lodgings but Sibella's boy and Robert Tricker had gone and it was just the two of us again, with no money again, so we went back to Stonham again. Back home with our tails between our legs and any remnants of dignity long gone.

I remember walking back through the doors of that cess-pit of a home I shared with Cage, hoping he would not be there, but he was.

They were all there, every one of my children, except Mary Ann; the one who got away. James was slumped upon his usual chair with his spindly legs splayed and his filthy boots, stinking and holed. His matted beard was mottled with grey and his lips, wet with beer. I almost vomited with hate and shame.

He did not say a word; just sat there sneering while my children stared passively. I was not pleased to be home, not even for them. The only one other than Sibella I had much time for by then, was Richard; but even that was wearing thin. So I walked through to the bedroom, opened up the floorboard where I had stashed a good quantity of opium pills, and took a handful. Within half an hour, it was bearable again.

I woke up the next day to the noise of scratching in a bedroom full of sleeping bodies, wincing as the rancid breath of James Cage wafted across my face. He slept so close to me that I could see his blackened teeth and count the coarse hairs on his chin. His chest rose and fell, too close to bear. I wished it would stop. The mattress was rank with lice and the scratching sound belonged to a sickly, under-nourished brown rat, scraping at the skirting in the corner of the bedroom. I could not summon up the will to shoo it away. It would have been more welcome in my bedroom than Cage ever was; but it put an idea in my head that would not go away. It was not an impulsive plan. I thought about it a few days before acting on it. I thought about all the horrid consequences and however bad they were, they did not fill me with the same dread as continuing my sorry existence.

I still had some of Robert Tricker's coins left, so I ventured to the chemist in the village. There were two other people inside when I arrived, so I delayed my purchase and looked about the store for a while until they were served. Mr Smith's shop had always fascinated me mainly because I could afford very little from it. But on the rare occasions I entered the glass-fronted cabinets with their intriguing variety of bottles, enthralled me. On the counter, Mr Smith kept quite the biggest bottle I had ever seen. Fashioned like a giant tear-drop with a spear-shaped stopper, it dominated the store. I imagined it full of honey, enough to last a decade. Beside it, he kept his weighing scales and his pock-faced assistant stood there now weighing quinine pills for Mrs Drew and her imagined ailments.

When she finally left the store I got to business and, without small talk, I asked him for two candles and some poison. He asked me what I wanted with poison and I said I had a problem with rats. Then he blushed to his toes and refused me. He would not let me have it. I was angry, but there was no point in persisting, as, clearly embarrassed, he hastened to the side room and out of my sight. I took the two candles without paying for them and marched out of the store.

I walked the street for a while considering the matter and decided it was time to pay my old friends at the farm a visit. Kitty had long gone, married to a decent man. They all married decent men except me, but Alice still remained - poor, ugly, spinster Alice, the fifty year old cow girl, with almost as sad an existence as my own. So I wandered over to the farm and engaged in small talk with Alice. When I left her, I stuck my head around the door of the barn to see if the rat poison kept there all those years ago, was still around. People are such creatures of habit, are they not? More than twenty years must have passed since I last worked at the farm but everything was exactly where it always had been. Better still, nobody was around, so I took a small pewter bowl and scooped what I hoped was rat poison out. It looked just like flour. I placed it in my basket and walked out and left the farm, just like that.

The older children were all at work when I returned. Sibella, now big with child, was minding her sister Emma. I sent them out and put the powder down in the corner for the rat. The rest I hid under the floorboard near my pills. The next morning I woke to find a dead rat in the corner of the room and two dead mice beside it, so I knew I had been right and it was poison.

The following morning I sent James to work with bread and butter and a little extra for his dockey. I took care to use only a small amount of poison for I wanted him to suffer, but not to die. I wanted him ill; very ill for a very long time. He would know something of the agonies I suffered. I cannot remember enjoying a day as much for a long time, revelling in the anticipation of his pain. It did not take long. James was brought back in a cart long before noon, writhing in agony and complaining of a fire in his stomach. Two men carried him in, one my son Richard. I ushered them to the bedroom and they laid him on the lice-ridden bed. When they left, I went to him. He clutched his stomach and asked me to fetch him water for he had an intolerable thirst. I did as I was bid and he drank half of it, clutched his stomach and dropped the rest to the floor.

James, never a clean man, stank like a fetid old goat. He had messed himself and it was over his trousers and now over our bed. I removed his vomit-stained jacket but that was as much assistance as I was prepared to give. "Help me woman," he screamed. I nearly gagged as the smell of vomit met the stink of human waste. He was a filthy human being and not worth my bother. Unable to spare a single drop of humanity for this loathsome man I had shared my life with I shut the door on him, deaf to his screams.

Sibella, who disliked her father almost as much as I did, complained bitterly. She was likely to give birth any time and should have taken the bed for her own, but said she could not enter that room at all now, and would have to make do with the one in the parlour with all the others around her. I patted her hand and told her I was sorry. I was. I had not considered her comfort. Richard was unsurprisingly sympathetic to his step-father. Richard had always known he was a bastard, yet of all my children he liked James the best. It disappointed me.

Richard recounted the moment James clutched his belly a half-hour after eating his bread, complaining of a sadly stomach. Before long, it became worse and, when he fell to the floor and began grinding himself into the earth in his pain, they thought it best to remove him home. On witnessing the severity of his symptoms, some of the men were anxious lest cholera had returned to the village. It pleased me, when I thought of the way those men had encouraged his mistreatment of me over the years and I was glad to have caused them concern, if only temporary.

By early evening, his incessant screaming was troubling the younger children, and I thought I would have to call the doctor out, which would be costly and risky. But by nightfall, he had ceased to cry out and appeared to be sleeping soundly. I thought it best to leave the powder where it lay beneath the floorboards for a few days.

James kept to his bed in the following days and appeared to rally. I feared he would mend, so I waited until they were all out and him asleep in his room, to remove the powder from the bedroom and re-locate it to its new home under a brick in the privy. The next morning I fetched him some ale with a little of the powder inside. This produced a new round of vomiting and diarrhoea and on the one occasion I looked in on him that day, James was curled in a foetal position on the bed, moaning. Though it was spring outside, the room was cold and dark; the dead rat still occupying its space on the floor, a suitable companion for my odious husband.

By the following day, James was making so much noise in his agonies the two middle boys, William and John, mithered at me to go to the doctor and get him some medicine. I welcomed an excuse to get out of the noisy, filthy rooms and took the long walk across the fields to Debenham, where I visited the rooms of Doctor Lock.

There were a number of others waiting to see him; two elderly women I did not recognise and Mary Jane Durrant who was carrying a sickly-looking infant with a rasping cough. She prattled on about how she feared it would die as the child had been unwell for most part of the year so far and, looking at its sallow, sunken face, I thought it might be better for all concerned if it did die. I could not say this, of course. People shun the truth. She was called through ahead of me and returned shortly after looking pale and worried. She carried a poultice and a glass bottle, filled with a liquid of some kind. The child flopped against her shoulder, looking at me through half-open eyes as they left the room. It did not look to me as if she would have too much longer left to worry.

Doctor Lock sat tall behind his solid, dark wood desk, peering at me over round-lensed glasses. He interviewed me at length about James' illness, with particular regard to the symptoms he displayed. I found it hard to concentrate for the sight of his bushy eyebrows moving above owl-like glasses with a life almost of their own. It was all I could do not to laugh aloud. After considering the matter, Doctor Lock concluded that James was suffering with a gastric ailment and poured a thick, creamy liquid from a large receptacle into a brown bottle which he sealed with a cork stopper and passed to me, charging me half a penny for the privilege. I reluctantly handed the money over and left the premises, choosing to walk back the long way round by the roadside in the hope of securing a ride back to my village on the way.

I did not meet anyone that day so arrived wearily back at Stonham Aspal mid-afternoon. The children were all working in the fields and Sibella was not at home even though she was close to her confinement. I heard low moans as soon as I reached the door of the bedroom, so decided to take a handful of pills from my hiding place and wait a while for them to take effect.

When I was suitably numb, I opened the bedroom door and the assault on my nostrils from the stench of him was almost too much to bear, even with the calming effects of the opiates. I took him water and the bottle of medicine given by Doctor Lock, as if I were a dutiful wife, and he sat up in his crumpled shirt decorated with vomit stains, and took a slug of medicine straight from the bottle.

He grimaced, then said, "I am in a great deal of pain, Mary," as if he hoped for sympathy from me. I could not help but laugh at him and I told him he deserved it and that I hoped his illness would be of a long duration. His yellowing, bloodshot eyes filled with tears as a fresh cramp assailed his guts and I walked from the room leaving him to his agonies.

The following evening, Richard interfered with my plans by sending word to Doctor Lock when the screams became too much for him to bear. The doctor could not attend until the next morning but the thought of his visit caused me sufficient concern that I dropped the remains of the powder down the privy and swilled out the pewter bowl. While Richard and Sibella waited at the house, the others being out in the fields, I went to Mrs Cooper's shop and asked her what she would give me for the pewter bowl. She gave me some coins which I concealed in my pockets, as it was rare for me to have money all to myself.

By the time I returned, Doctor Lock had arrived by carriage and stood in my front room holding a well-worn Gladstone bag, bulging with medical paraphernalia. By now James' screams had turned into low moans but they were still loud enough for the Doctor to find his patient without further direction. When he emerged from the room he fixed me with a narrow glare and barked orders to "clean the man up." Then turned to Richard and told him the patient was very sick indeed and must be better cared for and that his recovery would be impeded by the squalor about him. He said James must continue to take his medicine and he should be told at once if there was any change in his condition. Then he turned abruptly and left as quickly as he came. He could not have spent more than six or seven minutes the whole visit, but who could blame him. Any of us who could have left this hovel, would have.

I did not clean his bed sheets, his festering body or the vomit-stained floor that day or any of the three days that followed. Perhaps others did, but I cared not. On the fourth day he rallied, briefly left his bed and seemed improved. He cleaned himself and threw the filthy sheets in a pile on the floor. He called for me and I fetched him water and a little food. He grabbed my arm and leered at me, thrusting his lips towards mine. I turned away, sickened.

That night I dreamed he was on top of me again, pinning me down while his bristled jaw scraped my face as he thrust deep inside. By the morning, I had decided I could not let him fully recover. I excused myself from the house with the intent of fetching more medicine and walked briskly to Debenham, as fast as I might.

I returned again to Doctor Lock who glowered as he passed another bottle of medicine. He said he trusted his patient was residing in better conditions than he had previously endured, and I assured him he was. I never lied when I was Mary Moise, yet Mary Cage was an accomplished liar with little conscience. He dismissed me from his rooms with a flick of the wrist, wearing a pained expression on his weathered face and I left clutching the bottle, which I placed inside the pocket of my apron. As I walked past the chemist shop, I thought to go in and purchase some more poison to take James down another week or two, then thought the better of it; much too public given the proximity of Doctor Lock.

Then it came to mind that Elizabeth Lambert resided a short distance away and the whey-faced vixen owed me for treating me as a fool all those years ago, so I sought her out and found her at Mrs Parker's house. The house contained a family of two adults, their four children, Mrs Parker, Elizabeth and her two girls. Unfortunately most of them were present and Mrs Parker lay inconveniently in her bed in the corner of the room watching me through hawk eyes. She had not left her bed these last six years and the comings and goings of the household were her entire world. I thought it imprudent to talk to Elizabeth in front of her, so suggested a walk down the lane so the old woman could not hear us.

Elizabeth walked along, prattling about her tedious life and her deeply uninteresting family and I pretended to be fascinated. Not once did she ask me about any of my family which was useful as I did not want to bring the subject of James' illness and poison together in one conversation.

At the end of the lane, she told me she was pleased to see me and turned to go. I said I had forgotten an errand in Debenham, that I had promised Mary Ann I would get some poison for her to kill a troublesome rodent and then asked Elizabeth if she might fetch it for me. She said she would not and asked why I did not go myself. This presented a problem as I had not considered that she might decline, so I quickly feigned a malady and sat down on the ground, fanning my face with my hand. I told her I had felt faint all morning and that I could manage the walk home if I could only rest a while first. She was finally persuaded and took the money and set off for the chemist. I had been right; she was sufficiently stupid.

She could not have encountered any obstacles in her task as she returned far more swiftly than I expected carrying a small package marked with lettering I could not read. I thanked her, then cautioned her not to mention the transaction to nosy Mrs Parker and headed for Stonham.

When I arrived no one was at home, so I secreted the poison in my hiding place beneath the brick and put my head around the door of the bedroom to see how James was faring. He had been sick again and was pale and drawn. His recovery had not continued unabated, as I feared. I placed a glass of water by him but he grasped my wrist with dirty, clawed hands and asked me what I had put in his food. I was so taken aback I sat down momentarily on the bed. Watching me through crusty lashes, he searched my face for clues. My discomfort must have been apparent for he said he could see it written all over my face. I was trying to do him harm and he would take no more food or drink from me. I dashed his filthy hand away and told him he was hallucinating and that his illness had made him mad. I told him I hated him but not enough to risk my life and he lapsed into silence, considering my words. Then I left the room and perched upon the doorstep thinking about what he had said and I resolved to give him another dose to keep his loose mouth quiet.

I could not find any time the next day to introduce the powder into his food or drink. Sibella had taken to her bed in the front room in the early stages of childbirth and Kezia Oxborrow was nigetting

85

for her, coming in and out without a by-your-leave. Sibella's labour was long and hard. It was not until the next day she finally birthed her daughter, Jane. Richard asked me to bring bread and butter to James and, while they all clucked around the new baby, I took the plate to the privy to sprinkle the powder over.

I nearly dropped it such was my shock when I realised the brick had been moved. I lifted it up but there was nothing beneath. The powder had gone. I slipped the plate back on the table and surveyed the room in disbelief. Richard, Sibella, Emma and Betsy were at home. John and William were out. I had not seen the powder for two days and the privy was never locked. Anyone could have had it but I could not risk asking after it.

I passed the plate to Richard in stunned silence and he took it to the bedroom. Seconds later, the tin plate rattled to the floor as James spewed a stream of profanities. I opened the door and told him to quiet his filthy mouth. Bread and butter were strewn over the floor of the bedroom, too dirty for anyone else to eat. I asked Richard what happened and he said James refused to eat anything I had prepared, now or ever. He told Richard that I was an evil bitch, bent on his destruction. I said, in my defence, that James was losing his mind and Richard should not heed the ramblings of a daft old man. Richard scraped the bread and butter from the floor and passed it to me. I gave it to the cat and it licked the butter with relish. Then I left the house and wandered the street of Stonham contemplating the missing poison.

I was out for several hours. When I returned James had eaten and was resting quietly. Sibella and her daughter slept and the room enjoyed a peaceful calm I hardly recognised. Even when John and William returned, peace reigned for a while. Then, in the dark of the night, James screamed as if a thousand devils were torturing his soul. The screeches were as penetrating as the cry of an animal at abattoir and the whole house roused, beginning with the squalling baby.

I hastened into the bedroom, not to help but to try to quieten him. He clutched at his throat, scraping his skin with filthy nails. Then he sat up and vomited over himself, over the floor; green, viscous vomit everywhere. The wailing continued through the small hours turning, into moaning as the dawn broke. The children had gone back to sleep but Sibella, Richard and I could not.

A return to the doctor the next day was unavoidable. James had taken a serious turn for the worst. It would have excited far too much attention not to have seemed, at least publicly, to be tending to him as a devoted wife should. So I trudged the long walk to Debenham once more, using the last of my coins to purchase more medicine as James was swigging it from the bottle as if it were ale.

Doctor Lock said he would visit James the next day. I thanked him although I did not care one way or the other, but uncommonly met with good fortune when I encountered William Gunn in his cart. I knew William by sight, and thought I might prevail upon him to take me to Stonham Aspal. As it turned out, he was fitting windows at Mr Sparrow's building in Stonham, every detail of which I was subjected to on the ride home. William was clearly not a man comfortable with silence. When he was not talking about himself, he was prying about my life as if he felt he had some right to know. The village gossips had been out in force and he was not only possessed of the information that James was very sick, but was aware of my recent relationship with Robert Tricker. He offered his sympathies on the one hand while trying to glean information about Robert, on the other. He had the bad manners to ask me how I would manage if my husband died. What sort of a question is that to ask? It irritated me so much that I was rude in my reply, telling him that it was not his business to ask. This, pleasingly, annoyed him; but not enough to prevent him asking a succession of even more intrusive questions.

We finally reached Stonham and I removed myself from his presence with a brusque thank you before taking the medicine to James, who was twisting from side to side in the bed when I entered the room. I passed him the medicine and he dashed it to the floor. I told him that was the end of it. There would be no more medicine for I had no more money. He could scarcely speak, but managed to croak that he would refuse anything I had touched, so it did not matter. I raised my eyes heavenwards and left the room.

Kezia Oxborrow was in my front room by then, checking on Sibella and baby Jane. She told me James had been calling for Samuel Oxborrow all day and that he would come tomorrow, when he returned to the village. I told her Samuel could do as he pleased. I did not tell her I would much have preferred it if he did not. I did not like any friend of James and they had long since despaired of me.

By the time Doctor Lock arrived the next day, there had been a sudden change in James. He was much worse and his mind had wandered away irrevocably. He clutched at his stomach, complaining of creatures inside him. There was also a marked change in my attitude. I began to realise, for the first time, that James, who should have been recovering from his illness having received no further poison from me for several days, had deteriorated beyond all reason. I did not understand science but his worsened condition seemed inconsistent with the doses given. A creeping dread gnawed at the pit of my stomach. James was so much worse, he could easily die. The poison, I had persuaded Elizabeth Lambert to purchase was missing. All at once, the prospect of James becoming sicker was terrifying.

I joined the doctor in the bedroom, as he examined James, who was thrashing around on the bed screaming incoherently. The doctor scowled and ordered me out of the room. When he returned a few moments later, he gave me another lecture over the state of the room and the lack of bedding. Then he scribbled some words onto a sheet of paper and instructed me to present it to his assistant, without delay.

I left our rooms and rested on the stile in the field behind the house where I could watch to see when he left. There was no point in going to the doctor's rooms, for I had not a farthing left. I could not pay for the medicine and I could not see the purpose in trying to explain this to the doctor. He had eyes. He must have been able to see there was no food or drink in the house; no soap, no water and barely a stick of furniture. I had purchased as much medicine as I could afford, and if I had any money left I would have used it for opium pills, before I fed myself or the children. No doubt that sounds selfish, but Richard made this choice easier. He was a good son and used his earnings to support the other children.

No sooner had the doctor removed himself from the house, Samuel Oxborrow arrived and let himself in. I hastened back as I wanted to be around to hear their conversation. I was beginning to worry and did not want James to have the opportunity to accuse me of interfering with his food if he unexpectedly became coherent.

I stood at the door of the bedroom watching over Samuel's shoulder as he approached James. As much as I disliked my husband, what I saw in that room haunts me to this day. Blood dripped from

James face. It dribbled from his mouth in great, gobs of sputum. He screamed again and put most of his right hand in his mouth, scratching at his gums until the blood spurted down his chin. His left hand clawed at his stomach which was covered in bloody lesions. In between his fingers were shreds of meat.

Samuel grabbed James' hands and held them away from his body. He turned to me, words spilling out of his mouth in a torrent of horror as he explained that the shreds were strips of flesh James had wrenched from his own stomach. While he talked James, in his delirium, screamed of rats and ferrets. In one sickening spasm, he pulled his hand away and tore a strip of flesh as big as a fist from his stomach and thrust it down upon the mattress, claiming he had discovered the ferret.

I do not know how Samuel stayed in there. It finished me. I exited the room, shocked and stood trembling in the doorway. Kezia glared at me and asked what was wrong. She said it was no secret that I hated James, so why did I look so upset now he was dying? I answered that he was a wicked man and had ill-treated me the whole of our marriage but for what it once had been I hoped he would die and die quickly, for no man should suffer as he did. She sneered at me and told me I was the wicked one and would burn in hell for what I had done. Sibella admonished her but the words were out. Kezia tended to all birthing women in the village and was a gibble-gabble. I did not doubt there would be talk, as there was when my children died ten years ago. There was some justice in that, just as there was in this, but it was not the whole story. Yes, I had given him poison. Yes, I had made him sadly, but who had removed the poison? Had he been given more? He must have.

James lingered another two days. Doctor Lock visited one of the days but James had stopped screaming by then and lay quietly. By the time I rose and looked in on him the next day, he was gone; cold, bloody and ravaged. I knew I would be held to account. It was only the when of it.

Chapter Nine

A clash with the law

Louisa arrived at Claxton Hall by hansom cab, excited and happy. It had taken several days to recover from reading the contents of the diary, and she was contemplating whether to dispose of it. Louisa had encountered little unpleasantness in her life, and the grotesque descriptions laid bare in the diary were too graphic to leave her unmoved by the experience. Part of her considered Mary Emily Cage an inhumane monster comparable with Jack the Ripper and his recent reign of terror through the streets of London, but another part sympathised with the hopeful young girl, moulded into the cruel, selfish woman she became through unendurable hardships. Tonight however, she put these thoughts firmly from her mind to concentrate on the matter at hand.

When she alighted from the cab Louisa saw the familiar forms of Ada and Bessie Ridley waiting on the pavement in front of the arched entrance to Caxton Hall.

"Hello cousins," she cried jovially and reached to them, gently taking each of their hands in turn and kissing their cheeks.

"We are so pleased to see you," said Bessie. "How have you enjoyed London?"

"A great deal," replied Louisa. "My aunt has taken me to see a play and an opera already and I have shopped almost every day. It is a great shame I must go home next week."

"I am sure you miss your family," said Ada. "You will be glad to leave by the time it comes. London is too tiring after a while. Come inside. Meet some friends."

Louisa needed no introduction to Millicent Fawcett who she recognised as soon as she stepped into the large hall. She waved to her relative across the room as there was a throng of women around her preventing movement in that direction. Ada gently guided her towards a stern looking woman wearing a high collared lace shirt with navy blue satin dress over, and sporting an impervious expression.

"I would like to introduce you to Emmeline Pankhurst," said Ada.

"Pleased to meet you," said Louisa, making small talk for a few minutes, before Emmeline made her excuses and joined Millicent Fawcett on the stage. A younger, shorter version of Emmeline, who Bessie identified as Christabel Pankhurst, climbed the stairs to the stage. Finally, a solidly-built woman dressed in a dark, high-necked brocade dress in stark contrast to her white hair, edged in between Millicent and her companions, completing the four speakers.

"Charlotte Despard," said Ada reverently. "Poor Millicent is rather outnumbered tonight."

"How is that?" whispered Louisa as a rotund woman in high stiletto heels, joined the stage and began to introduce the speakers.

"They are all militants and she is not," explained Ada. "This debate could be a little one-sided."

The large woman finished her introduction and beckoned Christabel Pankhurst to come over. She stepped forward confidently and launched into a strident attack on the government.

"As you all know, we ceased militant action at the end of last year on the promise that the Conciliation Bill would go through. Whilst Prime Minister Asquith is making all the right assurances, I have it on exceedingly good authority that this bill will never be passed. He has not the smallest intention of granting us the vote and rumour has it that his priority will be to enfranchise all men first."

"You cannot know this," protested Millicent Fawcett from her podium. "I do not profess to know what machinations occur within government but we cannot take the position that they are liars before they have had the opportunity to discuss the bill, which we know cannot take place until May."

Emmeline joined her daughter on the opposite side of the stage.

"But we do know," she said. "It is openly discussed in parliament. They forget we have some male sympathisers and think their secrets will not be revealed but we have heard that this bill will not go through, despite their promises. We say act now and lose no time."

"Hear, hear," the hall filled with a roar of encouragement as a substantial part of the audience shouted their approval. The debate continued. Louisa listened enthralled, empathising with both points of view. As the Pankhursts continued their impassioned plea, the atmosphere in the hall grew ever more febrile. Some of the women became angry and agitated until Louisa witnessed language from some women she had never heard before from the coarsest of men. It was a very different atmosphere to the quiet, dignified night of the census evasion.

By the time the debate was concluded, passions were high. Ada took Louisa's hand and began to propel her to the front of the hall so they could commiserate with Millicent Fawcett, who had been on the less popular side of the argument. But in the excitable throng of women Louisa dropped her hand and became separated from her cousins.

Feeling faint in the stifling, crowded hall she squeezed past a gap of women and through a side door. She took in the cold air in deep staccato breaths, gasping audibly.

"Are you quite well," asked a well-spoken woman in a black evening dress and tailored coat. She drew deeply from a cigarette, smoke hanging in the air as she exhaled.

"I am better now," said Louisa. "It was stifling in there for a while."

The woman opened an elegant silver cigarette case. "Would you like one?" she asked.

"Thank you, no, I do not smoke," Louisa replied.

"More fool you," said her companion. "Cigarettes and alcohol make it all so much more bearable." She held out her hand. "I am Clara," she said.

"Pleased to meet you," said Louisa introducing herself. "I do not live in London but have travelled from Ipswich."

"How very provincial," said Clara, "have you been with us long?"

"With you?" asked Louisa, confused.

"With the suffragettes, you silly ass," said Clara.

"Not really," said Louisa. "I was part of the Ipswich census evasion though."

Clara laughed. "How militant of you," she said. "Have you been on a demonstration yet?"

"I do not know if my father would allow that."

Clara snorted. "Really," she exclaimed, "my father has no idea what I do; and I do not consider it any of his business."

"That is very brave," said Louisa uncertainly, the words tailing away.

"It is not brave," said Clara curling her lip. "The whole point about being a suffragette is to try to change this patriarchal system. We do not ask our fathers for permission. Have you never done anything wrong or broken the law?"

"No, never," said Louisa.

The side door banged open behind her and another two young women in long dresses and feather boas emerged, giggling.

"There you are," said Clara.

"Cynthia, Laura, I would like to introduce you to Louisa. She has never attended a demonstration nor broken the law."

"Pleased to meet you, "said Louisa, inching towards the door, "but I must go now. My cousins wait for me inside."

"You can spare five minutes, can you not?" asked Clara taking Louisa by the hand and dragging her towards the side street.

"I really cannot," said Louisa pulling away.

"Come on, quickly," said Laura. "Just up here."

"But..."

"Come on," cried Laura pulling Louisa by the hand and running towards a small crowd of about twenty women at the top of the narrow street.

Louisa opened her mouth again to protest but was propelled along by Laura. The crowd of women were obviously suffragettes as evidenced by their purple and green badges and a large placard with "votes for women" in bold black writing, just readable in the fading light.

"What are they doing?" asked Louisa.

"You will see," replied Clara darkly, reaching into her bag.

One of the women in the group, notably taller than her peers, clapped her hands, "quickly now girls," she said. "We do not want Millicent to get wind of this."

They hurried down a wide road, into a warren of alleyways, and presently found themselves at a street corner. The tall woman beckoned them to stop, and they stood quietly in the shadow of the wall.

"The police station is over there," she whispered. "As soon as you have let loose run as quickly as you can in different directions, like you did before. Are you ready?"

"Ready for what?" asked Louisa, but her voice was drowned by a sea of noise as the women ran towards the red-brick station, hurling a volley of stones into the windows of the building. They cracked like gunshots in the dusky night.

"Run," said Clara as the front door of the police station slammed open and a whiskered policeman ran out brandishing a stick.

"Oi, you women; stop at once" he commanded, as the women fled up the street. He ran behind them as several of his colleagues emerged behind him, joining the pursuit.

Louisa ran instinctively. She did not know where she was running to until she saw Laura ahead, feather boa trailing from her neck. Louisa ran in her direction; but she was not shod for fleetness of foot and went over badly on her ankle as she stepped into a pothole in the road. She stumbled and fell, just scrabbling to her feet when one of the younger constables caught up with her and grabbed her roughly by her coat.

"I have one of the bitches," he shouted up the street.

"Get off me," Louisa cried. "This has nothing to do with me."

The constable dragged her coat open, buttons pinging into the gutter. "What is this?" he asked, pointing to the purple and green button badge given to her by Constance Andrews.

She groaned inwardly, wishing she had not decided to wear the button beneath her coat tonight to show her support for the movement.

"You are coming with me," said the policeman, grabbing her roughly by the wrist. He dragged her behind him as he walked in strides too wide for her to match.

As they neared the police station, Louisa crunched through glass scattered across the street. Every window was cracked and broken. A policeman appeared from the dark of an alleyway pulling a woman behind him who was spitting and snarling like a wild cat. "I am not coming with you," she screamed and sat down in the road.

The policeman hauled her to her feet by her hair and slapped her twice in the face. "That is where you are wrong, he snarled. You walk or I will drag you."

"You bastard," screamed the woman who Louisa now recognised as Clara. "I will have your badge for this."

The policeman laughed at her and then spat on the ground close to her feet. "Get through that door now," he said. "We will see what my sergeant has to say about your behaviour."

Louisa and Clara were pushed unceremoniously through the door of the station, through a hallway, down a corridor and into a small room with bars across the window and a hatchway. The policeman pushed them roughly through the door and Louisa fell onto the floor sobbing.

"Pull yourself together you silly woman," hissed Clara. "Do not give them the satisfaction."

"I did not ask for any of this," snapped Louisa. "How has this happened? Why did you make me do this?"

"Nobody made you do anything," said Clara. "Either you are one of us or you are not."

She sat down on the metal bed and lit a cigarette from the bag she still carried. She took a long drag and blew the smoke in Louisa's direction.

"What happens now?" asked Louisa.

"How should I know," said Clara. "I have never been caught before."

"I need to speak to my aunt," said Louisa. "She will be wondering what has happened to me."

"You will be lucky," said Clara. "They will not let us out tonight."

Louisa put her head in her hands, wondering how she had been stupid enough to get caught up in this. They sat in silence while Clara smoked her cigarette. The cell was freezing cold and the only place to sit was on the bed, so she perched next to Clara shivering. Clara glared disdainfully.

Louisa jumped as the hatch on the door slammed back unexpectedly and a face appeared through the bars.

A voice rumbled in the background.

"Two of them," he said gruffly and a few seconds later, "glad to."

Keys jangled against the metal door which opened to reveal a sharp-faced man wearing a dusty cape over his suit and sporting a neatly clipped moustache.

"What have we here?" he asked, peering at the two women.

"Please, I need to telephone my aunt," said Louisa.

The man looked down his nose towards the young woman sitting on the bed, head bowed and staring at the floor.

He laughed a deep, unsympathetic laugh. "You get nothing," he sneered. "I have no windows left in my police station. You are going to pay dearly for what you have done."

"But I did nothing," cried Louisa jumping to her feet. "I threw no missile. I was just there at the wrong time."

Clara took another cigarette from her bag and placed it carelessly in the side of her mouth. "She never did a thing, the little mouse," she said. "She is not a suffragette, she is a child."

The sergeant snatched the cigarette from her mouth and ground it into the floor with an unpolished boot.

"No smoking in here," he said, removing her bag. "Yours too," he said reaching towards Louisa.

"Please, no" she said but he took it roughly from her hand.

"You are up in front of the magistrate tomorrow," he said to Louisa, before pointing at Clara. "You, come with me."

He dragged Clara from the cell. A door clanged nearby and Louisa heard Clara shouting from a nearby room. Ten minutes later she could hear the strains of the suffragette anthem from further down the corridor. "From the daughters of the nation, bursts a cry of indignation….." Clara was singing as loudly as she could.

She kept it up for several hours. When Louisa finally fell asleep, huddled on a thin bolster on the wooden bed in the freezing cell with no blankets, she could still hear the faint, tired strains of singing.

She was woken in the early dawn by the clang of the door bolt. A bowl of thick porridge was thrust towards her by a whiskered constable, who she had not encountered the previous night.

"Eat," he commanded, dropping a spoon into the bowl. Porridge splattered across the floor landing on Louisa's skirt. She was about to speak when the sound of metal clattering onto the stone floor distracted the constable, who darted into the corridor.

A loud roar came from the distance. "You filthy, little bitch," yelled a deep voice. "She has thrown her breakfast on the floor."

The door of Clara's cell opened and Louisa heard a slap followed by a high pitched scream. She covered her ears and wept.

Chapter Ten

Trapped

The experience of standing in the dock of the Magistrate's Court, next to a sullen Clara and trembling from head to foot, was one Louisa hoped never to repeat. The reprimand from the Judge, followed by a two week custodial sentence, bought Louisa to the lowest point of her young life.

After the judge rapped his gavel and dismissed the court, two female warders removed Louisa from the dock. They marched her through a white-washed corridor to the holding cells, where she stood in disbelief before spotting Laura and one of the Pankhurst women rushing towards them.

"Clara, Clara," shouted Laura. "Do not worry. We are trying to secure your release."

"A good thing too," snapped Clara.

"Will you help me?" cried Louisa.

"Who are you?" asked Laura.

"I am Louisa Russell. Tell Ada or Bessie Ridley that I am here," she said, "or Millicent Fawcett. They will wonder what has happened." Her voice faltered as she spoke, and tears pricked her eyes.

"I will," assured Laura.

The warders lead them past noisy cells, through a door at the end of the corridor, before herding them into a large, black automated cab. For one moment Louisa hoped they might be driven home; but after an uncomfortable ride they arrived outside the iron-railed gates of Holloway prison.

Louisa gasped at the size of the building as she emerged from the cab. To make matters worse, it was raining. Large droplets splashed onto her face, dripping from her nose. She wiped the rainy tears from her face, hands over her mouth, trying to stifle the sob that threatened to overwhelm her.

Louisa attempted to hold Clara's hand as the warders escorted them through a side gate and into the black and white squared corridor of the woman's prison, but Clara pushed her away. After registration, in a bleak, unheated reception room, they found themselves the occupants of single cells opposite each other, barred doors allowing a partial view into each other's cell.

Louisa placed her face against the metal bars. "I want to go home," she whispered.

"Darling, this cell is your home for the next few weeks," said Clara firmly, seemingly recovered from her ordeal.

"Can your friends secure our release?" asked Louisa.

"They will try but whether they will succeed is an entirely different matter," said Clara.

"Are you not worried?" asked Louisa.

"Not at all," she replied. "I am not afraid."

Around midday, a dour prison wardress placed a tin plate of unappetising, congealed meat through the cell door. She handed Louisa a spoon and Louisa picked through the mess eating only a small portion. Clara received the same meal but made no attempt to eat it. Instead, she hurled it against the window of her cell, laughing as it dripped down the brick walls.

"I will eat nothing from you," she screamed at the prison wardress. She behaved in the same manner for the evening meal and at breakfast the next day the wardress thrust a thin bowl of porridge at Clara. "This is your last chance," she hissed.

Clara picked up the bowl and spoon as if she intended to eat the meal but walked straight in front of the prison wardress before deliberately upending the bowl over the warder's shoes.

"You have done it now," snarled the warder pushing Clara onto the bed. Clara shook her head, glared at the warder and started to sing.

"Stop it," said Louisa from her cell. "You will be in terrible trouble."

Clara pressed her face to the bars. "I – do – not – care," she said slowly and precisely. Then shouted, "I do not care" over and over until her voice cracked from the strain.

As Clara ceased her vocal protest, footsteps clattered on the floor further up the corridor accompanied by the creak of something wheeled. Through the grille in the door, Louisa saw two men in white coats pushing a gurney containing tubes and a jug of dark green liquid. Even from a distance, she smelled the rancid odour of rotting cabbage. The men were accompanied by a hard-faced female warder and a well-dressed man in a smart suit and polished shoes.

The warder unlocked the door to Clara's cell and the men wheeled the gurney to the far end. The warder reached below and produced a bowl of porridge.

"You have one more chance to eat this," she said, "otherwise you will be made to eat it."

"Never," said Clara.

"Please eat," called Louisa, "please Clara."

"I will not," said Clara shaking her head stubbornly.

The suited man nodded while the white-coated men pushed Clara onto a wooden chair by the side of her bed. She screamed and thrashed her arms before being pinned to the chair by the stronger men. They worked in silence placing a metal gag over her face and jamming her mouth open. Clara wriggled and moaned, red-faced with exertion but for all the effort, she remained trapped.

"Hold her head," barked the man, nodding to the wardress.

"Yes doctor."

The men stood either side of Clara holding her shoulders until she was motionless. Then the doctor grabbed a dirty length of hose from the gurney and snapped it straight. Taking Clara's chin in his hand, he tipped her head backwards and rammed the tube into her gullet. Clara instinctively gagged causing lumps of vomit to stream either side of the metal gag, which spewed down her face.

"Stop it," screamed Louisa.

The doctor raised the tube high over Clara's head, inserted a funnel and poured the evil looking green liquid into the tube where it gushed into Clara's stomach.

But for a small part of the grille blocked by the warder, Louisa could see everything. She forced herself to watch as Clara vomited repeatedly, while the green liquid spurted from gaps between her mouth and the metal gag. When the jug was empty, the spectacle ceased. The doctor removed the restraints before lecturing Clara on the stupidity of refusing food. He told her he hoped she had learned her lesson and hoped he would never see her again and then gestured to the men to remove the gurney. They left the cell without a backward glance at Clara, sitting broken on the chair staring wordlessly at the mess on the cell floor.

"Talk to me Clara," said Louisa. "Can you speak?"

Clara stared with hate-filled eyes. "They will pay" she whispered, through swollen, battered lips. Her smart, black dress was coated with vomit and her loosened hair stuck to her shoulders. Sweat and liquid feed covered her skin and clothes.

"I am so sorry," said Louisa. "I cannot believe they treated you so badly."

"Then you are naïve," said Clara hoarsely. "Many of us have been made to endure force-feeding."

Louisa opened her mouth to sympathise but Clara said, "I cannot talk any longer." Standing gingerly, she limped around the chair hanging onto the back for stability. She crawled onto the bed where she laid face-down, immobile save for her shaking shoulders.

Louisa watched silently from her cell. Every so often she pressed her nose to the door bars, checking on Clara who lay prone on the bed. She remained shocked and angry at the scene she had witnessed, numbed to the noises of the prison which failed to register in her consciousness. When a wardress approached her cell in the early afternoon, Louisa was taken by surprise, oblivious to her presence and deaf to her footsteps.

The door clanged making Louisa jump. The wardress entered her cell and beckoned. "Come with me," she said.

Louisa followed uncertainly until they reached a small room, containing only a table and two wooden chairs.

"Wait here."

She waited an anxious five minutes, drumming her fingers on the table, until she heard more footsteps, and then watched as the door swung open. Standing next to the prison wardress was Daniel.

A mixture of relief at a familiar face, and shame at her circumstances, overwhelmed Louisa. She dropped her head in her hands and sobbed.

"Come now," said Daniel, patting her shoulder awkwardly.

"Have you come to help me?" asked Louisa between sobs. Daniel nodded.

"I am sorry," she sniffed, "but I did not do what they said. I was in the wrong place at the wrong time, caught up in something I did not understand."

"They know," said Daniel. "Some of the other women you were with that night insisted you were not part of it. The authorities were unconvinced at first but when your uncle intervened, they were persuaded."

"My uncle," gasped Louisa. "I will be in so much trouble. How did you come to be involved?"

"Mrs Fawcett was advised of your predicament," said Daniel. "She contacted your cousins who informed your aunt and uncle. I happened to be visiting Harrington Gardens because..," he looked at his feet, "because I felt it necessary to ensure you had returned safely from Caxton Hall following the debate. I called the next day and found your aunt and uncle recovering from their visit by the Misses Ridley."

"Was my uncle very angry?" asked Louisa.

"He was less than impressed," said Daniel, "but I explained our connection and asked if I could be of help. They spoke with me more openly than they might have done in other circumstances. You are fortunate that your uncle is such a highly regarded surgeon, for it was his influence that precipitated your release. He does not think it appropriate for a man in his position to visit Holloway Prison, so they agreed I should come and I am here now to escort you home."

"I am grateful," murmured Louisa. "Thank you for your kindness to my aunt and uncle; and to me."

"I did it for Sophia," said Daniel curtly. "Had she known of your predicament, she would have insisted we help."

"We will leave now," he said, turning to the wardress.

The hook-nosed woman grimaced as she led them out. She glared at Louisa through narrowed eyes before opening the heavy doors into the reception area where Louisa's bag was returned intact.

Louisa followed Daniel towards the exterior prison door, then grasped his arm and pulled him back. "I cannot leave Clara" she said.

"Then stay," said Daniel, "Clara's fate is in the hands of the Pankhurst's. I believe they are trying to secure her release, but it is not your problem and certainly not mine."

"They hurt her terribly," cried Louisa. "She is alone and in pain."

"I am sorry," said Daniel, "but I can do nothing for her. I am charged with your recovery and that is all."

Louisa stood still, looking back towards the reception area through haunted eyes.

"I will not waste precious time convincing you to leave," said Daniel with his hand on the door. "I am going now."

Louisa took a final glance before rushing to catch Daniel, as he strode towards a carriage parked outside the driveway of the prison grounds. He opened the carriage door just long enough for Louisa to enter and then slammed it shut. She sat down, chest heaving with the exertion of trying to reach him. He did not look her way.

Louisa remembered little of the journey from the prison to her aunt and uncle's house. She was tired, relieved and above all concerned about the likely reaction from her uncle. The journey barely registered in her consciousness before she found herself alighting from the carriage outside Harrington Gardens. Daniel, silent through the journey, opened the door of the carriage and took her hand as she descended, before guiding her up the steps and into the house. Her aunt and uncle were waiting in the drawing room.

Louisa opened her mouth to apologise but her uncle ignored her. Shaking Daniel by the hand he said, "thank you for returning my niece. Please join me in the study?"

"Thank you, sir," replied Daniel and the two men left the room.

Louisa turned to her aunt lowering her head, "Is uncle terribly angry?" she asked.

Her aunt sighed, "Yes, he is Louisa, I wish it were not so. It was all I could do to prevent him from sending word to your father. In this, I have succeeded, but he wishes you to leave the house at once."

"I am so sorry," cried Louisa. "I did not set out with the intention of any wrong-doing. I was naïve and stupid, perhaps even weak. I take full responsibility for that, but please believe me when I tell you that I never intended any harm."

"I do believe you," said her aunt, "but reputation is everything to your uncle. The slightest hint of a scandal is an anathema to him. You know he deplores the idea of suffrage. Your attendance at a suffragette rally is almost as bad as your detention in Holloway. I cannot convince him that this escapade was unplanned. Much as I will miss you, it is best if you return to Ipswich. I will have a better chance of smoothing matters when you are not here."

"But my father is not expecting me back until next week," said Louisa. "He will ask why you do not want me."

"While I hate to conceal anything from my brother, I can see no benefit in telling him what has occurred," said Aunt Beatrice. Not only will you be in trouble, but there will be a question over our guardianship while you were in our care. Ada and Bessie have convinced me of your innocence and I would not see you punished any further for your naivety. I believe you have suffered quite enough. I will write to Henry today and tell him I have been unwell and you are returning to Ipswich to avoid catching my illness. You will travel back tomorrow. The letter will be with him by the time you arrive."

"Thank you," said Louisa, "and thank you for believing in me. I am so sorry I let you down but I promise I will never place myself in such a position again. As strongly as I feel about our cause, I am more convinced than ever that Millicent's position is correct. We will only succeed through peaceful protest."

Aunt Beatrice smiled, "a useful lesson learned," she said as the door opened and Louisa's uncle entered alone.

"I am truly sorry, sir" said Louisa before he could speak. "I would not wish to bring embarrassment to your house, for all the world."

"No doubt," said her uncle curtly, "but the fact remains, that you have. Your foolishness has given rise to unanticipated consequences. You have demonstrated precisely those reasons why women should not be allowed to vote. Women lack the wisdom and rationality to make sensible choices."

Louisa bit her lip, trying not to let her uncle goad her into an argument over his unreasonable views. She managed to control herself. "I am sorry, sir," she said again.

"Indeed," continued her uncle. "But, I think it best you leave and return to the care of your father so there is no future temptation to involve yourself with this senseless cause. Mr Bannister returns to Ipswich by coach tomorrow and has offered to escort you home. I have agreed."

"Thank you uncle," said Louisa, "but I do not need a chaperone."

"Nevertheless you will have one," said her Uncle firmly. "You leave after breakfast tomorrow."

Chapter Eleven

To death with dignity

From the moment Louisa boarded the carriage the following day, her expectations were low. She anticipated little pleasantness from her travelling companion and this assessment was proved correct. Daniel was dour and wore a perpetual frown. He barely uttered a word as they travelled in uncomfortable silence.

After half an hour, Louisa felt so awkward that she attempted to start a conversation. "How is Sophia?" she asked.

"I do not know," Daniel replied. "It has been several days since my last contact with the family. My recent concerns have been with other matters. I have neglected the family a great deal considering the parlous health of Charles when I left."

"I am sorry if I have been one of the other matters to which you refer," said Louisa." I appear to have, unwittingly, taken up much of your time that would have been better spent in your duty to your family."

Daniel sighed. "Do you ever think of anyone but yourself, Louisa?" he asked. "I have been occupied, in the most, with business. The electrical consultation was not concluded satisfactorily.

Louisa blushed. "I did not mean to offend you," she snapped. "I was trying to apologise. And I am sure Mr Drummond will be quite well by the time you return."

"I will be greatly relieved if that is the case," replied Daniel, drifting into another brooding silence.

Louisa sighed. She had packed the diary into her bag in anticipation of any awkwardness on the journey, knowing that conversation could be politely avoided by reading. As she held the diary in her hand, the repulsion she felt towards Mary Cage left her unsure whether she could bear to read to the end. Given that the alternative was stilted conversation and uncomfortable silence, she decided it was the worst of two evils and opened the diary at the place marked with a purple ribbon.

The village gossips finished me in the end. We almost buried James. I thought it was over until Constables Grimwood and Whitehead strode through the Lychgate while we waited to toss the final sod into his grave. We surrounded the coffin like black-clad crows while Reverend Shorting read the litany. Before the last words were uttered, Constable Grimwood raised his hand towards the Reverend and beckoned him over. A whispered conversation ensued, then Reverend Shorting announced that the funeral would not take place today and there would be a coroner's inquest instead. The crows took flight, cackling together, filled with gleeful pleasure at my misfortune. Then Constable Whitehead asked me to follow him back to his house, which was also the village police station.

Kezia Oxborrow watched as I left the churchyard. She looked down her long nose with an air of satisfaction. "Now you will hang," she said.

I stayed the night at the police house with Constable Whitehead, which was not at all uncomfortable, considering the conditions I usually endured. They gave me three meals a day during my time there, which was two more than usual.

I returned home only once again. It was the following day and the doctors had finished picking over James, returning his body to the church to be decently buried. Constable Whitehead escorted me to the graveside and I watched my husband interred for the second time. Then Mr Grimwade told me they knew about the rat poison that Elizabeth Lambert purchased for me and asked me where it was now.

He escorted me back to the house and I told him he could look around to his heart's content, but that he would find no poison. He found a packet of orange-coloured powder in one of the cupboards which caused him great excitement and he passed it to another policeman who took it away. Quite how he found anything at all is a miracle. We had nothing. There was never any food or drink in the house.

Then he told me to follow him and he walked to the privy, opening the door with the edges of his fingers, curling his lips in disgust. I joined him, watching disinterestedly as he kicked the loose brick away from the floor with his foot. There, beneath the brick, was the missing packet of powder; but a lot less of it. I sat, before I fell, with the shock of it. How the powder came to be there, and from where, I could not imagine.

I remained with Constable Whitehead and his family until the inquest which was held about a week after James died. Phoebe Whitehead, an old acquaintance of mine for many years, kept me apprised of the tattle in the village during my confinement. It was she who told me when they removed James' bodily organs to test for poison and I knew it would not end well for me. Poor James could not sleep quietly in death any more than he had in the last weeks of his life, for they dug him up once again to remove his brain; so Phoebe said.

The inquest took place at the Ten Bells public house over the weekend. They called upon my two children, Mary Ann and Richard to give evidence. Richard, a good, loyal son, would not speak ill of me but Mary Ann went against me. It was not entirely unexpected. After all, I implicated Mary in my lie to Elizabeth and Mary was the type of woman to value the truth above her own mother's life.

I did not comprehend most of the evidence given at the inquest. There was much talk of tests and medical matters and a drawn-out discussion over the presence of poison in James stomach and bowel. After much debate, they concluded that James had died from ingesting arsenic. Then the Coroner pursed his lips and told me in a hushed voice that I would be remanded in custody to await the Ipswich summer assizes.

After the inquest, they moved me from my comfortable quarters in the prison room at Stonham to the cold, crowded cells of Ipswich Gaol. They placed me in a cell with three other women and set me to work in the prison laundry. The work was hard but I did not mind as I still received three meals a day. Breakfast was a paltry affair of bread and tea, but we received meat and potatoes every day for dinner, without the worry of having to pay for it. Working in the laundry bought an additional reward of a small piece of cheese with the supper meal. Some women complained of the hard, heavy labour, but it kept me warm and the food kept me full. It made my time in prison bearable, and whilst it was not the best, neither was it the worst time of my life.

I thought to be a pariah in prison, but unexpectedly made friendships. A particular friend was Polly, a girl in her third decade, slim and pretty but with only one arm, having lost the other in a childhood accident. Polly was clever and made up for the loss of her arm with tricks and wiles. She had a reputation for being able to procure anything and there was always a ready supply of gin and tobacco for those who wanted it. Polly became a true, loyal friend who did not judge me as others had, choosing to disregard gossip in favour of finding out information by asking. Though there were two decades between us we got along well, having lead similar lives. Before gaol, she lived with a cruel man who beat her so badly she lost a child and never conceived another. It bonded us.

I must have mentioned my fondness for opium pills during our time in prison because she presented me with a small packet before supper one night. I was delighted, not just because I desired them but because it was the first time in memory that anyone had been good to me, for no personal gain. Opiates were cheap, of course. How could poor women afford them otherwise? But it was still a rare kindness and I will never forget it.

Ipswich Gaol was not built to provide prisoners with views of the outside. Some cells had windows but mine did not, however there was a window on the way to the laundry room, so I noticed as the days became lighter and, before long, I felt them getting warmer too. Summer was on its way and along with it the Summer Assizes, at which I would be judged. As the time drew closer, I received the first of two visits from my attorney Mr Gudgeon. A pock-faced man of about forty summers, Gudgeon spoke in a deep, monotone voice. His features were obscured by a poorly trimmed beard and a full handlebar moustache. His natural air of gloom and despondency sapped my confidence on the first meeting and destroyed it completely on the second. Finally the day of the assizes arrived and I was called to the bar to face the judge with my attorney by my side, like a grounded albatross.

I was permitted to dress in my own clothes for the assizes. Someone took it upon themselves to launder them during my confinement in prison and they retrieved and mended my black bonnet too. I looked quite respectable for once; ironic given the circumstances. Court orderlies guided me to the dock, built for others taller than I. It was a challenge to see over. The jury, composed of stern-looking, middle-aged men, were sworn in. There was not a kind face amongst them. Proceedings began when the judge banged a gavel.

The prosecution started by summarising the last days of my husband, James, beginning with his breakdown in the field through to a graphic description of his final, agonising injuries. Then they introduced Elizabeth Lambert and called her to give evidence.

She stood, trembling on the stand, unfamiliar with the formality of her situation and I felt ashamed that my actions had bought her to this. She was asked to recount her story which she did in a faltering voice. I leaned forward to hear better and as I did, my legs buckled, and the wardress behind me shoved a wooden chair behind my legs, There I sat looking through the dock as Elizabeth continued to give her evidence.

On the day I visited her, it transpired that Elizabeth returned hotfoot to her lodgings to tell the bed-bound Mrs Parker all about the errand. Half of Debenham would have been aware of it by the end of that day if Mrs Parker had the opportunity to see anyone else. As it happened, Elizabeth's mother was the next visitor, having travelled from Wetheringsett for the day. Mrs Parker lost no time in relaying the gossip and Elizabeth's mother took it upon herself to tell Mr Grimwade.

Mr Smith, the chemist, was next to the stand. He fixed me with a cold stare as he gave his evidence, describing Elizabeth's visit in a dispassionate manner and stating that he had, at first, refused to serve her. When he was cross-examined, the prosecutor implied that he should have stuck with this course of action. Even I could tell he was discomforted by the notion that he might have saved a life had he shown more resolve. It is curious how many casualties there are from a crime, other than the criminal and victim.

After Mr Smith sat down, he continued to stare at me. I was hypnotised by the hatred manifested upon his face and could not wrest my eyes from his countenance until my eldest, Mary Ann, was bought to the bar. Her red-rimmed eyes were half slits in her face and she could barely stand. I leaned forward looking straight at her, silently mouthing my apologies. She did not look in my direction and stared at her feet as she spoke. Her voice trembled and the judge *asked her to speak up on more than one occasion. Her ordeal lasted but a short time, there being nothing much to say except to refute the story given to Elizabeth Lambert. She denied ever having spoken of rats, mice or poison and said it had been three months or more since she visited Stonham Aspal and was not aware of her father's illness, as the news had not travelled to her village, some three and a half miles away.*

William Gunn was called next. He took a long look at me and then purposely misquoted some of my words. Although I had long reconciled myself to the deceit and folly of my former life, I was unprepared for downright lies from another about my conduct on that fateful day. Gunn claimed I told him James was 'so ill he could keep nothing down and that it would soon go one way or the other'. That was indeed true, but I never told him that 'the other man was not far off,' yet that is how he quoted me in court, under oath. We parted on bad terms that day and it is clear he has neither forgiven, nor forgotten. His evidence served me ill. Perhaps I should have been more tolerant of him; after all, he did me a kindness in providing a ride without expectation of payment.

I was relieved to see my son, Richard on the stand after Gunn. I knew he would be loyal as he had already proved at the inquest. He told the truth, as he saw it, but when he confirmed that I was the only one who waited on James during his illness, I knew it to be another nail in my coffin. Somebody else waited on him. Somebody gave him at least one dose, if not several, from that poison I had off Elizabeth Lambert. I wish I could go back in time and re-live that day. It was a senseless waste, procuring poison without having the use of it.

Richard was at the stand for a long time and was questioned relentlessly. He called me attentive, kind and affectionate in his evidence, although I was none of those things. I realise now what a selfish, uncaring monster I had been. I wish I was still driven by the same bitter feelings towards James that motivated me before. Now, having had the benefit of shelter and nourishment even in these difficult circumstances, I no longer feel such hatred of the world. I will never forget how cruelly James treated me or how my life might have been different if he were a kinder man but the disgust that fuelled my every callous action, no longer fires me. My anger has dissolved and been replaced with sadness and shame.

Indeed, my shame was made public in court when Mr Power, the Prosecutor, asked Richard about Robert Tricker. Despite his loyalty, Richard was obliged to confirm I had gone away with Tricker on more than one occasion. An unfamiliar feeling of embarrassment covered me, until the colour rose in my cheeks and I was hot and flustered. For the first time, I understood why the faces of the jurors displayed puzzled disgust as they tried to comprehend how a mother could desert her young children for her lover, leaving them to fend for themselves. There were no poor people on the jury though. How could they know what it is to have no money and no choice?

There was a brief moment of hope when Mr Cooper, the defence, asked Richard about the cat. A cat may seem unimportant, but on the Wednesday before he died, I passed Richard some bread and butter to take to James. By then, James was filled with such mistrust he would not eat anything prepared by me even if it was given to him by another. James dashed the dish to the floor and refused to eat it, so Richard picked it up and bought it back to me. The food was too spoiled for anyone else, so we gave it to the cat. Richard explained that the cat ate the food and remained healthy, suffering no ill effects from its repast. The jury would surely realise that poison could not have been added to the bread and butter which might cast doubt on some of the other allegations.

The witness I dreaded most of all took the stand next. Samuel Oxborrow was a life-long friend of James. He attended our wedding and James attended his. I knew Samuel would not hold back but he gave a more balanced account than I thought he might. He did at least tell the jury that James had been gaoled for 'misusing' me, but talked about Robert Tricker again, reminding the jury of my faithlessness.

As Samuel began to speak, I remembered the horror of the last days of James' life which I had managed to keep suppressed until now. A wave of nausea flooded my gullet and goose-bumps stood cold upon my skin. In answer to careful questioning by the defence, Samuel described the moment James tore strips of flesh from his stomach and mouth in his mania, under the illusion he was curing himself of the ravaging pain. An elderly, corpulent man on the jury put his hand to his mouth and visibly wretched. The judge asked if the man would like to be excused but the juror declined, although he *remained ashen-grey for the rest of the testimony. As I slumped further down my hard wooden chair, I wished the judge would excuse me for a few moments as the guilt and the shame threatened to overwhelm me.*

While Samuel was unexpectedly fair in his account, his wife Kezia manipulated my words until she was as close to a mistruth, as is possible, without actually lying in court. She was asked about the events of the night before James died and told the jury that I said James was a very wicked man and prayed God would take him before morning. My actual words were that I hoped he would die that night because he was in so much pain. But what right do I have to argue the point when I introduced the poison into his system in the first place?

The next witness, Mr Image, puffed his chest out, resplendent with his own self-importance while relaying a barrage of scientific language, that meant nothing to me. I was as unable to comprehend the meaning of his evidence in the courtroom as I had been at the inquest. The little I understood revealed that arsenic was present in James stomach, though why it took quite so many words to say so, I will never know. Perhaps if I had benefitted from an education, I would have understood the evidence that would ultimately condemn me.

I wonder, Anna, as I recite this, whether it would have made any difference if I had been as honest with the defence as I have been with you. I had no confidence that Mr Cooper would succeed in defending me from the gallows, yet he fought valiantly on my behalf, giving the jury serious misgivings about my motivation for murder. After all, I had come and gone from the home freely during my marriage, whether my husband wished it or not and James had no money, so there was no financial gain. What might he have been able to do, had I confessed to purchasing the poison and admitted it was subsequently taken from me?

Not much, probably, as I would have been condemned for using poison in the first place but the real reason I did not tell the truth is that any of my children could have poisoned James. Richard had never showed anything but kindness to his step-father but appearances can deceive. He was, after all, a bastard and there was a stigma attached. Indeed, he may have blamed James for the loss of his real father who never returned to the village again. It was no secret that Sibella disliked her father intensely. She was dear to me, and I dear to her. Every time he abused me, she felt it keenly. I cannot think of a reason why the younger boys would have poisoned him, but both John and William were old enough to have done so, had they found the powder and realised what it was. James was a disagreeable man and John, in particular, had fallen foul of the law on several occasions. His lack of conscience was troubling; but the reality is that anyone could have taken the poison. It was no accident. The powder was wilfully removed and replaced. Who is to say whether it was one of my family or another unrelated individual, but I have been a poor excuse for a mother and if there is a chance that one of my children did this terrible thing, I must pay for it for making them that way.

Louisa looked up from the book, eyes filled with sudden tears. She felt a wholly unexpected sympathy for this woman who she had despised during her last reading of the diary.

Daniel noticed her head move as he watched the passing scenery. He turned his gaze towards her. "Are you well, Louisa?" he asked softly.

"Quite well," she said blinking away tears.

"It is over," said Daniel, misunderstanding her concern," your uncle will not discuss the matter with your father. You have nothing more to worry about as long as you do not get into any further trouble."

"Thank you, but that is not it," said Louisa. She was about to attempt to explain the diary and her unexpected surge of compassion for Mary, when there was a sudden jolt and the cab lurched forward. The impact threw Louisa towards Daniel sitting in the opposite seat. She fell, kneeling in front of him and he grasped her hands instinctively as he moved forward. He held her close, her face just a few inches from his. Their eyes locked and they remained there for several seconds as if hypnotised, then the carriage halted and righted itself. Daniel gently pushed her back onto the seat and dropped her hands.

"Are you hurt?" he asked.

"Not at all," she said, looking at the floor.

Daniel opened the door. "What happened?" he asked the cabman. "Nothing to worry about, sir" he replied. "The wheel ran right over a branch in the road. No harm done."

"Carry on then," said Daniel. The cabman checked the wheels, looked over the horse and took his position at the front of the cab. In a few moments, the cab began to move and the silence inside was punctuated with squeaking and grinding as the wheels ran over the uneven road surface.

Daniel sat down and picked up a newspaper. He looked towards Louisa, opening his mouth as if he were about to speak, but changed his mind. He folded the paper and resumed his examination of the Essex countryside.

Louisa's heart beat so quickly, she struggled to catch her breath. She could not look at Daniel for fear of blushing. Those few seconds where he held her hand and her gaze had provoked a flurry of emotions she neither anticipated nor desired. She felt awkward and uncomfortable, glad of the opportunity to retrieve the diary from the floor of the carriage where it had fallen; grateful to distance herself from the discomfort of the moment. There were only a few paragraphs of Mary's entries left to read.

I sat through the summing-up of both prosecution and defence with my head in my hands, weary of the words that would decide my future, crossing back and forth between educated men in a blur of incomprehension. Finally, the judge dismissed the jury and they set off to consider their verdict while I was released from the dock. I rested some twenty minutes and was given a cup of water to drink. The prison wardresses were kinder than usual and it felt like no time passed before I was called back again and made to stand in front of the judge. The clerk asked the jury if I was guilty or not guilty. The foreman got to his feet standing straight-backed and unflinching. He looked me in the face and said "guilty" in a firm voice.

I was not shocked. Indeed, if it had gone any other way, then I would have been. The verdict was exactly what I expected and was nothing less than I deserved. Other women are beaten; other women do not use poison to try to teach their errant husbands a lesson.

The judge fixed me with sorrowful eyes, peering through thick-lensed glasses. He said I was a dissolute, licentious woman. I did not understand what those words meant but they sounded wicked, so he was probably right in his assessment of my character. Then he placed a black cap over his wig and told me that I would be hanged by the neck until I was dead and asked the Lord God Almighty to have mercy on my soul. I clasped the rails by the dock, using them to stand upright, wobbly from the long day and the expanse of time that had passed since breakfast. I plodded wearily back to the cell and collapsed on the bed, with something closer to relief than distress. I never had any doubt it would end this way.

Chapter Twelve

The return

It was early evening before the cab reached the outskirts of Ipswich. Louisa was subjected to two stops at coaching inns to change the horses, and two meals eaten in awkward silence with Daniel. She was relieved to see the familiar sight of her home town and positively joyful when Christchurch Park loomed into view and she knew she was only a few short minutes from home. Her joyfulness turned to concern, as they approached the upper part of Ivry Street, where an unfamiliar motor vehicle and a windowless horse-drawn carriage were parked near the front of her house.

She hung out of the window on one side while Daniel opened the opposite window, both watching at first with interest, then fearfully as they closed the distance.

"Dear God" exclaimed Daniel and rapped loudly on the front of the cab. "Stop here," he commanded, throwing the door open before striding up the road. Louisa took another look and understood what Daniel had seen that she had not. The horse in front of the second vehicle wore a black plume; the colour of death.

Louisa stayed in the carriage while the cab driver trotted the horses the remaining twenty yards. He stopped the carriage opposite the unfamiliar vehicles and she opened the door and alighted without delay. It was now obvious that the vehicles were directly outside The Rowans. A wave of relief, tempered with guilt, washed over Louisa as she realised it was Sophia's family problem and not her own.

Without waiting for the cab driver to remove her luggage, Louisa raced up the driveway to Sophia's house in time to see the door closing on Daniel. She made to ring the bell and then reconsidered when she noticed a freshly made laurel wreath hanging from a hook on the front door. It was tied with black ribbon. Louisa watched in silence. Every curtain in the house was drawn. The inescapable conclusion was a death. Someone in or close to the household had recently departed.

Leaving her bags where they had been set at the side of the road, Louisa flew into her own house. "Mother, father – what has happened next door?" she called frantically opening doors as she sought out her family. Presently her mother descended downstairs.

"Thank the Lord you are home," she said embracing Louisa. "I fear Sophia will need your friendship more than ever."

"What has happened?" repeated Louisa. "Has somebody died?"

Marianne gestured towards the drawing room. "Sit down," she said, settling next to Louisa on the couch. She took her daughter's hands.

"It is Sophia's father," she said, "he passed away yesterday afternoon, thank God."

Louisa gasped. "Poor Sophia," she said. "Her father was ill when I left for London, but was surely not expected to die."

"No, dear, he was not" said Marianne. "Charles was extremely ill, but rallied after a few days. Then five days ago he was taken ill again with agonising stomach pains. His suffering was excruciating."

"What caused him to suffer so?" asked Louisa.

"They think it dysentery or some other condition of the bowel. Doctor Hill has been here every few days with medicines and potions of one kind or another, but he could not make him better."

"How is Sophia?" asked Louisa. "Have you seen her?"

"She kept to her room yesterday," said Marianne, "at least that is what Maggie tells me. The household are all at sixes and sevens. Jane Piggott cooks but nobody eats; Harold cannot get near the garden for running errands to the doctor and Minnie spends more time keeping our servants informed than at her own work."

Louisa smiled despite the sadness she felt for her friend. "Trust Maggie to arrange things so she does not miss out on any of the household intelligence," she said. "I am truly sorry for the Drummonds though, especially for Sophia and poor Mrs Drummond. They must be heartbroken."

"I have not seen them," said Marianne. "I should call to pay my respects. Perhaps you would like to join me?"

"I would," said Louisa. "Has my father visited yet?"

"He cannot. He is in Cambridge on business for a few days. He is not even aware of this death. We will both represent him tomorrow."

When Louisa woke the next morning, she realised with relief that her return from London had barely registered and her exploits would probably never be discovered. Her relief was heightened with guilt that her misdeeds were hidden behind another's misfortune. She felt a quiet dread for Sophia and nervousness at the thought of seeing Daniel again, assuming he permitted the visit at all. She was relieved to be attending with her mother as it was unlikely that Daniel would turn the two of them away.

She breakfasted with her mother and sister, pacing the back of the house until mid-morning when her mother deemed it an acceptable time to visit. They walked to the neighbouring house, clad in dark apparel.

Jane Piggott answered the door, acknowledging them with a nod and showed them into the drawing room to wait. The long, velvet curtains were drawn and the only light entered the room through a side window. The gloomy room contained too much dark, mahogany furniture giving a feeling of claustrophobia. They stood quietly, watching the door for signs of movement. After a few minutes it opened and Daniel entered the room.

"Mrs Russell, Miss Russell," he said nodding politely.

"We are so sorry to hear the sad news about your uncle," said Marianne, "and have come to pay our condolences to Mrs Drummond."

"Thank you," said Daniel. "She saw you walking up the driveway and asked me to tell you she will see you shortly. May I trouble you to wait here while I escort Miss Louisa to the morning room? Sophia is greatly distressed by her father's death and will appreciate a friendly face at this difficult time."

"Of course," smiled Marianne Russell.

"Thank you," said Louisa, before following Daniel down the tiled hallway in to the morning room.

"Louisa," cried Sophia, jumping to her feet. "Oh, Louisa," her red-rimmed eyes peered from a tear-streaked face framed by tousled hair hanging loose about her shoulders.

"Come here," said Louisa reaching out to her friend. She hugged Sophia tightly, stroking her hair as she cried into her shoulder.

117

Sophia sobbed for several minutes then her shoulders stopped shaking and she pulled away. Louisa guided her to a chair, drawing it close to her own. Holding her hand out towards her friend, she said. "I am so sorry about your father, Sophia. What can I do to help?"

"There is nothing you can do," sniffed Sophia. "It is my poor mother I am worried for."

"Yes," murmured Louisa, "she will miss your father dreadfully and I know it will not be easy. These things take time to mend".

The momentary look that passed between Sophia and Daniel, as he glanced across the Morning Room did not escape Louisa. It was a look she was familiar with, reflecting an understanding of a situation she was not privy to.

"My mother will offer any help she can," said Louisa uncertainly. "Ask anything of us; we only want to help."

Sophia gazed at Daniel as if she was looking for permission to speak, but no words were uttered and the moment passed. Louisa was left floundering for something else to say.

"Would you like to take a walk in the Park?" she asked.

"I would like that very much," replied Sophia, "but tomorrow would be better. Forgive me, but I do not think I could face being among strangers today."

"I quite understand," sympathised Louisa. "I will call for you tomorrow," she said. "I can see how upset you are and will not take up any more of your time today but do send Minnie to us if there is anything at all that we can do." She embraced Sophia again and joined her mother in the drawing room.

Mrs Elizabeth Drummond was a gentle, elegant woman with violet eyes and dark hair, streaked with the barest trace of grey. Her face was pale and her cheekbones high. Clad in black, she sat quietly by Marianne Russell in the drawing room talking softly in delicate tones. She projected an air of sophistication Louisa had not anticipated in an inhabitant of rural Wiltshire. She did not know Mrs Drummond well and had only exchanged a few words with her before today but sensed an air of fragility and understood why Sophia showed more concern for her mother's well-being than distress at her father's sudden death.

"We must not keep you any longer," said Marianne. "Thank you for seeing us at this difficult time and please ask if we can help in any way."

"Thank you for coming," said Elizabeth politely. "I appreciate it very much. I wish we had become acquainted in more favourable circumstances."

She escorted them to the door of the drawing room, where Daniel was waiting. He took over her duty, accompanying them through the front door and to the end of the driveway.

"Thank you for seeing my aunt," he said to Marianne Russell. "She is delicate and your visit will mean a great deal to her." Smiling, he took his leave.

"What a nice young man," said Marianne.

"He would not let me see Sophia last week," protested Louisa. "He is not usually this accommodating."

"He may have had good reason for denying your visit," said Marianne. "Not everything revolves around your needs," she teased.

"I cannot see why not," laughed Louisa, relieved at having left the tension of a bereaved household. "My needs are extremely important."

"Of course they are, my darling," said Marianne as they returned home.

The postman had been while they visited The Rowans and Louisa noticed a stack of letters on the hall table as soon as she came through the door. She flicked through them finding nothing addressed to her, so she went to her room to look for a book. Maggie knocked on her bedroom door to see whether she had finished unpacking.

"Can I take the cases back to the storage room? " She asked.

"There are a few things left to put away," replied Louisa. "But come in and help me then you can take the cases back downstairs when you go."

"What was London like?" asked Maggie, shaking the creases from a blouse.

"It was big, very noisy but pretty in places," said Louisa. "I was impressed with the underground railway system."

"Underground?" asked Maggie.

"Yes, deep beneath the streets of London. One descends using a moving staircase called an escalator, boards a train and returns up another set of moving stairs until the destination is reached."

Maggie frowned. "I do not like the sound of that," she said. "I would rather walk."

Maggie took a dress from Louisa and hung it in the second of the dark, wooden wardrobes.

"Mother and I went to The Rowans this morning," said Louisa.

"Is Miss Sophia any better?" asked Maggie. "She was very low yesterday."

"She is still distressed," replied Louisa, "but bearing up. She is more concerned about Mrs Drummond."

"As well she might be," said Maggie.

"What do you mean by that?"

"Minnie saw the doctor take some of Mr Drummond's sick away. He asked her for the sheet too," she said darkly.

Louisa gasped. "No," she exclaimed.

"I would not lie about such a thing," said Maggie indignantly, snatching a hangar from the bed.

"No, I know you would not, Maggie. I did not mean to imply you lied. But I know what it means for a doctor to test bodily fluids. If they have taken samples, they must suspect poison."

"Lawks, Miss Louisa," said Maggie. "They think he had dysentery. That is why they are testing but it must be horrid for Mrs Drummond, all the same. I cannot imagine they suspect us of putting things in his dinner." She chuckled to herself, "the very notion of poison in the soup."

Louisa blushed, angry at herself for speculating in front of Maggie.

"Mind you," Maggie continued in full flow, "he wanted poisoning that one, the way he treated poor Mrs Drummond. A proper brute, he was."

"Maggie," said Louisa disapprovingly, "what a thing to say. What can you mean?"

"Well, she said putting her finger to her lips conspiratorially. "He gave her a black eye once."

"Really, Maggie; that is enough," said Louisa.

"He did too, Minnie saw it. She tried to help Mrs Drummond after it happened, but Mrs Drummond sent her away. Next day she told Minnie she walked into a door, but it was not true. Mr Drummond hit her across the face and I believe Minnie."

"Thank you Maggie," said Louisa exasperated. "You can take the cases now."

Louisa sat on her bed with a bump, angry at herself for speaking out in front of Maggie and cross with Maggie for her indiscretion. The Drummond's housemaid, Minnie enjoyed more gossip than was good for her, and seemed unable to screen the truth from fiction. Louisa considered the matter a moment trying to decide whether she ought to do something about Minnie's tattling. The last thing the Drummonds needed, at this difficult time, was a housemaid with an overactive imagination. She wondered whether to discuss it with her mother or Charlotte. Eventually she opted for the wise counsel of Janet McGowan. Louisa sat at the table in the morning room, embroidering while she waited until Janet bustled in to set the lunch table, as was her routine.

"Can I talk to you about Maggie," she said without explanation.

"Of course you can," Janet replied. "What has the silly, young thing done now?"

"It is not what she has done," said Louisa, "it is what she has said."

Janet listened while Louisa explained. When she was sure Louisa had finished, she took a deep breath.

"There are two things you should know," said Janet. "Maggie is much too fond of talking for my liking but she is generally quite truthful. If she says Minnie has told her this, then she has. Now whether Minnie is a stranger to the truth is anyone's guess. I cannot tell you myself as I have only ever spoken a few words to her. The other thing you should know is that I spoke briefly with Jane Piggott yesterday to enquire how Mrs Drummond fared. Mrs Piggott was concerned, fearing for Mrs Drummond's health. She told me that Mrs Drummond did not fare well at all and was very distressed but that at least, now, she would know some peace. Make of that what you will, Miss Louisa."

"It could mean anything," said Louisa doubtfully.

"Yes it could," Janet agreed, "but it was the way she said it, you know, the intonation. I got the impression that the importance lay in what she did not say."

"I too," exclaimed Louisa, "I had that exact same feeling when Daniel Bannister spoke to me; as if he was not telling something of great magnitude."

"Would you like me to have a word with Maggie about her behaviour today?"

"No," said Louisa, "if you think Maggie truthful, it may be useful to hear what she has to say in the coming days."

Janet raised an eyebrow.

"Well I will not encourage her to gossip, of course," said Louisa. "Neither will I deter her by remonstrating unfairly if she does."

Louisa retired to bed that evening, mulling over the matter and spent a restless night battling with rational and irrational thoughts. There was nothing of great significance that made her anxious about the death of Mr Drummond but there was an air of secrecy in The Rowans. The atmosphere was heavy with unspoken words. She was glad when dawn broke and she had the distraction of breakfast. She ate a little, and then spent some time in the garden cutting fresh flowers and arranging them in her mother's heavy, cut-crystal vases.

By the time she was ready to call on Sophia, Louisa was in turmoil, desperate for someone to talk to about her fears. She realised that Sophia was the wrong choice and elected to bite her lip and talk of other things.

She rang the doorbell and Sophia emerged immediately, dressed in light coat and hat. She had evidently been waiting by the door.

"I am glad you are here," she said as soon as they left the house. "It is unbearable at home."

"It must be dreadful," sympathised Louisa. "I feel for you all."

"Everyone behaves so strangely," Sophia continued. "Mother is anxious, Daniel is like a cat on hot coals and Minnie has turned the house upside down looking for something but will not say what it is."

"I am sorry," murmured Louisa.

"And a policeman arrived unannounced last night," continued Sophia. "Daniel received him and said it was nothing to worry about, but would not say what the policeman wanted. Anyone would think it is his house and not my mother's."

"What could a policeman possibly want?" asked Louisa.

"I do not know," said Sophia tersely, "that is the point. Daniel will not tell me."

"Could I ask you an indelicate question?" asked Louisa, "You must not reply if it upsets you and you think it too soon to ask."

"You may ask of me what you will," replied Sophia, "although there is every chance I will not know."

"Will you tell me more of your father's illness, if you feel you can talk about it? I was away, you see, and know nothing of his medical condition and how his health deteriorated so rapidly."

"I see," sighed Sophia. "He took unwell in the weeks before you left but recovered somewhat. Then he was almost better for a whole week before becoming ill again. The second time was worse. He was in so much pain it was unbearable to listen to. He did not recover."

"And what were his symptoms?"

Sophia frowned. "He had a raging fever from the very first," she said, "and the most awful vomiting and diarrhoea. I cannot tell you any more than that. I heard him but did not see him."

"You did not see him?" asked Louisa, "not at all?"

"Not at all," confirmed Sophia.

"My goodness," said Louisa. "If my father was ill, I would have visited every day."

"Good for you," snapped Sophia. "But I did not."

"I am sorry," said Louisa. "I did not mean to offend you, not at all. Every family is different, of course."

Sophia stared at the ground and continued to walk. They were in Christchurch Park now. The cloudy sky broke momentarily letting slivers of sunlight through and then just as quickly closed over to block them out again.

Sophia shivered. "We should return," she said.

"Of course," said Louisa, then, "What was the doctor's opinion of your father's illness?"

"He thought it a stomach ailment," Sophia replied, "probably dysentery or food-poisoning, although mother said he expressed some concern over father's low spirits. He told her that he thought father was depressed. She told him she thought it most unlikely."

"Do you remember that diary I read?" asked Louisa.

"I shall never forget it," said Sophia, "you were glued to the wretched thing while we were all jolly and singing."

"Well it put me in mind of something. But I do not know if I can speak it."

"Do not play with me," said Sophia. "If you wish to speak, then speak now."

"It is sensitive," said Louisa.

"Have I not demonstrated sufficient fortitude as a suffragist?" asked Sophia. "Do you not think I can bear what you have to say?"

"I know you are resilient, you demonstrated it amply at the census evasion, but this requires more mental fortitude than physical."

"I do not see what this has to do with the diary. You mentioned the diary. What of it?"

"It recounted the last days of a woman who was accused of killing her husband with poison," said Louisa.

Sophia stopped suddenly. "I hope you are not implying what I think you might be," she said open-mouthed.

"No, Sophia. Not your mother. I did not mean that. I merely wondered whether it could have been caused by poison but of course it could not....."

"Louisa, I thought you were my friend but I tell you now, I do not like the way this conversation has gone between us and I think it better if we part company."

Sophia stood pale and trembling. She took a tearful glance towards Louisa, then shook her head and hurried away.

"Sophia, I am sorry," called Louisa, "wait."

"Please go," shouted Sophia over her shoulder, walking briskly now. "Leave me alone."

Louisa sat on a nearby bench holding her head in her hands, wondering what possessed her to speak so frankly about the diary at this most inappropriate time. How would she be able to repair the friendship? She sat anxiously for ten minutes, then rose unsteadily to her feet, walking slowly back to The Poplars.

She had not quite reached the driveway to her house, when she heard heavy footsteps behind her. She turned to see who the footfall belonged to.

"What the devil have you done to Sophia," Daniel thundered. "What have you said to her?"

"I am sorry," said Louisa in a faltering voice. "I was stupid. I did not think..."

"She is distraught," said Daniel. "I thought you were her friend. Why is she so upset?"

Louisa stared at her feet, blinking away tears. "I read a diary about a poisoner. I should not have mentioned it in context with her father's illness, but I did. I am sorrier than you can know."

"You stupid woman," barked Daniel. "What were you thinking? I have tried to keep this from her. How could you possibly have known?"

"I did not know," said Louisa, "but I read an account of something like it, very recently."

"I have done everything in my power to keep Sophia and her mother protected," said Daniel tossing a cigarette to the ground and grinding it to powder, "then you come along and reverse all my attempts to keep this family's business out of the public domain. You should not have interfered. Do not visit The Rowans and stay away from Sophia. I will not tell you again."

He strode angrily back up the street.

Louisa burst through the doors of her house, ran upstairs and threw herself onto the bed sobbing. She must have cried herself to sleep for she awoke a few hours later with red-rimmed eyes and a tear-stained face, heart heavy with the loss of her friend and the injustice of Daniel's remarks. His tirade seemed especially harsh considering he obviously suspected the same thing himself.

She washed her face, changed her dress and walked downstairs and into the hallway. A cacophony of excited voices came from below stairs, the volume suggesting they were oblivious to her presence. Louisa only heard snippets of conversation but the tone implied news of great importance. She rushed downstairs to find out what was going on.

"They are there now," said Maggie gesturing towards the front of the house. "There are two of them."

"Two of who?" asked Janet.

"Two motor vehicles," said Maggie, "pulled up next door. There are policemen everywhere but I do not know why."

125

Louisa's eyes widened, "It cannot be true," she said.

"It is true," scowled Maggie. "I saw them."

"Can you find out why they are here?"

"I do not think so," said Maggie, "not yet. I will see Minnie later, but I have no wish to go near a house full of policemen. My father says not to talk to coppers."

By the time Louisa returned upstairs, her mother and sister had reached the drawing room and were watching discreetly through the window as the scene unfolded. The rear of the second vehicle was visible behind the gated driveway with its doors hanging open. A policeman stood motionless beside the vehicle. The tension in the air was palpable.

As they watched, Maggie emerged from the side of the house and strode towards the front gate.

"What is Margaret doing out there?" asked Marianne.

"I think she is seeking information," said Louisa.

"I wish she would try to be little less conspicuous," said Charlotte. "She will never make a spy."

Maggie came to a halt, loitering at the end of the driveway. She stared into the house next door with a total lack of discretion. The three women watched her gesture towards the policeman, before engaging him in conversation."

"Oh dear," sighed Marianne. "Not only does this make our household look terribly nosy, but the laundry will not wash itself."

Maggie remained outside for half an hour as Marianne began to lose her patience. "It is not what she is paid for," she complained, as the clock chimed the hour.

Just when Louisa was on the verge of going outside to retrieve the housemaid, Maggie turned and ran up the driveway at speed.

Showing a lack of propriety, even by her usual lax standards, Maggie flung open the front door, slamming it against the inner doorstop.

"Margaret," admonished Marianne. "You will break something."

"I'm sorry Ma'am, cried Maggie, "but they have taken her away. She is gone."

"Who is gone?" asked Louisa.

"Mrs Drummond. They have put her in a black cab and taken her to the police station."

126

Louisa looked speechlessly towards her mother.

"Why?" asked Charlotte.

"She stands accused of murdering Mr Drummond," said Maggie dramatically. She turned to Louisa, "He was poisoned - just like you said, Miss."

Chapter Thirteen

A friendship mends

Breakfast the next day was a trial for Louisa. She was still sitting at the table pushing a congealed slice of bacon around her plate, long after the rest of the family had finished. She was relieved when the door opened and Janet entered.

"Cheer up, Miss Louisa," she said with a broad smile, "you have a visitor."

"Who is it?" asked Louisa, gazing over the lawn.

"Miss Sophia," said Janet. "Shall I show her through?"

"Sophia, oh thank goodness. Yes, please tell her to come in."

Louisa jumped to her feet as Sophia came through the door, clasping her hands nervously.

"Thank you for seeing me," she whispered. "I did not know if you would."

"Of course I want to see you," cried Louisa. "It was my fault. I should not have spoken quite so directly. It was not my place to speculate."

"On the contrary," said Sophia. "You had every right. I was awake most of the night considering your words. You gave me much to think about but there are things you do not know. Things I should have confronted before and chose to ignore instead."

"You must not feel obliged to delve into any distressing matters because of my ill-considered opinions," said Louisa. "Please, forget I said any of those things."

"May I sit," asked Sophia. "I have hardly eaten these last days and I am feeling quite faint."

"Of course, I will ring for some tea and toast," Louisa said, summoning Maggie. "Now, what can I do to make things better?"

"You can listen," said Sophia, "which you are very good at. I think you would have heard me a long time ago, had I been ready to speak."

Louisa nodded, waiting for Sophia to begin.

Sophia opened her mouth, took a breath and stopped. She composed herself and tried again.

"They...they came for mother last night," she said, faltering. "It was not wholly unexpected, at least by Daniel. I did not know myself."

"Does Daniel know you are here?" asked Louisa, in spite of her determined intent to listen without interrupting.

"No, he does not," admitted Sophia. "There is something about you that brings out the worst in Daniel. It must be hard for you to appreciate what a kind man he really is."

"It is unfathomable," said Louisa bluntly.

"Anyway, it appears that Daniel knew something that I did not know. He was aware that Minnie had watched the doctor remove bed sheets from my father's room. He also knew the Doctor was observed scraping vomit samples from the rug. But that is not the worst of it."

Sophia took a deep breath and stared at the back of her hands. She spun a delicate gold ring round her finger as she considered her words.

"Minnie saw my mother take a small vial from the bedroom before the doctor arrived. She does not know what was in it and she has not seen it since."

"That is not so very odd," said Louisa. "It could have contained any useful medicine or tincture. Why would Minnie assume a problem?"

Sophia covered her face with her hands. It was several minutes before she spoke again. Louisa waited, not sure whether to speak or remain silent.

"Minnie would assume a problem because she knows our family is riven with problems," said Sophia raising her head and looking directly at Louisa. "Daniel has also known for a long time. He watched over us from the moment he first arrived, dismayed to be called to London during the onset of my father's illness at the most inopportune of times. He would have remained here with us had his work with the electricity company not been of such vital importance."

"I suppose my conduct in London could not have helped matters," sighed Louisa.

"I do not know anything of your conduct in London," said Sophia. "Other than that you returned in the same carriage as Daniel."

"I will tell you another time," said Louisa, making a mental note to thank Daniel for his discretion, "but I still do not understand why your mother was taken from you."

"A few nights ago a policeman called at the house. He spoke with Daniel and took a short statement about those persons present during the last days of my father's life. Daniel was told that they had taken some samples from my father's bedroom and were in the process of testing them. As Daniel is fully conversant with our unfortunate domestic situation, he suspected the worst."

"Your situation?" asked Louisa.

Sophia exhaled, fixing her gaze on the garden in the distance. "My father was not a pleasant man," she said finally. "He hid behind a demeanour of respectability. He was hard-working and wealthy, bringing much comfort to our physical living conditions but he was cruel, bad-tempered and unkind, particularly to my mother. He was quick to temper and when in a rage, he would, he would…," Sophia faltered and her eyes filled with tears. "This is not easy," she said, "I am ashamed."

Louisa reached out and took Sophia's hand. She rallied and continued.

"He would hit her," said Sophia. "There, I have said it now. My father would hit my mother, quite deliberately and often."

Louisa bit her lip. "I cannot pretend I am not shocked," she said. "One hears these things, but normally from families driven to despair through poverty. How you must have suffered, Sophia."

"We did not suffer any physical pain. Our hurt was watching our mother endure her constant humiliation."

"Could she not leave him?" asked Louisa.

"She could, in principle" said Sophia. "She had an inheritance of her own and the law allows her to retain it in her own right, but it is the disgrace of it, Louisa, and the loss of her family. Father would have fought her for John Edward. Mother could never part with him. He is her youngest. She has borne father's violence for such a long time, for all of our sakes; which is why I simply cannot believe she would act now. Why now? What gain would there be?"

"I do not know," said Louisa, "but I agree it sounds unlikely after all she has endured. Still, it does not explain why the police have taken her away."

"It is because the doctor was suspicious of my father's symptoms in his final days. That is why he took samples. We would not have known it without Minnie, but Minnie saw it and what Minnie sees, she says, however unwise. They tested it, Louisa, and found a substance called Antimony. It is a poison."

"It is exactly what I feared," said Louisa, casting caution aside, now that Sophia appeared willing to talk openly. It must be fate that I found the diary. It educated me in the ways of the poisoner and the effects poison has on a human being. Although it was a different substance, in the case of Mary Cage, it produced similar effects. And Sophia, I hardly dare tell you this next thing."

"You must, interrupted Sophia. You can and must tell me everything you know."

"It is the reason for the poisoning. Mary was terribly abused by her husband."

Sophia's face fell. "I cannot believe mother did this. I will not," she declared.

"It is an odd thing that Mary Cage was convicted of the murder but denied it to the very end, even when she confessed to other equally disgusting crimes."

"You must tell me how it ended for her," said Sophia, face pale and anxious.

"It ended on the gallows," whispered Louisa. "I am sorry."

"That will not happen to my mother," declared Sophia. "Daniel has secured a barrister, well-known to his father. She will have the best legal representation."

"I still cannot understand why they fix this crime upon her."

"It is the vial Minnie saw that she could not keep quiet about. She gossiped to half the household and somebody passed the information to the police. They questioned Minnie and, of course, she told them all about it and a lot more besides. That is the problem with new servants. They lack the loyalty of those who have been with the family for a long time. Both Harold and Jane have served us many years and their discretion has been exemplary. Minnie has only been with us a few months and has no care for the consequences of her chatter."

"Housemaids are all the same, in my experience," said Louisa wryly. "We have the same problems with Maggie."

"We have always been lucky," said Sophia. "Jane was a housemaid at my mother's home before she met my father, coming to Wiltshire with them when they married. Harold was employed soon after and though he is close to retirement, we have never needed to employ another gardener. He does the work of two men."

"How does your mother explain the vial?" asked Louisa.

"She does not. She refuses to talk of it. Daniel has asked her on several occasions. She will not even discuss it with the barrister."

"Will she give an explanation if you ask her?"

"I do not think so."

"Perhaps she feels a responsibility to you and Daniel because you are younger. I wonder…"

"What?"

"I wonder if she would speak to my mother."

"She does not know her," said Sophia doubtfully.

"Precisely," said Louisa. "She owes my mother no duty of care, as they are so little acquainted. I could ask her to visit. My mother excels at putting people at their ease."

"I do not see how it would help," said Sophia, "if she is not prepared tell her counsel what is the point of having the information, even if she was prepared to tell your mother?"

"It could not worsen her position though."

"No, it could hardly be any worse than it is. In that case, please ask your mother to see her. You have my permission to tell her anything you think she ought to know in advance of her visit."

"Thank you," said Louisa, "and thank you for forgiving my clumsiness yesterday."

"It is all forgotten," said Sophia. "I am indebted to you for making me confront our secrets. There is no shame in being a victim of violence, only in concealing it. I grieve for my poor mother but feel relieved now this cloak of secrecy is lifted."

"I will seek you out as soon as I have news to tell."

"Come to Ethel's house then," asked Sophia. "I will be there for the next day or two. Two of her children are poorly with influenza and I have promised to help. It will take our minds off poor mother."

They embraced and said goodbye. Louisa hurried to locate her mother and found her writing letters in the drawing room. Marianne listened quietly as Louisa recounted all the necessary details of Sophia's story.

"Of course I will visit," she said when Louisa finished. "That poor woman should feel she has some support after the difficulties she has endured."

"Do you think she did it?" asked Louisa.

"She has suffered great provocation but I am inclined to agree with Sophia. What would she gain from taking action now?"

"I knew you would understand," said Louisa hugging her mother. "I am lucky to have such a wise mother."

Marianne smiled. "I feel for poor Sophia. She must have felt powerless watching her mother suffer, unable to offer any help. No wonder she is drawn to suffrage. She must yearn to have some control over her life. There is no point in delaying this mission. Where can I find Mrs Drummond?"

"She was at the police station," said Louisa. "She may still be there but Daniel will know."

"I shall call on him before I leave," said Marianne. "We will talk later." Folding her letter and placing it on the hall stand, she swept upstairs to get ready.

Chapter Fourteen

The Visit

By the time Marianne located Daniel and discovered that Elizabeth Drummond had been moved to Ipswich gaol, it was too late in the day to arrange a visit by normal means. Fortunately, Henry Russell returned home in time to use his influence to secure a private visit for Marianne the following day.

Daniel met Marianne Russell and escorted her to the prison, leaving her with a wardress at the entrance to the gaol. They decided he should not go any further to give Marianne the opportunity to speak freely alone with his aunt.

The wardress guided her to the holding cell, where she found Mrs Drummond sitting quietly on a wooden chair. She leaned over a writing desk penning a letter in small, precise strokes.

"Good morning," said Marianne. "Will you receive a visitor?"

Elizabeth Drummond looked up. "Good morning Mrs Russell," she said. "I am surprised to see you."

"I hope I do not intrude upon your task," said Marianne.

"I did not expect you but that does not make your visit unwelcome," Elizabeth replied, smiling. She snapped the lid onto her fountain pen and placed it on the desk. "Please sit," she said gesturing to a plain wooden chair on the opposite side of the table.

Marianne turned to face the wardress positioned in the corner of the cell. "Will you leave us?" she asked. The wardress pursed her lips but did not move.

"I was promised privacy," said Marianne, raising an eyebrow.

The wardress shook her head and left without speaking.

"How are my children?" whispered Elizabeth.

"They are well, but missing you," said Marianne. "Sophia is looking after John Edward and Ethel has returned to manage the house in your absence. Daniel keeps watch over all of them."

Elizabeth smiled weakly. "He is a good boy," she murmured.

"I think so too," agreed Marianne.

There was an awkward silence which Marianne filled. "I am charged with a task," she said, "and I do not know how best to fulfil it, save by asking you an indelicate question without knowing if you will answer me or be offended by my asking it."

Elizabeth nodded her head imperceptibly. "I do not promise to answer," she said "but I will hear your question."

"Before I ask it, I will tell you for better or worse that I know what you have endured and I sympathise."

Elizabeth sighed. "It is shameful," she said. "How can you know? Who has talked of this?"

"It does not matter," said Marianne, "suffice to say that it is not in the least bit shameful. You have suffered enough through matters not of your own making and should not feel worse because others now know what you have endured."

"It will not help me in court," said Elizabeth bitterly. "It gives me motive in their eyes."

"As the police are already aware of the violence, there is little more you could disclose that could harm you," said Marianne.

"What do you wish to know?" asked Elizabeth.

"What was in the vial?" asked Marianne, seeing no reason to prevaricate.

"Do you know everything of my life?" asked Elizabeth.

"I do not but I will be glad to know more, if you wish to tell me."

"You are very blunt, Mrs Russell."

"I want only to help you, Mrs Drummond."

Elizabeth's violet eyes sparkled. "I believe you do," she said, "but I do not know if you will think the same if I tell you more."

"There is only one way we can establish that," said Marianne, smiling.

"Very well, I will tell you. The substance in the glass vial was potassium bromide."

"What use is that?"

"No use to Charles but of great importance to me," said Elizabeth. "It gave me peace."

"I may be married to a chemist," said Marianne, "but I know nothing of chemistry. I do not understand your meaning."

Elizabeth sighed. "It is embarrassing," she said, "it would be even more so if we were better acquainted, so perhaps it is as well that this is a fledgling friendship."

"I am glad to hear you speak of a friendship at all after my most impertinent questions," said Marianne." Please do continue."

"You are sufficiently informed of our troubles to know that Charles ill-used me. I will not mince my words. He beat me badly and often."

"I know," said Marianne sympathetically, "it must have been dreadful."

"He took my self-respect and my confidence. He also took other things that married men think they have a right to whether they are willingly given or not."

"I understand," said Marianne. "He enforced his spousal rights regardless of your wishes."

Elizabeth nodded.

"I came from a wealthy family but we were encouraged to work and make ourselves useful. Before I married, I spent many years nursing and still have medical contacts. One of these colleagues helped me procure a bottle of bromide a few years ago. When I was a nurse, we used it to treat epilepsy and also to calm certain male urges. I have given it to Charles regularly since then and have known, if not perfect peace, then much less disturbance."

"I see," said Marianne. "This bottle you removed contained a drug to prevent your husband becoming aroused?"

"Exactly; but how can I tell anyone this? They will think if I can add one thing to his drink without his knowledge, I can easily add another."

"It is a dilemma," agreed Marianne, "but surely all you need to do is present the bottle for testing, so they can establish whether there is poison in it."

"They could and perhaps it would help but I repeat, how much more likely is it that they will think I gave him something more?"

"You should tell them so they may find this bottle."

"I cannot. I will not and you are not authorised to speak to anyone of this."

Marianne considered the matter for a few moments.

"Elizabeth my dear, if you did not poison your husband and somebody else did, that very person could be in your house with your family, even as we speak."

There was a long silence.

"Marianne, I have not for one second considered this prospect," whispered Elizabeth. "I have been entirely absorbed in how it affects me. When the doctor first expressed his concerns over Charles, I panicked and assumed something had gone wrong with the bromide dose. I thought that I might have been the cause of his symptoms. I have given no thought to the possibility of it being another."

"Well I think you should consider it now," said Marianne.

"The glass vial is in the linen cupboard," said Elizabeth. "I did not have time to dispose of it, just to hide it. If you can find it, I will confess to administering it, if you think it will help."

"I do not think it could make matters worse," said Marianne. "I will speak to Daniel and visit you again tomorrow to tell you of our progress."

"I am sincerely grateful for your help," said Elizabeth.

"Until tomorrow, then," said Marianne patting Elizabeth's hand.

She called out and after a few moments the wardress, wearing a sullen expression, appeared at the door and escorted her back through the prison and into the entrance hall where Daniel waited impatiently.

"Well?" he asked.

"We can talk in the cab," said Marianne.

They walked to the bottom of the drive and hailed a cab at the gate.

As soon as they were settled into the carriage Marianne spoke. "I talked with your aunt," she said. "I believe her innocent."

"I too," said Daniel, "but there is the small matter of the vial."

"If I tell you that there was no poison in that glass bottle, will you refrain from quizzing me about the contents?"

"If I must, although I would prefer to know."

"I would prefer not to tell you, unless absolutely necessary. Trust me when I tell you that it is not necessary for you to know at this time in order for us to prove your aunt's innocence."

"Very well, then I agree."

"Your aunt tells me the vial is in the laundry cupboard on the upstairs landing of your house. If you can retrieve it, have Minnie identify it and give it to the police for testing, your aunt's innocence should be rapidly established."

"Thank you," said Daniel. "That is excellent news. I will procure it without delay."

The cab alighted outside their respective properties and Daniel said goodbye, running up the driveway with undue haste.

Marianne opened the door to The Poplars as Louisa was coming downstairs.

"Did you see her?" she asked, before Marianne had taken two steps over the threshold.

"I did, but let me remove my coat and shoes before I tell you more."

Louisa paced the hallway waiting for her mother.

"Sit down," said Marianne beckoning her into the drawing room. She moved the Times from where it was carelessly discarded on the couch and set it beneath the coffee table.

"Would she speak with you," asked Louisa.

"She spoke openly," Marianne replied.

"What did you discover?"

"I am certain she did not poison her husband," said Marianne.

"Did she admit to having the bottle?"

"She did but….."

There was a rapid knock at the door, a ring of the bell, followed by another succession of knocks.

Louisa jumped up and ran to the window.

"It is Daniel," she said.

"Let him in," replied Marianne.

Louisa opened the door and Daniel strode through. "Good day," he said, "where is Mrs Russell?"

Louisa gestured to the drawing room.

"It is not there," he said upon seeing Marianne.

"Not in the laundry cupboard?"

"No. I have searched it top to bottom."

"What is not there?" asked Louisa, "what are you talking of?"

"The bottle Elizabeth disposed of," said Marianne. "She said it was hidden in the laundry cupboard. Is there another laundry cupboard?"

"I do not think so," said Daniel, "there is a laundry room; but it is not my house, so I could not say if there is another cupboard in another location."

"Can you ask one of the servants?" asked Louisa.

"I would suggest not," Marianne interrupted. "Charles Drummond was poisoned and that is a fact. We all three believe in Elizabeth's innocence which means the poisoner is someone else, quite possibly an occupant of your household."

She turned to Daniel, "Would you not agree?"

"It is what I fear," he replied.

"You should not alert any other person to this knowledge. We should use the utmost discretion trying to prove that Elizabeth did not poison her husband. Proving her innocence will not suit everyone."

"But surely I must tell my cousins?" asked Daniel.

"You should limit the information as far as you are able," counselled Marianne. "It is all too easy to let a secret slip."

"Then I must return and make a search of the house at once. There is no time to lose."

"You must be discreet" said Louisa. "It may be difficult for you to search the house without drawing attention to yourself and to do a thorough job you may need to search every room."

"I suppose I must," said Daniel. "Although I think it unseemly to rummage through my cousins' possessions, or those of the live-in servants."

"I will help, if you wish," said Louisa.

"I do wish," replied Daniel. "It would feel like less of an impropriety."

"When do your servants take their half days?" asked Marianne.

"Minnie's is today. No doubt she will already have left," said Daniel. "Harold will work outside and I could send Mrs Piggott out on an errand."

"That is wise," said Marianne. "So you will deal with Mrs Piggott then search those rooms occupied by men while Louisa checks your cousins' rooms and those of the servants."

"I am not comfortable with the thought of checking my cousins' rooms." said Daniel. "It is an invasion of their privacy."

"Anybody could have removed the bottle with the most innocent of motives," said Marianne. "Search your cousin's rooms, but do it last. With luck you will find what you are looking for elsewhere. Do not omit any search for the sake of good manners. Nothing could be worse than losing the opportunity to help Elizabeth."

"You are right," agreed Daniel. "And fortune favours a search today with Sophia and John Edward at Ethel's house and usefully absent from home. Louisa, allow me half an hour to send Mrs Piggott to Ipswich on an errand, then join me for the search if you are still willing to assist?"

"Of course," said Louisa. "I will do all I can to help."

"Thank you," said Daniel, as he left.

Louisa wandered aimlessly, killing time until the half hour had passed. When the clock hand finally dragged itself to the appointed hour, she departed to The Rowans and tapped on the door. Daniel was standing by the study window at the front and noticed her immediately.

He let her in. "Where would you like to start?" he asked.

"We should be methodical," said Louisa. "The rubbish cart has not been for three days, so it would seem logical to start at the bin store."

Daniel pulled a face. "I should change out of these clothes then," he said.

"You should," Louisa agreed. "That suit is too nice to ruin. If you cannot find the bottle in the rubbish, check all the basement rooms and the family rooms up here. I will check the bedrooms and the servant's quarters in the attic."

"That sounds sensible," he said. "Thank you Louisa, I am grateful."

Louisa smiled, as she ascended the stairs, pleased to be the recipient of a few kind words, at last.

A large picture of a racehorse filled an entire wall at the top of the stairs. The bedrooms were set around a galleried landing and she turned left into the nearest bedroom, which appeared to belong to a man. The square room was sparsely furnished, containing a dark, wooden bookcase running from floor to ceiling. Opposite stood a polished mahogany desk on which a trio of ivory elephants had been carefully placed, arranged from largest to smallest. A double-posted bed sat centrally within the room. The bed, stripped bare of linen, stood incongruously upon the carpet on which several discolorations were still visible, despite evidence of recent cleaning.

Louisa grimaced. Starting with the bookcase she systematically began her search of the room. There were few personal effects and little furniture, but there were sufficient clues to identify the room as Charles Drummond's bed chamber.

When she opened the heavy wooden doors of the wardrobe, she balked at the thought of searching through a dead man's clothes; but she did it anyway. Louisa tried to open the top drawer of Mr Drummond's desk, but it was firmly locked. She made a lucky guess and located the key beneath a plant pot on the window ledge without expending undue energy in fruitless search. The contents of the desk were disappointing. Louisa pulled out drawer after drawer but found only paperwork relating to Charles Drummond's trade as a corn merchant. She sighed. It would have been fortuitous had the bottle been located in the first room searched but she was nevertheless disappointed.

The feeling of frustration continued as she searched the remaining rooms on the first floor, finding nothing of note. She avoided Daniel's room, deeming a search unnecessary but located the laundry cupboard, removed every piece of linen and searched again. The bottle remained stubbornly absent.

Louisa found the staircase to the servant's quarters through a narrow door near to the main staircase. She climbed the steps, treading on a squeaky board mid-way up the staircase where the steps bowed. At the top of the house were three rooms and a bathroom. Louisa performed a meticulous search of the bathroom and the empty bedroom, before moving on to the smaller of the remaining bedrooms.

The bed was covered with a yellow counterpane and a small vase of daffodils graced the windowsill. A selection of nail polish pots and laundered handkerchiefs sat on top of the desk, so she guessed the room belonged to Minnie. This was confirmed when she read an unsent letter in Minnie's spidery hand-writing, addressed to a young man. Minnie, showing a typical lack of caution and propriety, had written urging him to meet her the following week. Her fountain pen lay in a pool of ink beside the letter.

"My goodness," exclaimed Louisa, opening Minnie's wardrobe. There were many more outfits than Louisa expected a housemaid to own, and they were all well made. Although there was no evidence of a bottle, Louisa made a mental note to mention the outfits to Daniel, as they implied Minnie had access to more money than she ought to. Closing the door, Louisa entered the final bedroom which, by process of elimination, must belong to Jane Piggott.

The dark green curtains in the housekeeper's room were closed. Not quite wide enough for the window, they left a gap just large enough to allow a chink of light which fell across a tidily-made single bed, illuminating a wooden cross on the wall above. The room contained an identical desk to Minnie's, but it was placed against the opposite wall. Several reading books, a newspaper and an old bible lay upon it. Louisa opened the desk draw containing a few dog-eared letters and some writing paper, a tin of buttons and a half full bottle of ink. She picked up the books, two by Jane Austen and opened the bible lovingly inscribed "the dying gift of my dear mother." She was about to open the wardrobe when she heard a voice down the corridor.

"Come Louisa, I have found it."

"She hurried from the room to find Daniel at the end of the corridor with his finger to his lips. "Do not speak. Jane Piggott has returned," he whispered. "I do not want her to see you up here."

Daniel peered round the door and seeing no one below, he beckoned her through.

As they descended the stairs, a squeak burst from the bottom step before they had a chance to reach the landing. They stood stock still, waiting for Mrs Piggott to hear them but nobody came. They tip-toed quietly through the landing and made their way downstairs just as Mrs Piggott emerged from through the kitchen door.

"Good day, Sir," she said before looking straight into Louisa's eyes. "I have taken the box of fruit to Mrs Lucas as you asked."

"Good, thank you," said Daniel watching Louisa blush to the roots of her hair. "Are they well?"

"Mrs Lucas and Miss Sophia are quite well," said the housekeeper, "but the children are still sadly. The littlest one coughs so."

"The fruit will help, I am sure," he murmured. "Thank you."

Jane Piggott returned to the kitchen while Daniel escorted Louisa to the study.

"What must she think of me?" asked Louisa. "She saw us coming down the stairs together. She will assume the worst."

"I am sorry," said Daniel. "I do not know what to say to make this better."

"It is too humiliating," said Louisa burying her face in her hands.

"I will speak with her."

"You will not," said Louisa. "It will make matters worse. Never mind. She will have to think of me what she will. Do you have the bottle or not?"

"I think so," said Daniel. "I must ask Minnie to identify it. He put his hand in his pocket and retrieved a bottle from a brown paper bag. Manufactured from clear glass, the bottle was sealed with a glass stopper. Droplets of a clear liquid were just visible inside."

"That must be it," said Louisa. "Where did you find it?"

"On the floor of the pantry," said Daniel. "I nearly missed it; there were so many other bottles. It had been set down with the jam jars. "

"That is marvellous," said Louisa. "What will you do now?"

"I will speak with Minnie and make sure it is the same vial, then take it to the police station and demand they test it."

"Please bring news back as soon as you can." asked Louisa.

"I will," promised Daniel. "I am most grateful to you, Louisa. Thank you." He took her hand and brushed his lips lightly against her fingers."

Louisa shivered as a sensation like moth-wings shimmered along her spine. She did not speak. She could not. Daniel held her gaze; neither moved. Then Jane Piggott's footsteps advanced along the tiled hallway and the moment was lost.

Murmuring goodbye, Louisa left the house and returned to The Poplars to tell Marianne the good news.

The days dragged by as they waited for news of the tests. Neither Daniel nor Sophia visited The Poplars but Maggie and Minnie saw each other daily. Maggie passed on any news with great alacrity, notifying them as soon as Daniel summoned Police Sergeant Gordon to the house to witness Minnie's identification of the bottle. The sergeant, to his credit, was cooperative and understanding of the need to analyse the contents, although he was not prepared to accept Daniels' word that there was no poison in the bottle. He insisted on visiting The Poplars where he interviewed Marianne Russell at length.

She told him all she knew, at the end of which she asked, "Will they release Elizabeth?"

"If there is no poison to be found, I would release her," said the sergeant, "but I am not in charge. We will have to see what the inspector decides".

After two days waiting for news and receiving none, Daniel took matters into his own hands. He strode down to the Police Station on Prince's Street passing several "Wanted" posters pasted to the stone block walls and became increasingly irritated by their presence. It angered him to think of his innocent aunt imprisoned in gaol, while fugitives of the most callous nature were at large. Entering the establishment, he approached the front desk and demanded to see the Chief Inspector in charge. Daniel was directed to a hard, wooden bench upon which he sat while watching the occupants of the busy Police Station. After a short while he spied the familiar figure of Sergeant Gordon.

"Good day Sir," said the Sergeant tipping his helmet.

"Good day Gordon," said Daniel. "Have you any news of the tests."

"No Sir," said Gordon, "They have been conducted but the results are under consideration."

"Under consideration, by whom?" asked Daniel.

Gordon pulled a face. "Chief Inspector Briggs is deciding," he said.

"I have asked to see the man in charge," said Daniel, "I dare say it will be Briggs."

Eventually, a half-glazed door opened in front of him and a Police Constable emerged.

"Come through, sir," he said, ushering Daniel down the corridor into a comfortably furnished room at the end.

Daniel entered the room to find the corpulent figure of Chief Inspector Briggs, squeezed into a well-padded leather chair. Above him, a clock with a large, round pendulum ticked sonorously from its position on the wall. The air was heavy with tobacco smoke, which Briggs drew rhythmically from a battered, wooden pipe. The Chief inspector stared at Daniel through heavy-lidded eyes.

"Take a seat," he said gesturing to the left of a pair of red leather chairs.

Daniel sat. The Chief smiled and flipped open the lid of a long, narrow box which he offered to Daniel. "Cigar?" he asked.

Daniel waved a hand to decline and reached for his cigarette case. He extracted a cigarette and snapped the lid closed.

Daniel waited, watching the Chief inspector intently while he marshalled his thoughts.

"Why is Elizabeth Drummond still in prison?" he asked curtly. "You have new evidence to hand. She should have been returned to her home by now, not left languishing in gaol with common criminals. What is the delay? I anticipated her release long before now."

The Chief inspector exhaled a puff of smoke and spoke in measured tones.

"We tested the bottle and it is, indeed, potassium bromide just as Mrs Russell advised," confirmed the Inspector. "Clearly that liquid did not cause Mr Drummond's death."

"That is excellent news," said Daniel. "When will my aunt be released?"

"Slow down," said the Chief Inspector. "It is not as simple as that."

"I cannot see why."

"There is a distinct lack of motive for anyone other than your aunt," Briggs replied.

"My aunt had no motive," said Daniel leaning forward, raising his voice a notch.

"On the contrary, she had an extremely powerful motive as you are well aware."

"No, she did not." Daniel declared. "If you refer to my Uncle's appalling treatment of her, you should know that he has always treated her so. She has never retaliated. She only needed to wait for her youngest son to reach maturity and she could have left."

"Not without a scandal," said Chief Inspector Briggs.

"So you are holding her on purely circumstantial evidence?" asked Daniel.

"She was present at the crime scene and lived with the victim for the duration of his illness. She was in the habit of doctoring his food, had ample motivation for the crime and most of all, there are no other suspects; not one."

"This is shocking," Daniel shouted, slamming his hand on the inspector's desk. "There is a poisoner loose about our residence and you lock up an innocent woman. Other lives could be in peril."

"Other lives could be in peril if she is allowed to return," said the Chief Inspector. "That is the decision we have made. Now, I am sorry it is not what you wanted to hear, but there it is."

Daniel marched from the room and left the Police Station, striding angrily up Princes Street, clods of dry earth billowing beneath his feet. A half-full tram stood outside the chemist and he jumped aboard making his way to the quieter top deck. There he sat watching passing horses, lost in thought. Daniel flexed his fingers together contemplating the horrible lack of progress made so far. The efforts of the barrister supplied by his father had come to nothing, despite his vast experience. An infrequent visitor to Elizabeth, the barrister was likely unaware of this latest development, so Daniel decided to give him one last chance by informing him of Elizabeth's continued detainment without delay.

He left the upper level and loitered at the rear of the tram. Within minutes it juddered to a halt and he pushed past the waiting travellers and doubled back to his club in Church Lane. The red, yellow and blue of the tiled flag-bearer marked his way as he hastened up the narrow alley and into the Conservative Club. He gave his hat and coat to the attendant, purchased a whisky from the bar and asked for the club telephone. Standing in the foyer with his hand in his pocket, he dialled the exchange and asked for Sir Roderick Yates.

The ensuing conversation did not improve Daniel's faith in the legal system. Although the barrister was confident of procuring a not guilty verdict in court, he thought it considerably less likely that he would be able to influence the release of his client without her standing trial first. Daniel mulled over the matter smoking a cigarette, imbibed another whisky then walked his frustrations off during his return to Ivry Street.

Back at The Rowans, Sophia and John Edward had returned from her sister's house. She saw Daniel from her bedroom window and was in the hallway catching her breath by the time he reached the front door.

"What news, Daniel? I saw mother this morning and she is so thin and frail. Louisa tells me you have hopes of her release."

"It appears my hopes were premature," he frowned. "Inspector Briggs will not countenance her release until they find another viable suspect."

"That is outrageous," said Sophia. "They have no reason to keep her now. It is not her fault they have been unable to find someone else with a motive."

"It is as she feared," he sighed, "they believe her predisposition for doctoring his water gives her the means and motive to poison. In the absence of any other suspect, they pin their hopes of resolving the murder entirely upon her. But there is some small reason to hope. I have spoken with her barrister and although he thinks it unlikely he will secure her release before trial, he will nonetheless make his approaches to the constabulary tomorrow."

"She is so frail, Daniel. I fear for her if she remains in those conditions much longer. She has no experience of living so poorly. She shivers and does not eat."

"She is much stronger than you give her credit for," said Daniel. "Marianne Russell thought her quite indomitable and was much impressed with her resilience."

"She is my mother and she is suffering," insisted Sophia. "She was wracked with coughing this morning, Daniel. She is truly sickening for something."

"I cannot do any more than this," said Daniel. "I wish it were not so."

"It is so unfair," cried Sophia. "She would not be in that cell if she were a man. There is no reason to confine her, no evidence against her. They do it because they can."

"I am sorry Sophia."

"I am sorrier," she left the room, pushing the door behind her so it slammed into the frame and without hat or coat she ran up the driveway of The Poplars and hammered on the door.

"Hello Maggie," she said when she saw the housemaid. "I need to see Louisa."

Maggie did not have time to open her mouth, much less respond, when Sophia strode towards the drawing room and flung open the door.

She stopped, looking around the room in embarrassment, as she noticed the drawing room was full of women, many of whom she did not know.

"I am so sorry," she whispered putting her hands to her mouth. "I have interrupted you, please forgive me."

Louisa set down her coffee cup and walked across the room. She put her hand around her friend's shoulders.

"Whatever is the matter Sophia?" she said.

The room fell silent and Marianne Russell looked up. "Do tell, Sophia," she said gently. "You are among friends."

As Sophia took a closer look, she spotted Ada and Bessie Ridley in the room which gave her the confidence to talk freely.

"They will not release my mother," she said.

"Even with the new evidence?" asked Louisa.

"Not even with that," she said. Daniel can do no more and my mother languishes inside Ipswich gaol like a common criminal. She began to cry in gulping sobs.

"Oh Sophia," said Louisa, guiding her to the armchair she had previously occupied. She gestured to Sophia to sit down.

"Disgraceful," said Ada Ridley. "Tell me all."

Sophia recounted the tale though sobs. She spoke angrily in parts, lost her composure at times and most especially when she described her father's cruelty to her mother.

"Now she is in gaol and we know she is innocent. She would not be treated so harshly if she were a man," she finished.

Bessie Ridley spoke. "And she is represented by a barrister?" she asked.

"Yes, and Daniel says he is confident he can represent her to a successful conclusion but he does not think he can influence her release before trial," said Sophia.

"Is there nothing we can do?" asked Louisa, turning to Ada Ridley.

"We can draw attention to the injustice," said Ada. "We can use the oxygen of publicity to promote the unfairness of this confinement. It may help Sophia's poor mother." Her eyes shone with fervour.

"She knows few people of influence," said Sophia, "Daniel's father, perhaps, but few others."

"Yes, my dear," smiled Ada, "but you know women of influence do you not?"

Sophia frowned. Ada and Bessie exchanged glances. "What do you think Bessie?"

Bessie smiled. "Your mother has been badly used and if women had more power, she may not have felt compelled to tolerate this cruelty for so long. Where there are outrages against women, your suffragist sisters can be depended upon. We will help you, if you wish it."

"My mother is not a suffragist," said Sophia.

"But you are, and your mother is a victim of inequality. We are not without influence, Sophia. Would you like our help?"

"I would welcome any help you can give. I do not know what can be done to bring pressure to bear."

"I cannot make any promises," said Ada, "but we can speak to our sisters about your dilemma and see what they suggest."

"And it will be conducted peacefully?" said Sophia.

"Of course," Ada replied.

"Then by all means do so."

Chapter Fifteen

A Time for Action

Ada was a driven woman, working tirelessly over the week to promote public awareness of the injustice perpetrated towards Elizabeth Drummond. She contacted Constance Andrews and Grace Roe who found time to break away from their arrangements for the Coronation procession, just three weeks away, to lobby at the police station.

Ada wrote to Millicent Fawcett to seek her intervention and support together with a number of the other suffragists she had come to know over the years. She did all this while working with the WSPU to finish their Coronation banner.

Louisa watched her with tremendous admiration. She had long admired Ada's artistry which was of an extremely high standard. Ada could paint and sew exquisitely. The more time Louisa spent with Ada, the more she came to regard her.

Bessie, too, was determined to spread the word, visiting her club in Dover Street without Ada who could not leave Ipswich. There were several prominent suffragettes living at The Empress and she determined to consult with them to see what could be done about Elizabeth's plight.

The women worked quickly using any and all of their local contacts. The initial publicity from the murder had subsided but with their intervention it was not long until the Suffolk Free Press took an interest in Elizabeth's story and ran the first of several articles criticising the local police force. As suffragette militant activity was considerably quieter than usual while they awaited the outcome of the Conciliation Bill, the press seized any opportunity to report on the subject. The London newspapers rapidly picked up the story, guided by some of Bessie's colleagues, and within a few days it made the front page of the Times.

Soon after, Daniel, Sophia and Louisa were sitting together in the morning room of The Rowans pouring through the latest edition of the paper when there was a series of knocks at the door. A subdued Jane Piggott entered, accompanied by Chief Inspector Briggs.

Daniel stood to greet him.

"May I sit?" asked Briggs as a bead of sweat dripped from temple to cheek and wobbled precariously, threatening further descent.

"Please do," said Daniel gesturing to the fireside chair. "Do you have any news?" he asked.

"I do not, Sir," said the Chief Inspector. "May we talk privately?"

"No, we may not," said Daniel. "Sophia here," he gestured to his cousin, "is the daughter of the accused and has, if anything, more right to hear the news than I do."

"Very well," said Briggs, adjusting his tie around his portly neck. "I am here today charged with the task of telling you to cease harassing my police force at once. Your association with publicity-hungry Suffragettes does not advance your cause at all and will inevitably damage your aunt's prospects of release."

"I beg to differ," said Daniel coldly. "My aunt remains inside a gaol, charged on the most flimsy evidence and becoming more unwell, with each passing day. If she goes to trial, we have been told it will likely be after August, if she survives that long. Her health is poor, her spirits are low, so do not tell me to turn away the only offer of hope that remains unless you have an alternative to offer."

"I do not think you understand the seriousness of this situation," said Chief Inspector Briggs. "I have just returned from Winston Churchill's office in Westminster, having been summoned there last night; and it was not a pleasant interview, let me tell you. The liberal party are being pilloried from all positions by these blasted Suffragettes and the last thing the government needs is a high profile poisoning case linked to the Suffragette cause. I warn you, it will not end well."

"Chief Inspector, you are badly informed if you believe this case to have been hi-jacked by the Suffragettes. All action taken has been eminently peaceful. My cousins and their friends are suffragists, not suffragettes and even where more militant members have joined in promoting my aunt's cause, they have behaved impeccably. No law has been broken and there have been no public order disturbances. I fail to see how we could have conducted ourselves with more decency."

"Nevertheless," said Briggs, "it is not politically expedient and you must desist at once."

"If we agree, will you release my aunt?"

"You know I cannot do that."

"Then not only do I refuse but I warn you there is a demonstration planned later in the week, during which you will most certainly see a very public association between suffragists and my aunt's unwarranted imprisonment. So I suggest you communicate that to your ministers and start looking at another suspect for this crime."

"You will regret this Mr Bannister," said Briggs, heaving himself to his feet. "Good day," he said and turning to the ladies, he doffed his hat and shuffled up the hallway and out of the house.

"Daniel, you were simply marvellous," said Sophia. "I thought you were against women having the vote and suddenly you are supporting suffragists in the face of the establishment."

"I have had cause to reconsider my opinion during the last few weeks," he said, looking directly at Louisa. "All the kindnesses shown to my aunt have come from women. The most skilled barrister of my acquaintance is unable to free her and yet women who do not even know my aunt, work tirelessly for her release and to highlight the injustice she faces. It has given me much room for thought."

"I am pleased to hear it," laughed Louisa, a broad smile across her pretty face. "It is good to know you are converted to the cause."

"I would not go that far," smiled Daniel. "Anyway, back to it. The demonstration outside the gaol is on Thursday?" he asked.

Louisa nodded.

"I will come along too, obviously" said Daniel.

"And join all the other men devoted to our cause," laughed Louisa.

"I must be present on this occasion but I can make no promises for future events," he said, with twinkling blue eyes.

Louisa blushed while Sophia smiled. "There is such a change in you, cousin," she said. "I remember the first week you arrived with us and caught me leaving for the census evasion. You were furious at my conduct. Look at you now, practically one of us!"

"Yes, I did behave in a rather patriarchal manner," admitted Daniel. "I suppose I was trying to do the right thing by Charles."

At the mention of Charles Drummond, Louisa frowned. Turning to Sophia she asked "Do you ever miss your father?"

Sophia sighed. "I feel like I should, Louisa, but he was not a kind man. He treated our mother badly and we witnessed it often, even when we were very young. Father employed a nursemaid when we were small so we barely saw him except when we spent a few hours with mother in the afternoon. Then he would come home and that was the time he would abuse mother, especially if he had a difficult day. I cannot remember a time when he showed any interest in us or displayed any affection at all. He was a little kinder to John Edward but had to suffer three girls before his son arrived. I never felt loved, none of us did; not even John Edward."

"I am sorry," said Louisa simply.

Sophia continued. "He was never a pleasant man, but I might have been more upset had he not been in such an awful mood the week he died. Any little thing could set him off but that week he was particularly angry with the servants and that, of course, meant trouble for mother."

"Poor Sophia," Louisa took her hand. "I should not have asked."

"Not at all," said Sophia. "We have hidden our family secrets for quite long enough."

Daniel, who was sitting quietly watching a Nuthatch doing battle with a caterpillar on the wall of the kitchen garden, turned to face Sophia.

"What was Charles angry about?" he asked.

"When?" asked Sophia. "He was always angry."

"You said he was angry with the servants."

"Yes, he was in a frightful rage. One of them had disturbed some papers, perhaps even taken something. He mentioned dismissing them several times."

"Who was he talking about?"

"I do not know. He never said; just ranted about a lack of trust and that he could well do without them."

"Does Elizabeth know who upset him?" asked Daniel.

"I do not know if she is even aware anyone upset him," said Sophia. "She was quite poorly that last week, if you remember, and kept to her room most of the time."

"That changes everything," said Louisa.

153

"Indeed it does," Daniel agreed.

"I do not see how," said Sophia, furrowing her brow.

"It is the first time we have heard of another motive for the murder," said Daniel. "Now think, are you certain he did not say which servant?"

"How frustrating," Sophia signed. "Is it very important? I do not believe he mentioned a name. He was so angry he only spoke in broad terms about the deceitfulness of servants in general. Did you not hear him complain yourself?"

"Not that I can remember," Daniel admitted. "I gave him something of a wide berth. Although your mother did not own to her cruel treatment, it was known amongst her family. My mother was greatly relieved to hear I was to board with you. She asked me to look out for her sister and disclosed details of the wretched treatment she endured at the hands of her husband. I was polite to Charles but could not bring myself to make a friend of him."

"Should we not inform the police?" asked Louisa.

"Ordinarily I would say yes," said Daniel, "but I am wary of giving them anything further while they threaten us. The behaviour of the Police Inspector today is almost unprecedented. The government have nothing to fear from us and they surely cannot be that worried about further publicity going to the suffrage cause as a result of Elizabeth's confinement."

"It is interesting you think so," said Louisa. "For when I attended the meeting at Caxton Hall, Emily Pankhurst had received intelligence from inside the government that, contrary to assurances, they would shortly renege on their promise to advance the bill for enfranchisement. She was certain of this. If they are about to make such a declaration, they can expect a great deal more trouble and I can see why they would prefer to avoid publicity of any kind where inequality could be deemed a factor."

"That makes a lot of sense," said Daniel. "So, I think we should discuss this away from the house," he nodded to the door, "away from servants and anyone else who might have cause to listen."

"You are welcome to come to The Poplars to talk," said Louisa.

"Better not," said Daniel in a low voice. "If there is one thing I have learned since my arrival, it is that the servants seem to know a great deal more about household matters than the householders themselves."

"You are quite right," agreed Louisa, "Minnie and Maggie share everything. Where shall we go then?"

"It is a beautiful day," said Daniel. "We can walk to the park and I will buy you both an ice cream."

"That would be a guilty treat with mother shut away in such an awful place," said Sophia sadly.

"Your mother would wish you to carry on as best you can," Daniel declared. "Do not punish yourself for her benefit."

They left The Rowans, pausing only for Sophia to find a parasol to protect her pale skin. They walked down Ivry Street and left into Henley Road where they entered Christchurch Park, stopping to purchase ice-creams from the vendor positioned by the Brett Fountain. The area around the fountain was planted with cosmos and larkspurs providing a pleasant palette of pastel colours with which to enjoy their walk.

They strolled along the pathway going south through the park and crossed the well-mown lawns to the shelter in the lower arboretum, where they sat beneath its sharply pitched roof. The park was busy with people enjoying the spring sunshine but the shelter was shaded and they enjoyed complete privacy.

"So," said Daniel taking charge. "Charles was angry with one of the servants. Which servants must we consider our suspects?"

"All of ours," said Sophia.

"And ours?" asked Louisa.

"I cannot see why your servants would have upset Uncle Charles," said Daniel.

"No, I suppose not," said Louisa, then turned pale at the thought that next entered her mind. "But the poison would have been readily accessible to our servants."

"How so?" asked Daniel.

"My father is a chemist," she replied, "an industrial chemist. He keeps a small laboratory in the house so he can conduct experiments away from the factory. There are many samples to be found in his rooms."

"Does he not lock them?" asked Sophia.

"He does," nodded Louisa. "He keeps a key about his person and a spare in the house. Anyone could gain access if they were sufficiently determined."

"It is true that your servants could have acquired poison, but there is no reason why they should wish any harm to my father."

"No," agreed Louisa," especially now we know that your father intended to dismiss one of the servants."

"He actually said he would have one of the servants dismissed."

"So he was not explicit that it would be one of his own servants."

"Not at all," said Sophia.

"We are going around in circles with this," grumbled Daniel. "He cannot mean another householder's servants.

"Well," Louisa mulled over the statement, "he could, you know."

"How so?"

"Our Maggie is in and out of your property, most days Janet pays the occasional visit to Jane and I know Minnie has made several friends of other housemaids in this street. If somebody else's servant had taken something, your uncle could have threatened to have them dismissed by their employer."

"That complicates matters," sighed Daniel. "Just when I thought we had a concise list of possible suspects."

"We should definitely consider your servants," said Louisa, "so Minnie, Jane Piggott and Harold Turner are on the list. I suppose I should put Maggie on too."

"What about your cook?"

"Janet McGowan? She is as straight, as the day is long," exclaimed Louisa, "and it is hard to imagine any of our servants committing such a crime after knowing your family so little time."

Daniel raised an eyebrow, "As you say, your servants had easier access to poison so they should go on the list too. Are there any more?"

"You must put Joan Bradley and Sarah Simmonds on the list," said Sophia. "I often find those two waiting in the house when Minnie has a half day. I suppose they could have gone into my father's study, although for what reason I cannot imagine."

"Well we now have a list to work from but the idea that this dismissal is a motive constitutes a tenuous proposition. I do not think it substantial enough to put before the authorities. What can we do to improve our prospects of finding the culprit? How do we find out what they did to anger Uncle Charles?"

"We have searched the house already," said Louisa, "there is nothing there to help."

"I do not think we are looking for an object so much as information," said Daniel. "Perhaps it would be better to question the domestics?"

"They may be reluctant to answer," said Sophia uncertainly.

"Probably," agreed Daniel, "but we will be subtle. Shall I speak with Harold?"

"Yes, you will get a better response as one man to another," said Sophia. "I suppose that means I will have to talk to Minnie and Mrs Piggott; two conversations that do not fill me with pleasure."

"Minnie will be easy to get information from," said Louisa.

"It is not getting her to talk, I am concerned with," smiled Sophia, "it is getting her to stop. And I shall be dreary for the rest of the day if I have to speak too long with the dour Mrs Piggott."

"Then I will speak with Janet and Maggie, for all the good it will do," said Louisa, "I am by no means convinced they should be included."

"Good, now we are properly organised, we can return," said Sophia looking anxiously at an ominous grey cloud drifting across the sky.

"Yes," agreed Louisa, getting to her feet. "We will find opportunities for questioning today and tomorrow. We will be much too busy after that when we join the demonstration on Thursday. At least it feels like we are doing something constructive now."

They walked briskly back to Ivry Street lest the cloud should burst open and returned to their respective homes. Marianne Russell was leaving The Poplars just as Louisa arrived.

"Where are you going, Mother?" asked Louisa.

"I have permission to visit Elizabeth," said Marianne.

"Good, Sophia is very worried about her."

"Understandably," said Marianne, "I am concerned for her too. She is in much lower spirits than she was the first few times I saw her. She is too polite to say so, but feels that giving up the vial has worked against her. I am fortunate she is still prepared to see me."

157

"She is fortunate you are taking such an interest," said Louisa. "It must be frustrating to have her hopes dashed so cruelly. Does she take no comfort from the proposed march?"

"She has allowed it, but I would not say she is enthusiastic for it," said Marianne. "Everything about this experience humiliates her, but she cannot bear a long stay in gaol and is willing to take a chance."

"Chief Inspector Briggs visited Daniel earlier, to tell him to call off the suffragettes," said Louisa sullenly. "He says we have angered the parliamentarians."

"I will inform Elizabeth," said Marianne, "as I am obliged to; but if I have learned anything about her, I judge this news will strengthen her resolve."

Louisa bid her mother goodbye and, deciding there was no time like the present, thought she would begin by interviewing Maggie whom she deemed a much easier prospect than Janet McGowan.

She was just heading downstairs when the door opened and her father emerged from his study, a pained expression across his face.

"What is the matter, father?" asked Louisa.

"Where is your mother? Something has happened I cannot account for," he said.

"She has gone to the gaol to visit Mrs Drummond. What is the problem?"

"Come in and I will tell you."

Louisa entered the study and shut the door. Henry Russell pulled out the chair to the front of his desk and she sat down. He scribbled nervously on a notepad as he considered his thoughts, his features pale and drawn.

"When I found out Charles Drummond was poisoned, I checked my supplies - all of them" he said, tearing the scribbled page from his notebook which he crumpled and tossed into a waste bin. He rolled the pencil across the desk with his finger.

"I keep quite a lot of compounds here, as you know," he continued. "Quite frankly, I was not sure whether they had been tampered with. I have never been concerned for the safety of my laboratory before. Why would I be? It is always locked. But since this blasted affair with Drummond, I have been a great deal more vigilant." He stopped, picked up the pencil and tapped the end against the desk.

"This morning I required Sodium Sulphate for an experiment and carried out a quick visual inventory of my chemicals while I was about it. Some tartar emetic is missing."

"Are you sure?" asked Louisa.

"Quite certain," said Henry Russell. "It is my habit to tap bottles on the counter after use so the contents are uniformly spread. The tartar emetic has been tipped out but not evened. There is an obvious powder mark on the neck of the bottle and the contents are irregularly spread."

"Perhaps you forgot to tap the bottle."

"I never forget. It is a habit, Louisa; quite besides which there is less substance in the bottle than there was when I last looked."

"What will you do?"

"I must tell the authorities. This is a serious matter," said Henry getting to his feet and reaching for his hat atop the stand.

"Are you going now?"

"Yes, it cannot be delayed."

"Then tell me, when did you last check the laboratory? Was it before or after Elizabeth Drummond was arrested?"

"I cannot say, Louisa. I was away on business when she was taken." Henry Russell strode to the door and then turned back. "If I have not made my concerns crystal clear to you Louisa, Tartar emetic is extremely poisonous. If somebody is trying to harm your friends next door, you ought to warn them this substance is missing."

"I will, at once," said Louisa, alarmed. She ran round to The Rowans in unseemly haste, almost knocking Harold off his feet as she rushed up the driveway.

"Careful Miss," he grumbled.

She knocked at the door, gasping with exertion. Minnie answered.

"Can I speak to Mr Daniel or Miss Sophia?" she asked.

She waited in the hallway until the handsome form of Daniel appeared seconds later. "What is it?" he asked.

"I need to talk to you," she said, surreptitiously pointing to the study, while watching Minnie clean a non-existent mark from the oak hall stand.

"Oh, I see," said Daniel. "Come inside," he ushered her in and closed the door. They walked to the front of the room and looked out across the front garden, where Harold was busy pulling weeds.

"My father has just set off for the police station," whispered Louisa.

"Good Lord, why?"

"There is some tartar emetic missing from his store cupboard."

"Is he sure," asked Daniel.

"Completely certain."

"Do you know that tartar emetic contains antimony?" asked Daniel.

Louisa shook her head. "I did not know," she said.

"That may well be what poisoned Charles in the first place, said Daniel, "and we must consider the possibility that this chemical has been taken to facilitate another poisoning."

"I know. My father fears this. We must be vigilant," said Louisa.

"I cannot see how Chief Inspector Briggs can ignore this," said Daniel. "Surely Aunt Elizabeth will be released now."

"No," said Louisa. "Father cannot be sure when the poison was taken. It does not help."

"Then we should question as many of the staff as possible before the police arrive," said Daniel. "I no longer have any faith in the police force and even less in the government."

"I will go and speak with them now."

"And Louisa," he said, grabbing her wrist and pulling her close. He paused and looked directly into her eyes, "be careful."

He walked away without another word. She touched her cheek; it was burning.

She left The Rowans in a trance-like state then meandered down the hallway and downstairs to the basement kitchen.

Janet was stirring the contents of a large ceramic bowl while Maggie poured boiling water into jam jars.

"Hello, Miss Louisa," smiled Janet, "what can we do for you?"

"Can I borrow Maggie for a moment?" she asked.

"Where are we going?" asked Maggie.

"Just outside to the garden. I want to cut some flowers but I have hurt my wrist. Can you get the secateurs from the shed and cut them for me?"

"Of course, Miss," said Maggie, "it will be good to get away from the kitchen for a few minutes. It is much too hot down here today."

Louisa and Maggie walked down the garden to the bottom flower bed where white roses bloomed against a trellis. They opened the shed door at the foot of the path, collecting secateurs and gardening gloves."

"Maggie, do you remember the week leading up to Mr Drummond's death?" asked Louisa, rubbing her wrists while she feigned soreness.

"I should, Miss, it was my birthday. It was a lovely week. Mrs McGowan helped with my chores and my half day fell on my birthday, so I went to mother's house for tea. Fairly pushed the boat out, she did. She made me a seed cake and we had hot, buttered toast and jam."

"It sounds lovely," said Louisa, "and did you see Minnie that day?"

"Oh yes, she bought me a pretty little keepsake box as a birthday present and even Jane Piggott put in some ribbons and a book."

"That was nice," said Louisa, "You have not known them long. It is kind that they gave you presents."

"I haven't really, have I?" agreed Maggie," but Minnie and I get along so well that I was not at all surprised. It was very thoughtful of her, considering she was having such a horrid week."

"How so?"

"She knocked a vase over, I think. Something like that anyway," said Maggie, pulling her hand away with a start. She removed her gardening glove and examined her hands mournfully. A scarlet teardrop swelled across her thumb.

"Spiteful things, roses," she said, "I have never liked them."

"And everyone else was in good spirits?" asked Louisa.

"I suppose so," said Maggie. "Why are you asking all these questions?"

"No reason," murmured Louisa. "I was away in London that week and I wondered what it was like in the days leading up to Charles Drummond's death."

Maggie frowned, "just like normal really; perhaps a bit more tense, I suppose. I know you do not like me talking about my betters, but Minnie told me that Mr Drummond was even nastier to Mrs Drummond than usual"

"I asked you the question so you may answer honestly," said Louisa.

"Well," said Maggie conspiratorially," there was a big argument because some of Mr Drummond's papers went missing and he blamed Mrs Drummond, because he blamed her for everything. Minnie said he struck her so hard, she hit her head and took to her bed for the rest of the day, but Minnie did not actually see it. She only heard about it."

"Who saw it?" asked Louisa.

"I do not know," said Maggie. "Perhaps Mrs Piggott; she is devoted to Mrs Drummond but then again, perhaps not. I cannot imagine her telling anything to Minnie. Much as I like Minnie, she is a shocking gossip."

Louisa raised an eyebrow and restrained herself from saying "pots and kettles."

"Who do you think poisoned Mr Drummond?" she asked.

"I am sorry to say it," said Maggie, "but I think it must have been Mrs Drummond. Why would anyone else want to poison him?"

"I do not know," replied Louisa, "but I am certain it was not her."

Maggie shrugged. "I hope you are right; just because they have not hung a woman in sixty years, does not mean they never will," she said darkly.

"Maggie," exclaimed Louisa. "That is enough of that kind of talk. Miss Sophia or John Edward might hear you."

"I would not say it in front of them," said Maggie sulkily.

"I know," said Louisa trying to coax Maggie round. "Of course you would not; and you have been very helpful. Thank you."

Maggie brightened, "can I go in now," she asked. "I really must help Janet."

"Yes, of course," replied Louisa, taking the wicker trug full of sweet-smelling rose stems into the house.

She arranged the flowers across several vases and sat down in the morning room, thinking about how best to tackle Janet McGowan.

The opportunity did not present itself until the next day. She breakfasted with Marianne and Charlotte. Even Albert made an unexpected appearance, having caught the overnight train from London.

"Bessie Ridley told me about your march tomorrow," he said, when asked why he was present, "and I had a few days off due so decided to come and lend my support."

"Thank you, darling," said Louisa squeezing her brother's hand. "They will appreciate it. I will introduce you to Daniel Bannister later today. I think you have already met Sophia. He is her cousin."

"Oh yes, I have met the lovely Sophia and it is my pleasure to meet any relative of hers," grinned Albert. "However, I must drag myself away from your company and visit my tailor in town. I had a little accident on the train," he said ruefully, unrolling a double-breasted jacket and pointing to a pocket curling away from the suit.

One by one Louisa's relatives left the room, until Louisa sat alone. Eventually Janet McGowan appeared and Louisa took a breath in preparation for a question, exhaling deeply when a volley of knocks at the front door shattered the silence. The door to Henry Russell's study swung open almost immediately as Henry uncharacteristically answered the door.

"Come in," he said beckoning a trio of policemen to his study; two in uniform and one in plain clothes. By the time Louisa turned back to talk to Janet McGowan, she was gone.

Annoyed at the missed opportunity and frustrated at the door barrier between her and what was going on in her father's study, she decided to visit Sophia and report her conversation with Maggie, keen to let her know the police were at the house.

Daniel and Sophia had managed to speak with all three of their domestics and were sharing information when Louisa arrived. They showed her into the library and drew the door closed. Daniel pulled up an armchair and the two women settled on a leather couch. They talked quickly, in hushed voices.

"The police are with my father," whispered Louisa, "we may not have much time."

"Who have you spoken to?" asked Sophia.

"Only Maggie, I have not been able to see Janet alone."

"What did you learn?" asked Daniel.

"Not a great deal," sighed Louisa, "and some of it is difficult to talk about."

"You must tell us everything," said Sophia placing her hand over Louisa's.

"Maggie said Minnie was upset that week. She had knocked a vase over. She also said Minnie told her that," she paused, "this is awkward."

"Please Louisa,"

"She said your father hit your mother so hard that she banged her head and took to her bed for the rest of the day."

Sophia sighed and looked at her feet. "I do not doubt it," she said. "I cannot confirm it myself. My mother took pains to conceal these things from us."

"Did she say anything else?" asked Daniel.

"Just that she received gifts from Minnie and Jane Piggott for her birthday and that Jane Piggott was devoted to your mother."

"We know," smiled Sophia. "Jane is a treasure, for all her dour exterior. She has been with my mother since mother was a young woman."

"What information did you acquire?" asked Louisa.

"Similar stories from Minnie, who I ended up interviewing in the end," said Daniel. "She mentioned the problems between Sophia's mother and father. She said there was a previous incident a few weeks before. She was dusting in my aunt's room and saw bruises over her arms."

Sophia sighed, "My poor mother, If only we could have done something to make her life easier."

"You are not responsible for any of this," said Daniel, gently. He went on, "Minnie gave quite a graphic account of both Charles' bouts of illness, which were similar in nature although the first was shorter and less intense than the second. I did not press her for details, as the police already have this information."

"She told you nothing more?" asked Louisa.

"Nothing useful," said Daniel.

Louisa turned to Sophia, "and Jane Piggott?"

"She said very little," replied Sophia, "it was hard to get her to talk without asking a direct question. Perhaps Daniel should have tackled her. She might have been more receptive to a man."

"Did she say anything?"

"She confirmed that Mr Drummond was in a disagreeable mood before he became ill and asked her if she had removed any papers from his study. She said she was cross with him for asking, but answered politely saying that she had not. Then I asked her who she thought may have poisoned Mr Drummond and she said she did not know, but could personally guarantee it was not Mrs Drummond. She was upset at the very idea of it. Jane loves mother and became tearful at the mention of her. It was very touching......"

Sophia was interrupted in full flow, as the door to the house flew open and Maggie ran through the hallway without knocking, yelling Louisa's name.

Louisa rushed to the study door and threw it open, "Maggie," she thundered. "How dare you."

"They have taken her," cried Maggie, trembling from head to foot.

"Calm down girl," said Daniel, taking control. "Who have they taken?"

"Mrs McGowan," she replied and burst into tears.

Chapter Sixteen

Another Arrest

Sophia rang the bell and summoned Minnie.

"Get her some water," she said then watching Maggie's trembling hand changed her mind. "Actually, get her some brandy instead."

Maggie cupped the brandy glass, breathing in the fumes. The glass wobbled in her shaking hands.

"Now Maggie, tell us exactly what happened," said Louisa squeezing the housemaid's hand.

Maggie took a deep breath and composed herself. In a faltering voice she began to explain.

"Three policemen arrived at the house," she said.

"I know," replied Louisa. "They arrived before I left."

"Well not long after they came, Mr Russell summoned me and Janet to his office. The three men with him said they were policemen and were going to search the house. They asked us if we had anything to say before they started. I asked what they were looking for and they said Mr Russell had reported that some of his chemicals were missing. I said I had nothing to tell them and Janet said the same."

"What happened next?" asked Louisa.

"He told us we must stay in the study while they searched the house."

"All of you?" asked Daniel.

"Yes, Janet and I, Miss Charlotte and Mrs Russell remained in the study with one of the policemen while they conducted the search. Everyone else was out, you see. They were only away from the room for about a quarter of an hour when one of the policemen returned. He called Mr Russell outside then came back to the study. They asked me to leave but I waited in the hallway. Miss Charlotte and Mrs Russell left the room, leaving Janet alone with Mr Russell and the policeman.

I sat on the stairs until the door opened again. They came outside, holding Janet by the arm. I asked what was happening and Mr Russell said they had arrested Janet." Maggie covered her face with her hands, her silent crying only evident by the shaking of her shoulders.

"Why was she arrested?" asked Daniel.

"They found the missing chemicals in her cupboard in the kitchen."

"Well that does not look good for her," said Sophia. "Was the cupboard locked?"

"Yes, it is always locked and she is the only one with the key, except that I know where the key is kept but I did not tell them in case they took me away too," stammered Maggie. "Will I go to prison?" she continued plaintively.

"No Maggie," reassured Daniel. "You will not and nor should she. Once again, they have arrested someone on purely circumstantial evidence. What possible motive could a housekeeper have for murdering someone who was not even her employer?"

"Minnie, take Maggie into the kitchen and give her a cup of cocoa," said Sophia walking to the door.

"Thank you Miss," said Maggie, glad to leave the room. Her eyes were still watering and she bit her lip, trying to stem the tears.

When the two housemaids were safely out of ear-shot Sophia spoke," Will they release mother now?"

"One would think so," replied Daniel. "But based on what we have witnessed so far, we cannot be sure."

"The march is tomorrow," said Louisa. "A great deal of organisation has gone into it. There are women coming from as far away as Colchester and Norwich. Bessie is even bringing a delegation from London. Ada implied there may be some well-known suffragettes among them."

"The march should still continue," said Daniel. "Even if Aunt Elizabeth is released, it is not right that your housekeeper is in custody on so little evidence. She has far less influence as a servant and I am sure the women will be equally supportive of her cause."

"They will be," nodded Louisa. "Sylvia Pankhurst works tirelessly for the working class women in the East End. She would certainly be concerned to right such an injustice for a woman less able to defend herself."

"It is settled then," said Daniel. "You go to the march as planned tomorrow, and I," he said, eyes twinkling, "will come along and supervise".

Louisa left the Rowans and hurried up Henley Road to Ada Ridley's home. She spent half an hour apprising her of the changed situation and was relieved to hear that Ada was as supportive of Mrs McGowan, in principle, as she was of Mrs Drummond.

Before Louisa left, Ada cautioned her. "Like you, dear Louisa, I am inclined to believe both women innocent. The evidence against them is flimsy, at best. But you should prepare yourself for the possibility that one or the other could be guilty. Just because the evidence is circumstantial does not mean it is wrong, but we fight it because on its own it is not good enough. For your own sake, Louisa, keep an open mind."

Louisa thought about this all the way home. She considered Ada's words while Charlotte told her more about the police visit and the dramatic moment the constable made Janet get the key to the locked cupboard, producing the bottle of tartar emetic from its hiding place in the salt cellar.

She thought about Ada's words as her father told her how sad he had been to identify the bottle of powder as his missing poison and how he had tried to prevent the police taking Janet away for questioning. Even though her father had promised to send legal help for Janet, Ada's words remained with Louisa and by the time she retired for the night, she began to question Janet McGowan's innocence.

Louisa liked Janet. Their relationship had evolved easily in the six months since she joined the family and Louisa considered her much more than an employee and someone she could turn to for counsel. She wracked her brain, trying to think of a reason why Janet may have taken and concealed her father's poison, but could think of nothing. She decided to go upstairs to the attic rooms to see if Maggie was awake.

She tapped on the door and Maggie answered. Her eyes were still swollen.

"I hope I have not woken you," said Louisa, eyeing her pallid face with concern.

"No, Miss," said Maggie. "It is too early to sleep and I do not think I could anyway. I have been reading," she pointed to a battered book, fly cover hanging off. "Why can she not see John Thornton is a good man?" she sighed, "I would marry him in a flash, if he asked me."

Louisa smiled. "You like Elizabeth Gaskell?" she asked.

"Oh, very much Miss.

"Then I will lend you some more of her books."

"Thank you," beamed Maggie. "I would like that very much."

"Are you feeling any better?" asked Louisa. "I realise how distressing Janet's arrest is for you," she continued.

"I am better," said Maggie. "Do you think they will let me see her?"

"I expect so," said Louisa. "Do you know there is a march by the suffragists tomorrow to draw public attention to the plight of Mrs Drummond?"

"I had heard," said Maggie.

"Well, they will also march for Mrs McGowan," said Louisa.

"Even though the poison was found in her cupboard?" asked Maggie.

"Yes," said Louisa. "It is not a good enough reason to detain her, if that is the only reason and I cannot think of another. Tell me, what do you know of Mrs McGowan?"

"I know she came from a small town in Scotland; Falkirk, I think. She has been a cook or housekeeper all her working life."

"Does she have children?"

"She has never mentioned any."

"Did she ever speak of her husband?"

"Not to me," said Maggie. "Funny, I never thought of her having a husband, but I suppose she must have if she is a Mrs."

"Hmm," agreed Louisa. "What did she keep in her cupboard?"

"It was just a housekeeping cupboard, Miss. She kept spare crockery and cleaning things; so if we ran out of something, I would ask her and she would usually have a spare in her cupboard. She had a weekly allowance from Mrs Russell for the food which she also kept there and I think there were some vases and silver and that sort of thing."

"That sounds reasonable," said Louisa. "Who knew where the key was kept?"

"I did," said Maggie. "But anyone else may have. It was kept in a drawer in the kitchen. She was not particularly careful of it."

"I did not know the key even existed," mused Louisa, "although I have lived in this house all my life."

"No Miss, but you do not spend much time in the kitchen. Any of the regulars like the baker or chimney sweep or the odd job boy might have a cup of tea in the kitchen with us on their rounds, and they could easily see it taken or put back in the drawer."

"Oh dear," sighed Louisa, "this does not help at all."

"Sorry Miss," said Maggie, "but surely they must release Mrs McGowan when so many people could have access to her cupboard."

"I think they must," smiled Louisa, "It has helped me to know that the finding of the poison in her cupboard does not convict her, by any means. I have kept you long enough, Maggie. Thank you for your help and I hope you can sleep properly tonight."

Louisa retired to her room and to bed but could not sleep at all. She tried, to no avail, but eventually gave up and lit a candle, deciding instead to look for the two Elizabeth Gaskell novels she kept in her bookcase. She located them with ease and was contemplating re-reading Cranford before giving it to Maggie when her eyes were drawn to the battered black-covered diary belonging to Anna Tomkins that she had removed from The Old Museum all those weeks before.

"I should take this back," she thought removing it from the bookcase. She flicked through and noticed that there was another entry at the back of the diary in Anna's hand but written in her own words. The previous entry she read was in Mary's words. She thought back to when she last saw the diary, blushing as she remembered the awkward encounter with Daniel in the carriage. This was probably the reason she did not turn the page after Mary's last account.

Dear Daniel. Her feelings towards him had changed so much in the last few weeks. The beating in her heart whenever she thought of him, was difficult to ignore. Sometimes she felt his eyes on her and wondered if he felt the same way, but if he did, why did he not act upon it? Was she mistaken? He treated her in the same easy manner as he treated Sophia, which was good in its way. They were definitely friends now; but did she want to be treated the same as his cousin? No, emphatically not.

Thinking of Daniel was not going to help her sleep so she turned to Anna's final diary entry, devouring the page with her eyes.

She is dead. My friend is no more and perhaps I could have stopped it but she made me promise never to tell. She wanted the truth known, but one person in the know was good enough for Mary, so I watched her go to the gallows in the certain knowledge that for all she contributed to the death of James Cage, another was equally guilty.

She was given an execution date of 16th August which allowed us only a week together from when I found her in the cell. We made a lot of that week and she told me all of her life, however horrible, and I wrote until my fingers were sore to get it all down. Some of it was unbearable to listen to. I thought her cruel, sad, loose, insane; she conjured manifest emotions in me as I heard her story, but most of all, I thought her truthful. I am certain that she has given me all the facts, withholding nothing of her life in this account.

What a wretched life she bore. I never knew the consequences of abject poverty and how it might alter a decent human being and make them an unconscionable monster, before I heard Mary's story. I would like to think I might have conducted myself differently if I had lived her life, but how can I know? Few of us experience so much bad fortune and so little good.

I was with her most part of the day, each of the days she passed between trial and execution and every day we were joined by the prison chaplain who prayed with her and read passages from the bible to bring her comfort. She did not seem to need much attention and bore her situation with a quiet dignity, I had not seen in her before. She seemed fully reconciled to her imminent death and did not fear it. The only time she broke was when she was told they could not perform the execution on the set date, as Mr Calcroft, the executioner, was otherwise occupied. She did not view this short stay of execution with any kind of relief and thought it cruel to prolong the ordeal. But she soon rallied and prepared herself for the new date to meet her maker.

Day after day the prison chaplain implored her to confess to the murder of James Cage but he did not know what I knew, and could not make her say it. He could not understand why she would risk her mortal soul in this way, especially when she was so contrite about all her other misdemeanours. It did not occur to him for one moment that she could not confess, because in all probability, the death was at another's hands.

The chaplain was a kind man. After one of their meetings, he procured bibles and testaments for her benefit, so she might give them to her children to remember her by. He arranged for the children to see her one more time and sat with her as she dictated a final message which he wrote in every volume. Each was inscribed "The dying gift of my dear mother."

I was not in the cell when they spent their last hours together, but passed them in the corridor as they left. Richard, pale and wan, held the hands of the two younger girls who watched with detachment. William walked alone, his brother John had not even come to say goodbye. Only Mary Ann and Sibella shed a tear, Mary crying silently and Sibella with great racking sobs I could still hear down the corridor many minutes later.

By the time I reached the cell, Mary had regained any composure she may have lost at the sight of her children. She told me that she was happy and ready to die. She had not taken any pills for some weeks and could think with a greater clarity than for many years. She could feel properly again and was able to acknowledge the strength of the love she had for her children which made her strong enough to face any obstacle.

She told me that giving them bibles and reaffirming her faith had inspired a deep calm. The chaplain had taught her a little reading in her final days which enabled her to read the inscription in each of the bibles she presented. That she could finally read, after all the years of wishing for an education, filled her with pride.

Mary faced her final journey with spirit and fortitude, on 19th August, early in the morning. I stayed at home, hiding behind my curtains, wracked with anguish; unable to find the strength of character to watch the death of my childhood friend. Alfred, as my proxy, remained to the end and accompanied the under-sheriff to Mary's cell, where he ceremoniously demanded the body of the culprit. I shook with horror and rage when Alfred told this to me. How cruel and inhuman to carry out this ritual when we are supposed to be an enlightened nation.

Mary was made to walk in a procession from her cell, through the courtyard and up to the scaffold. She climbed the ladder on her own, faltering a little but standing on her own two feet without any support from the turnkeys. Then the bolt was thrown and she was gone.

There are some things in life that should be put away in a little box and never removed. My memories of Mary are forever tarnished by the violence of her death. She has burdened me not only with the intimate detail of her crimes, but with the knowledge that she was, in all probability, innocent of the murder of James Cage. The only thing I can do for her now is keep my promise. I will keep this journal for one year after her death and then I will burn it. I have not even told Mary's story to Alfred, nor will I ever do so.

Like her life, this journal ends today.

As Louisa read and re-read the final paragraph, she realised that if sleep was proving difficult before, it would be near impossible now. There were so many unanswered questions in the little book. Why had the diary been kept, when Anna resolved to destroy it? What happened to Anna that she had not done so? Most importantly of all, who killed James Cage? The parallels between his murder and that of Charles Drummond were astonishing. And there was something else in the back of her mind; something she could not quite grab hold of, that was bothering her.

Chapter Seventeen

The Penny drops

It bothered her all night and after a scant three hours sleep she rose again, dressed and went downstairs for breakfast. The whole family were sitting at the table. Minnie managed a competent job in Mrs McGowan's absence, cooking toast, scrambled eggs and sausages enough for all.

A smartly-dressed Henry Russell was sitting in his usual place at the top of the table.

"Do you have a business meeting?" asked Louisa.

"No, my dear," he said. "Albert and I are coming with you."

Louisa smiled broadly. "I believe we have converted you," she declared.

"Not entirely," he said, "but this is important and I want to see Janet properly represented, whether or not she has done this terrible thing. I am not happy with the idea of her confined to a gaol, while they make up their minds. I called upon your friend Daniel early this morning," he continued. "Elizabeth Drummond has not been released. Perhaps I would have reconsidered if one or the other of them had been; but this is beyond the pale and I feel I must act."

"Good for you papa," said Louisa.

"Even I am going," said Charlotte.

Louisa was astonished. Charlotte's apathy to the cause was a source of great consternation to her.

"Are we all going to protest?" she asked.

"Even Maggie," confirmed Marianne Russell. "She comes too, as does young Minnie, I believe."

"This should really draw attention to the case," said Louisa, "despite what Chief Inspector Briggs has to say on the subject."

"Yes, I heard all about it from him yesterday," said Henry Russell. "He warned me off, as he did young Mr Bannister. It is one of the many reasons I decided to attend today."

It was rare for the whole family to leave The Poplars without at least one of the servants being home, so they took the unprecedented step of locking all the doors. Henry, Marianne and Albert elected to take a carriage to the prison while the remainder opted to walk, it being such a glorious day.

Louisa did not join them, for she had made arrangements to go with Daniel and Sophia. She called at The Rowans, tired but with a heart full of optimism for the coming day.

Daniel and Sophia were waiting in the study, watching out for her from the window. Minnie emerged from the side door and walked up the path with Maggie.

"Is this all of us?" asked Louisa.

"Ethel is going separately," said Sophia, "she goes alone and against her husband's instructions. He does not approve of the association with the suffragettes."

"How selfish," said Louisa. "It is not about suffrage. They help us only because of the injustice against your mother and only then because you are personally known to some influential local suffragists."

"I know," agreed Sophia. "There is no convincing him though. Ethel has tried."

"I am sorry for her," said Louisa. "I hope she does not suffer for her involvement."

"He is not cruel," said Sophia, grasping an entirely different meaning to the one Louisa intended.

"Oh, no, I did not mean to imply that," said Louisa, wide eyed.

"Of course you did not," reassured Sophia. "They will probably not speak for a few days, her housekeeping budget will be cut in the short term and he will have plain food for a week, then it will all right itself. That is usually the way of it."

Louisa laughed. "Ready?" she asked turning to Daniel.

"I am. Come now ladies," he smiled holding both arms out for them to take.

Goosebumps scattered across Louisa's skin as she held his arm. They walked quietly together for a few minutes then, desperate to break the silence, Louisa said, "no Jane Piggott or Harold then?"

"Good Lord, no," laughed Daniel. "Harold would be appalled at the very idea, and Jane is religious and thinks suffragettes are ungodly. Harold is gardening and Jane has gone out on an errand."

"Which only leaves Catherine and John Edward, who is at school today" said Sophia. "Catherine could not leave her convent, not even for this. It is a cruel God who gets in the way of the love for a mother."

"The love for a mother, the gift of a mother" mused Louisa, then, "oh my goodness," she exclaimed. "That is what has been bothering me."

"What?" asked Daniel.

"I cannot say, it cannot be so, it is too unlikely. Just give me a few minutes, please go ahead. I need to check something. I promise I will be back in ten minutes. Walk ahead and I will catch you up."

"No, Louisa....." said Daniel, but she was gone, hurrying up the road at speed, pulling her olive green dress a few inches from the ground as she ran.

"Shall we wait," he asked Sophia, sighing in frustration.

"No, we have only just entered Henley Road. If we walk slowly, she will be caught up in no time."

"What do you suppose she is doing?"

"I cannot say," said Sophia, "but rest assured, this protest is so vital to her, she will not delay her return. Whatever she has gone to do must be of the utmost importance."

Louisa was breathless with exertion by the time she arrived at the door of The Rowans. She had already noted that neither Daniel nor Sophia locked the door prior to leaving. She walked hastily up the driveway, hoping that Harold would not be in sight. He was not.

She opened the door and closed it quietly, then tiptoed up the grand staircase to the galleried landing and up the further flight of steps to the servant's quarters. The staircase creaked again, just as it had the first time she climbed it. It did not worry her though as the house was empty.

She walked past Minnie's room, opening the door beyond. Jane Piggott's room was tidy and sparse. The only difference this time was that the far window had been flung wide open with a clothes horse set beneath, upon which hung a few smalls drying in the breeze.

Louisa walked to the desk and examined the pile of books. There it was; a small burgundy-coloured bible. She opened it, hoping she had misremembered, but she had not. The inscription, in faded blue ink, read "The dying gift of my dear mother." August, 1851.

Louisa took the bible and sat down hard upon the bed. It was either a remarkable coincidence or the bible Jane Piggott carried was one of the bibles given by Mary Cage on her death. But what of it? Did it matter?

Louisa flicked through the pages of the bible wondering. Mary Cage died in 1851. She must have been in her forties, so could Jane Piggott be one of her younger children? She supposed it was possible although that would make her nearly seventy and she did not look that old.

"Who are you?" she whispered aloud.

"What are you doing in my room?" hissed a voice.

Louisa looked up with a start. Jane Piggott leaned against the door frame, face as grey as the worsted dress she wore. "That belongs to me," she said, snatching the bible. She crossed herself then advanced towards Louisa, face contorted in rage.

"I am sorry," stuttered Louisa, "but who are you? What connection do you have with Mary Cage?"

Jane stopped, holding the bible to her chest. "She was my grandmother," she said hoarsely.

"You were baby Jane." declared Louisa, "of course."

"How do you know?" snapped Jane.

"You never knew her."

"I was born a few months before she died."

"I am sorry. Your mother was her daughter Sibella."

"She gave birth to me," said Jane bitterly. "She was not much of a mother once she had her other children."

"She gave you her bible," said Louisa, "it must have meant a great deal to her."

"I stole her bible," said Jane. "She gave me nothing. She still lives, you know, but we do not speak."

"I am sorry for you," said Louisa.

"No you are not, you suspect me. It is why you are here."

"I saw your bible before. The inscription made me think, I did wonder if........"

"...and you would be right," said Jane, "and they will all suspect me too, if they find out where I came from. I have been with Mrs Drummond for over forty years and she has never asked difficult questions of me. I found a new life in Wiltshire, far away from the shame of my background."

"Your background?" muttered Louisa.

"Oh yes," said Jane. "I have tried to be good and god-fearing, unlike the rest of my family. Some people are just born rotten. It turns out I am one of them, after all."

"Nothing is inevitable," whispered Louisa.

"What do you know?" snarled Jane. "Evil is in my genes. I am as wicked as my Uncle John who was transported for rape and my brother Arthur who was convicted for assault and my brothers Frederick and William who have been in and out of gaol their whole lives. Why did I think I could rise above it?

"Did you kill Charles Drummond?" asked Louisa, trying to disguise the trembling in her voice.

"I did and I would again," said Jane Piggott. "He was a vile man, quite the worst kind of bully. He hurt Mrs Drummond once too often. She....her family were the only people who ever showed me any kindness. I would have died for her. I will die for her if it becomes necessary."

Louisa gulped, "but he mistreated her for years. What moved you to act now, after all this time?"

"He nearly killed her last time he assaulted her," said Jane Piggott through clenched teeth. "He would have killed her eventually. She already lost two children because of him. You will not have known that. Nobody knows that but me."

She sighed before continuing, "I can read, you know. Mrs Marshall, Mrs Drummond's late mother, taught me herself. So I read newspapers whenever I can. I know all about poison through my reading. I thought about poisoning Drummond a long time ago." She stared dreamily at the window.

"I dismissed the thought but it kept returning until it took hold of me. When I found out we were leaving Wiltshire for Suffolk, I was terrified lest the wickedness of my family return to taint me. But it came as a great relief to find we were settled next door to a chemist with a household of staff, careless about leaving things around."

178

"You stole the poison from my father?" gasped Louisa.

"It was easy," said Jane in her thick, Suffolk drawl. "We are up and about long before you arise from your beds and your servants allow anybody in their scullery. You would not believe how easy it is to get around your house unnoticed. I located the key to your father's study after only a few visits and once I knew where it was, I helped myself to the poison. It was all very nicely labelled for me. I read about tartar emetic in the George Chapman case. He was hanged for it. I will not be."

"Then why did Janet get caught with the poison?" asked Louisa.

Jane Piggott raised her eyes to the ceiling, "because I put it there," she spat. "I love Mrs Drummond. I had not anticipated she would be blamed. I did not know she dosed his food with bromide".

For a fleeting moment she looked sad, "I thought she told me everything," she said. "I could not let her fester in that awful place when my only purpose was to protect her. Then it came to me. I could hide the poison somewhere else where it would be found. I was clever enough to make sure it was not noticed the first time but quite deliberately careless of it the second. I wanted your father to find the poison missing. I wanted them to search the house. I thought they would free Mrs Drummond and I would not be suspected. And it worked."

"They have not freed her though, have they?" asked Louisa. "She lingers in the gaol house and it is your fault."

"She will never be convicted now," said Jane, "I am certain of it. There is too much doubt, since Janet was found with the poison."

"She could die first. She is unwell and delicate. You must tell them you did it," said Louisa.

Jane Piggott laughed a long, cynical laugh. "Never," she said. "I will not die for this. My mistress Elizabeth will soon be free and I will look after her as always. No, my dear, today is your day to die."

Louisa sprang from the bed, and then shrank towards the window in horror, watching the steely glint of a pair of razor sharp shears as Jane Piggott snatched them from her wide apron pocket. Without moving her gimlet-grey eyes from Louisa, the housekeeper reached behind her back and twisted the key in the door lock. Louisa was trapped.

"No," she screamed, "Get away from me."

"Scream all you like," said Jane. "The house is empty. There is no-one to hear you and they believe I am absent from the house on an errand. When they discover your remains, they will not think of me."

"You are quite mad," whispered Louisa, edging towards the window.

Jane advanced quickly, pointing the shears towards Louisa who grabbed the bolster from the bed and hurled it at the housekeeper's head, knocking the shears from her hand. Cursing, she bent to retrieve them, as Louisa climbed on the bed, hurled open the sash window and slithered onto the pitched roof below.

Tiles crunched beneath her feet, falling, clattering down the roof like casualties from a tropical storm. She grabbed the window sill to stop herself falling with the tiles, watching as the manic face of Jane Piggott loomed through the window.

"Even better," she spat, banging the end of the shears against Louisa's clenched knuckles.

"No," cried Louisa as the pain ripped through her fingers. Jane smashed again, first one knuckle, then the next. Louisa's fragile grip on consciousness almost abandoned her as she felt bone shatter and a stab of pain flashed up her arm.

One more smash on her right knuckle and her tenuous hold upon the window sill gave way. Her chin crashed against the bay fronted window and she slipped down the pitched roof, scrabbling against the tiles. The sharp pitch of the roof did nothing to stall her descent. "I am going to die," she thought before being saved by the dual fortune of her dress snagging against a pipe as her foot found the gutter.

She came to a halt, flat against the roof, hardly daring to breathe while the gutter pitched and swayed beneath her feet. She tugged gently at her dress to test how firmly it held her to the roof but it did not feel strong. She waited for a few seconds, trembling, terrified and sick to the stomach. Then a rush of water sloshed towards her splashing into the gutter which wobbled precariously. She could not see where the water came from but heard Jane Piggott grunting as a further torrent of water spilled down the roof.

Louisa screamed as loudly as he could. "Harold," she cried. "Help me, please help me."

She stopped screaming and listened hopefully for a reply. All was quiet and still and she realised the deluge of water had ceased. Her relief was short-lived.

"Die, damn you," shouted Jane Piggott. Something crashed onto the roof above Louisa setting tiles jangling into the gutter and spraying sharp shards of clay over her face and neck. Another loud clatter of tiles ensued and she saw a heavy silver tin roll into the gutter, as a section of gutter detached from the roof and smashed on the pathway below. Jane had given up trying to dislodge Louisa with water and was launching tins of food taken from the pantry to destroy her fragile grip on the roof. The undamaged gutter had formed a stable hold for Louisa's foot before but she was now supported precariously against the wobbling, weakened structure.

Louisa screamed again; her piercing shrieks accompanied by another volley of tins. One hit her directly in the arm and a fresh wave of nausea assailed her as she heard her bone crack. She clung to consciousness through a hazy mist. In the distance she thought she could hear a familiar voice penetrate the fog marring her clarity.

"Hold on Louisa, hold on. I am coming for you."

It was Daniel. Daniel and Sophia; she could hear them both now, calling for her. "Daniel," she cried weakly.

Another tin clattered past her head, smacking into her shoulder. A crimson welt of blood seeped from under her dress but she found the strength to cling on, knowing help was near.

"Daniel, hurry," she whispered.

The sound of raised voices emerged from the window above. Then the window slammed open and Daniel threw a chain of sheets down the roof and began clambering down towards her.

"Louisa, hold on. I am here now." He reached her, breathless with effort and put a strong arm around her waist. Louisa's eyes fluttered as she heard Harold and Sophia calling from above.

"It's all over. You are safe now," said Daniel.

"Thank you," whispered Louisa and that was the last thing she remembered.

Chapter Eighteen

Whatever happened to baby Jane?

When Louisa woke the next day her senses sprang to life, as she inhaled the smell of freshly-laundered sheets, followed quickly by the delicate odour of sweet peas, her favourite flower. The sun shone through the window of her bedroom, casting warm rays over her skin and the bed quilt engulfed her body like a comforting friend.

As sleep fell away, she became aware of a nagging ache from her knuckles. She pulled her hands from the bedclothes, watching them with drowsy eyes, wondering why they were both swathed in bandages. She looked like a pugilist ready for a fight. She tried to sit up, but the effort of placing her hand on the bed to raise herself was too painful. Her eyes snapped open and she looked about the room.

"You are awake," said Charlotte. "Thank goodness, we were all so worried."

"What happened?" asked Louisa.

"Do you not remember?"

Louisa rubbed her head with her bandaged hands. "Yes, it is coming back. Jane Piggott, she poisoned Charles Drummond."

"We know," said Charlotte, "something must have snapped in her mind. She was raving when they found her. She admitted to everything. She was really quite proud of herself and saw herself as Elizabeth Drummond's protector."

"She tried to kill me," said Louisa shivering beneath the bedclothes.

"Daniel stopped her," said Charlotte. "I am afraid he had to restrain her in a very ungentlemanly manner. She was determined to dislodge you from the rooftop. Harold and Sophia had to hold her while Daniel went to get you."

"Where is Daniel?" asked Louisa. "I must thank him."

"You have been unconscious for two days Louisa. You have hardly been in a position to thank anyone. Anyway, he has gone back to London," said Charlotte.

"Oh," replied Louisa, taken aback. "How long has he gone for?"

"I do not know," said Charlotte, "but Sophia will. She asked me to tell her as soon as you were awake. She has been very worried."

Charlotte held a glass of water to Louisa's lips. "Drink this," she said. "Now, are you up to visitors?"

Louisa nodded and within a few moments a succession of people visited her room. First was Marianne who gave her daughter a hug, before telling her that the protest had been extremely successful, attracting a great deal of attention both locally and nationally.

It would have undoubtedly improved Elizabeth's chance of release had the arrest of Jane Piggott not already done so. Louisa forgot all about her aches and pains as soon as she heard Elizabeth Drummond was safely back home.

"Thank goodness," she murmured.

"Ada has sent you a message," smiled Marianne, before telling Louisa that Ada did not consider the state of unconsciousness to be an adequate excuse for missing such an important march.

When Marianne left, Maggie arrived followed by a grateful Janet who was just recovering from her ordeal, having only been released the day before.

Later that afternoon there was a knock at the door. Louisa looked up to see Sophia peering into the room, wearing a wide smile across her handsome face.

"Hello, said Louisa as Sophia rushed to her side.

"We wondered when you would wake up," she said. "You were unconscious for so long. Daniel was out of his mind with worry."

"Not so much worry it stopped him going to London," said Louisa waspishly.

"It is work, silly," said Sophia. "He has gone back to the electric company."

"How long for?" asked Louisa.

"He was not sure. He has no idea of returning soon. He did explain but it was all terribly boring. He seemed to think it would be at least a few months."

Louisa's heart lurched as a familiar feeling of nausea returned, which she now realised came from the searing pain of dashed hopes. Just as she was finally able to acknowledge her feelings, it appeared certain that Daniel's were only of friendship. He had not considered her health of sufficient importance to remain in Suffolk and await her safe recovery.

Louisa went through the motions of conversation with Sophia, barely listening, as she described how Daniel had insisted on returning to the house when Louisa did not come back after the promised ten minutes, only to hear shouting from the rooftops. They had rushed to the rear of the house to see Louisa hanging precariously from the roof. They advanced to the Housekeeper's room followed by Harold before making the rescue.

"You are quiet, said Sophia. "Are you still feeling unwell?"

"I am a little better, just tired," said Louisa, unable to tell Sophia the real reason for her quietness and her feelings of complete wretchedness.

"You will be better soon," said Sophia. "The doctor said you would be out of danger as soon as you woke. He never doubted your speedy recovery which is why Daniel felt able to leave."

"He checked with the doctor?" asked Louisa hopefully.

"We both did," said Sophia. "We are your friends Louisa. We were terribly concerned."

Sophia stayed a few moments longer, but Louisa slipped further into melancholy, which Sophia interpreted as sickness and she left, promising to visit the next day. As soon as the door closed, Louisa put her poor bandaged hands to her eyes and sobbed until the bandages were damp with her tears.

It took a few more days for Louisa to feel well enough to leave her bed, and a few more still besides until her physical injuries began to heal. Her knuckles were smashed and would never be quite right again but she found, to her relief, that she could pick up a pen and use it, even though her writing was shaky.

She received a steady stream of visitors but nothing improved her mood. She read Mary Cage's diary from cover to cover, trying to understand why Jane Piggott had behaved so badly. It was a mystery to Louisa. Jane was a tiny baby when Mary was hanged and had lived outside the sphere of influence of her family for many years. There was no explanation for why she felt moved to commit the same monstrous crime, unless the wickedness of her family provoked a self-fulfilling prophecy. Perhaps evil ran through generations.

It bothered Louisa and continued to bother her. Eventually she decided to visit the repository in Ipswich and waded through several decades of the Ipswich Journal quarter sessions, where she discovered how much trouble could follow one family. Every one of Jane's half-brothers had been charged with larceny or assault; one was stabbed to death and her Uncle John transported for rape. It was all true; virtually every man in Jane's family had been in trouble with the law. Her predisposition to crime was almost a given.

Louisa continued to fret about the origins of the diary, wondering how it had fallen into the hands of the Ipswich museum when it had not been destined to be read by another human soul. She consulted her father who suggested a visit to the parish priest. A week later Louisa walked to St Margaret's church on the south side of Christchurch Park, seeking access to the parish register.

She was in luck. The vicar was in the vestry and listened to her request sympathetically. He asked her what records she wanted and at her reply, he produced a dusty, red-bound book and laid it on the altar. She thanked him, turned a few pages and found the entry she had half expected.

"Anna Tompkins of this parish, wife of Alfred was buried April 12th 1852 aged 49." Scribbled in the margin was a single word, "tuberculosis."

It was a mystery solved and an itch scratched. Louisa knew from the earnestness of Anna's promise, that only something unforeseen could possibly have kept her from destroying Mary's diary. She wished there was a way to discover the other unsolved matter from Mary's diary. The matter of who killed James Cage? Some mysteries were not destined to be solved – perhaps this was one of them.

Chapter Nineteen

Twilight years

Woolverstone – April 1911. In the tiny village of Woolverstone, nestled on the banks of the River Orwell south of Ipswich, Abraham Barker trudged wearily down the dirt track of a farm, into the front yard of the decrepit stone cottage he shared with his disagreeable landlady and her granddaughter.

He entered the front door of the cottage, stooping to avoid the lintel as he passed from dwindling sunshine into the cold, dank interior of the dwelling. He walked toward the kitchen, rubbing tired eyes with calloused hands. His once handsome face was weathered and etched with the lines of disappointment gained from a hard life, not relieved by the comforts of old age. At 73 years old he had hoped to have sufficient means to retire but fate had been cruel and he was destined to labour in the fields every day if he wanted to eat. He worked rain or shine, despite his stiff back and the painful gout in his left foot.

Abraham opened the latch door to the back room feeling the same surge of resentment he felt every day. The fire was unlit as usual, there was no food cooking as usual and the room was filthy; nothing had changed and never would. Not until the old girl died anyway. And once she was gone, he would probably lose his lodgings, so he would be no better off. Nothing was ever likely to improve.

He sat heavily on the wooden kitchen chair, watching her recumbent form sprawled across a mattress on the floor. A dirty, fraying blanket covered her. She opened her eyes and searched his face.

"Where is Rose?" she demanded.

"I do not know," he muttered. "There is no food again."

"Rose gave me food earlier," she said triumphantly.

"And left nothing for me?"

"I told her not to bother. You do not pay enough," her eyes sparkled with pleasure at the unkind words.

He stood wearily to his feet and shuffled towards a wooden kitchen cupboard. The door hung uselessly from a broken hinge. He peered inside. There was a loaf of mouldy bread and a chunk of cheese. He removed a penknife from his pocket and sliced the cheese, picking the worst of the mould spores from the bread.

"I will have this," he said gruffly.

"It's mine," she growled, narrowing her eyes. "You cannot have it."

He sighed. Another night; another long night, arguing with this mad, bad old woman as the last vestiges of her mind crumbled.

"You cannot stop me," he said shaking his head. He took a mouthful of the dry bread and grimaced.

"I'll stop you," she said, "just like I stopped him. I'll poison you until you scream for mercy."

Her face contorted; spittle flew from her mouth with the force of her words.

He carried on eating. He heard this almost every night now. Rat poison, dead father, hanged mother, transported brother. It was sad to see a mind disintegrate this fast.

She carried on. "I'll get the arsenic out the privy again. Just you wait".

He finished the scant meal. No point in waiting up to listen to the ramblings of a decayed mind. He might as well get an early night, ready for the daily grind in the fields tomorrow. That is if her incessant, spiteful chatter allowed him the luxury of a good night's sleep.

He shook his head as he climbed the creaky stairs to his mattress in the tiny back bedroom, regretting the poor decisions he had made in his life. When he was looking for lodgings two years ago, he was given a choice between this room and a ground floor room at the house of the widow Johnson. The rent was the same but when his old friend Richard Cage said his sister had a room available, he felt obliged. Bad choice, he thought now listening to the irrational screams coming from the back room. He rued the day he crossed the path of Sibella Studd.

187

Chapter Twenty

The final conspiracy

Once Louisa discovered Anna's fate, she was disappointed not to have her research to look forward to as a distraction from the pain of missing Daniel. Every day was endless and filled with despair. She found no pleasure in the company of others and began to take long, solitary walks to fill her time. After about a week of walking around Ipswich, she decided to visit Ada and Bessie Ridley. A morning with them lifted her spirits immensely and she returned to The Poplars in an unusually good mood.

On entering the house, she made her way towards the morning room, conscious of the sound of voices through the door of her father's study.

"Who is father speaking to?" she asked Charlotte who was sitting sewing in the morning room.

"Have a cup of tea," said Charlotte gesturing to the tea pot. She was accompanied by Marianne and Elizabeth Drummond. "I do not know who father entertains," she continued, "do you mother?"

Marianne took a sip of tea and exchanged glances with Elizabeth Drummond. "I am sure I have no idea," she said.

Louisa sighed and poured herself a cup of weak tea. She sat down and stirred the brew morosely with a silver apostle spoon.

"How are you Louisa?" asked Elizabeth Drummond, much thinner than when Louisa had last seen her but looking well for all her recent experiences.

"I am better," sighed Louisa, "just a little tired still."

There was a sharp rap at the door and Maggie entered, accompanied by Sophia.

"Where is....?"

"Hello my dear," said Elizabeth, standing to greet her daughter. She put a finger to her lips.

"Oh," said Sophia.

"Are you well Louisa?"

"I am fine, I was just telling your mother I am well, but tired."

"Good," said Sophia absently. All five women were sitting in silence, sipping tea. The conversation faltered badly. Louisa was puzzled.

"Is everything all right?" she asked.

Sophia opened her mouth to speak and then the door to the study opened.

From her vantage point opposite the morning room door, Marianne saw Henry Russell emerge, accompanied by Daniel.

"Elizabeth and I are going for a walk around the garden." She said. "Come and join us?"

"No thanks," said Charlotte.

"Come on," said Sophia. "I am going too."

"I'll go with you," said Louisa.

"No, not you," said Sophia, "you are tired and do not look well. Charlotte will come." She took Charlotte's arm and practically dragged her out the glazed door and on to the lawn.

Louisa sat alone in the corner of the morning room, watching the four women walking in the garden, chatting together. Sophia was talking animatedly to Charlotte, who kept looking back at the house.

Louisa did not hear the door pushed too, nor see Daniel enter the room. She was so intent trying to decipher what was passing between Sophia and Charlotte, that she knew nothing until Daniel put his hand on her shoulder.

"Louisa," he whispered.

She looked up, the colour draining from her face as her heart thumped wildly against her chest.

"Daniel, where have you been?" As hard as she tried, she could not stem the tears welling up in her eyes. She lowered her head and tried vainly to disguise her hurt.

He knelt down beside her, placed a gentle hand on her chin, and then tipped her face until she looked directly into his eyes. Time disappeared in the intensity of his gaze until he kissed her gently on the lips and the clocks began to tick once more.

"Dear Louisa," he murmured kissing her over and over, lips like butterfly wings across her skin. "Be my wife."

And she thought her heart would burst with joy.

Daniel and Louisa were so preoccupied they did not see the four women watching them from the garden, smiling and clapping.

189

Epilogue

14 December 1918

Louisa looked into the oval mirror in the hallway, adjusting the brim of her dusky-pink hat. She smoothed imaginary hairs from her matching coat.

"Will I do?" she asked.

"You will do very well," said Daniel putting an arm around her waist. He kissed her neck.

"Come here Emily," he said to the pretty four year old sitting at the foot of the stairs. She ran to her father and he held her hand smiling.

"Thank you," said Louisa as the nanny pushed a large wheeled perambulator towards her. She looked in and smiled at her sleeping son, stroking his cheek with her finger.

"Good luck then," said Mrs Pierce, the nanny.

"Thank you," said Louisa. "I am truly sorry that you cannot come with us, but it is a start."

"It is," said Mrs Pierce, and it will be my turn soon.

Daniel opened the door and they walked down Henley Road towards the polling booth to cast their votes.

Note:

When the vote was given to women in 1918, only women over thirty owning property or married to men owning property were eligible. The remainder were compelled to wait until 1928. Suffragists and suffragettes alike, ceased all activity during the war, but campaigned again when the war was over, eventually securing their long-held dream of enfranchisement.

THE END

Afterword

My great, great Uncle, **Alfred Bird** married Rosa Jane Studd, granddaughter of Sibella Cage and great Granddaughter of Mary Emily Cage nee Moise. I first read about the murder of James Cage while researching my Bird family history in Stonham Aspal and was intrigued by the story. Mary Emily was truly remorseful for her actions and although she acknowledged the deficiencies in her conduct, she flatly denied murdering her husband. I wondered what drove her to her heinous deeds and how much the dreadful, gnawing poverty contributed to her crimes.

Ada and Bessie Ridley are also my genetic relatives. They were at the other end of the social scale, leading privileged, middle-class lives. They were both active in the suffragette movement with Ada, a fine seamstress, credited with creating the 1911 WSPU Coronation Banner. The women's 1911 census evasion in Ipswich Museum was a real event. Ada and Bessie Ridley may well have been there, as they were absent on the 1911 census.

Some of the characters in this book are real; some are invented. I have taken artistic licence with many of the events described. There are several accounts of the Cage murder available on the internet and in the Ipswich record office as it was widely covered in newspapers during 1851. I consulted several excellent books about suffragism, read numerous accounts on the internet & sought authenticity by reading historical newspaper articles. However, I am no expert and, notwithstanding the census evasion, 1911 was a quiet year for suffragette activity, so I have stretched a few historical points to fit the story into this year. Although I live in Gloucestershire, my heritage is East Anglian. I have a Suffolk genealogy going back to the early 1500's and family still living there, so I know my way around Ipswich. It was a pleasure to set the book around Christchurch Park.

This book should be considered part fact, part fiction, especially where Jane and Sibella Cage are concerned. I do not know who killed James Cage, if not Mary and have only speculated on Sibella's guilt and wickedness of character. Equally, I did not find Jane Cage in the census records after 1861 but that does not mean she is not there. It may be that a better genealogist than I will find her alive and well in a future census, perhaps living in another country.

My extensive family history can be found at:
http://eastanglianancestors.co.uk with links to records of the Cage & Moise family.

More details for Alfred Bird can be found here:
http://eastanglianancestors.co.uk/fam2666.html

Jacqueline Beard, Cheltenham, 2015

17998940R00114

Printed in Poland
by Amazon Fulfillment
Poland Sp. z o.o., Wrocław